THE CAPTAIN'S KISS

"Surely you know you can trust me to keep you safe."

As soon as the words were out of his mouth, Alexander wished he could take them back. What an idiot he was. The way he had bullied and manipulated Vanessa into co-operating with his plan, he probably was the last man on earth she trusted.

She tilted her head up and looked at him.

"Yes," she said, sounding surprised. "I believe I do. Isn't that curious?"

The look of dismay on her face was so adorable that Alexander laughed. When he gestured for her to come forward again, she did so without hesitation. Without knowing quite how it happened, he found her in his arms.

Alexander lost all interest in the riding lesson.

Staring into Vanessa's eyes, holding her narrow waist between his hands, he couldn't resist kissing her. And, wonder of all wonders, she kissed him back. Not very expertly, to be sure, but the sweetness of her response made up for it. When he drew back to look at her, she raised one gloved hand to her swollen lips. Her eyes had gone all soft and smoky.

I am *not* in love with Vanessa Whittaker, Alexander told himself, feeling a little desperate. He *refused* to be in love with her.

BOOK YOUR PLACE ON OUR WEBSITE AND MAKE THE READING CONNECTION!

We've created a customized website just for our very special readers, where you can get the inside scoop on everything that's going on with Zebra, Pinnacle and Kensington books.

When you come online, you'll have the exciting opportunity to:

- View covers of upcoming books
- Read sample chapters
- Learn about our future publishing schedule (listed by publication month *and author*)
- Find out when your favorite authors will be visiting a city near you
- Search for and order backlist books from our online catalog
- Check out author bios and background information
- Send e-mail to your favorite authors
- Meet the Kensington staff online
- Join us in weekly chats with authors, readers and other guests
- Get writing guidelines
- AND MUCH MORE!

Visit our website at
http://www.zebrabooks.com

THE CAPTAIN'S COURTSHIP

KATE HUNTINGTON

Zebra Books
Kensington Publishing Corp.

http://www.zebrabooks.com

ZEBRA BOOKS are published by

Kensington Publishing Corp.
850 Third Avenue
New York, NY 10022

Zebra and the Z logo Reg. U.S. Pat. & TM Off.

First Printing: March, 1999
10 9 8 7 6 5 4 3 2 1

Printed in the United States of America

ONE

August, 1812
England, during the War with Napoleon

Vanessa Whittaker took her duties seriously, unlike the other patriotic young ladies who volunteered at Chelsea Hospital and spent most of their time either flirting with the soldiers or complaining to the unresponsive nurses about the smells. So when the wounded officer yawned and irritably told her to go to the devil, she gave his shoulder another gentle tap.

While Vanessa disapproved of the hospital's policy of dispensing strong spirits to those patients who looked big enough to make a fuss if they took a notion to object to the conditions, she had to admit that in some ways the practice was humane as well as expedient. She supposed it must be virtually impossible to sleep in this overcrowded ward with the groans of the other patients ringing in one's ears. The poor man must be very drunk, indeed, if he had managed to achieve it. But Vanessa could hardly permit him to miss the only meal he was likely to be served for the rest of the day.

"I've brought your tray, Captain," she persisted. Vanessa had gotten quite good at telling a patient's rank by the remnants of his uniform.

"Go away," he said without opening his eyes, "or I shall

be delighted to offer a strong suggestion as to what you
may do with your bloody tray.''

His state of inebriation, apparently, had done little to
impair his faculties. His clipped, aristocratic speech was
not in the least slurred, so Vanessa was encouraged to think
he might respond to reason.

"Do try to eat something or you never will get well,"
she coaxed.

The officer slowly sat up on the cot, clenching his jaw
against what appeared to be a considerable amount of
pain. Vanessa backed off a little at the fierce expression in
his compelling, if shadowed, dark eyes.

When she had answered the appeal in the *Morning Post*
for Gentlewomen to Cheer Our Gallant Wounded in the
understaffed and overcrowded hospital, this formidable
man wasn't quite what she had envisioned. His lean, muscular body was too long for the cot, and his strong jaw was
shadowed with stubble. He could have been the devil himself with his dark, wicked eyes and all the thick, black hair
partially hidden by a bloodstained bandage.

The sight of so many maimed and broken men nearly
had overpowered Vanessa when she first arrived at the hospital. If she had been rich, she gladly would have expended
her entire fortune to take them all home and make them
comfortable in clean, cheerful surroundings. Vanessa
wanted to weep for all the pathetic men she had seen lying
hurt and broken with all the life gone from their eyes.

However, there was nothing in the least pathetic about
this man, and there was plenty of life left in *his* eyes. Instinctively Vanessa knew that he was a predator, all the
more dangerous for having been wounded.

Despite the primitive thrill of fear that shot through her,
Vanessa held her ground. He might look dangerous, but
he was hurt. And probably hungry as well.

"Well, well. What have we here?" he drawled, looking
her up and down. His tone was as insolent as his eyes.

Vanessa stiffened her spine. *This* she could deal with. As
a young lady of passable looks and no fortune who often

was regarded as fair game by idle London aristocrats, she had seen this expression often.

"Gruel," she said as she placed the tray on a low table. "And bread."

"Gruel," he repeated, looking at the plate with an expression of disgust on his face. He gave her a wolfish smile. "My good girl, I wouldn't eat that slop if I were starving." He patted a place on the cot next to him suggestively. "Now if you truly are interested in satisfying one of my appetites . . ."

Vanessa favored him with what she hoped was a dignified stare.

"I thought not," he said with a mock sigh of regret. "Pity."

"You will have to eat something, Captain," Vanessa repeated.

"Perhaps," he agreed, "but not that. Now do take yourself off like a good girl and find some other helpless sot to perpetrate your Christian duty upon before I forget I was born a gentleman."

"If you refuse to eat, I shall have to feed you," Vanessa said, picking up the spoon.

The smile on the captain's face hardened and became something quite menacing as he grasped Vanessa's wrist and hauled her closer to the bed. The spoon clattered against the filthy wooden floor.

"Listen, *sweetheart*, I am not hungry," he said, enunciating every word clearly, as if to an idiot. "I am drunk. And if you had seen what *I* have seen for the past four months, you would be drunk, too."

"Unhand me at once! You may have been born a gentleman, sir, but you certainly do not behave as one," Vanessa said, struggling in vain to pull away from him.

"If that were true, m'dear, I'd have had you flat on this bed and stripped by now." He gave a mirthless chuckle. "I haven't seen an English girl in months who wasn't a whore."

Vanessa gasped in outrage and splayed her free hand against his muscular chest to push him away. Something dangerous moved behind those hard, cynical eyes, and he grabbed that wrist as well.

"If you don't let go of me, I shall scream!" she said between clenched teeth as she renewed her efforts to extricate herself. He had a surprisingly strong grip for an injured man. One of her knees struck the steel bed frame as he drew her close, and the sudden pain brought angry tears to her eyes.

"As an angel of mercy, my sweet, you leave much to be desired," he said as he ended the undignified struggle by suddenly releasing her.

She staggered and would have fallen if someone hadn't caught her shoulders from behind to steady her. Vanessa turned and thanked the elegantly dressed middle-aged gentleman for saving her from a nasty fall, favored the captain with a last scornful glare, and stalked away as his mocking laughter rang unpleasantly in her ears.

"It appears you've lost your touch with the ladies, my dear son," said Cedric Logan, the Earl of Stoneham.

Captain Alexander Logan, Viscount Blakely, ignored his father as he watched the girl flounce away. She was a cool, raven-haired beauty with lovely dark blue eyes under delicately arched black brows, and flawless, typically English rose and ivory skin. Alexander watched her stop to speak to a blinded young soldier. Her fashionable jonquil muslin gown looked out of place in this hellish prison of unspeakable sounds and smells, but the captain wholeheartedly approved of the perfectly ladylike way in which it displayed her slim, regal figure. The faintest wisp of orange blossom scent had teased his nostrils while she had stood there, trying earnestly to inflict her gruel and bread upon him.

She couldn't be more than eighteen or so. What were her parents thinking of to let her come to this place alone?

The captain reluctantly took his eyes away from the vision in jonquil muslin when his father touched his shoulder. The earl looked taken aback by his son's appearance, and Alexander could hardly blame him.

Alexander's hastily stitched head wound had broken open, causing it to bleed through its filthy bandages during the journey home to England by government transport from the Spanish Peninsula. No one had bothered to change the dressings, not even after he contracted a fever and nearly died of it. He guessed he must be quite a gruesome sight by now. Mercifully, his leg wound was hidden by the thin, dirty sheet.

"I say, Alexander, I do hope that isn't as bad as it looks," the earl said, sounding dismayed. "I shall find someone in authority at once to ask how soon you may be removed from here."

"Stubble it, Cedric," Alex growled. "And don't play the concerned parent with me. It doesn't become you."

"My, my. We *are* testy today, are we not?" The earl raised his quizzing glass and regarded his son through it. Then he sniffed the air in distaste. "Foxed! That explains it. Alexander, my dear boy, it is shockingly bad *ton* to be castaway this early in the day."

"Not if you've had a ball dug from your leg by a surgeon who hadn't slept for three days," Alex pointed out. "He did almost as much damage as the frogs."

"Your leg, too?" Cedric frowned at the sheet covering Alexander's legs and moved to lift it.

"I wouldn't," the captain said ruefully. "Believe me, it isn't pretty."

"You have no one to blame but yourself," the earl declared, giving his son a fierce look. "I used every bit of my considerable influence to get you a snug situation with the Tenth Hussars, but were you grateful? No, you were not! As soon as my back was turned, you applied to the Prince Regent for a transfer to General Wellesley's army in Spain. Letitia was vaporish for almost a week."

Alex rolled his eyes.

"Not *that* again!" he said with a weary sigh. "In my six months with his Highness's toy soldiers I did nothing but parade through Brighton in my impeccably tailored blue uniform and go to assemblies. As for my aunt . . ."

The captain felt a reluctant smile tug at his lips and had to admit that he had missed his frivolous aunt very much, although he didn't flatter himself that she had given him a serious thought. Letitia, though she had lived with him and the earl through most of Alexander's growing-up years, was the least maternal female of his acquaintance, bless her.

"Alexander," Stoneham protested. "I'll have you know Letitia was inconsolable when she learned you had gone to Spain."

"Good of her," the captain acknowledged, "but I fear she was less horrified by the prospect of my demise than by the truly hideous possibility that she might have to go into mourning."

The earl gave a crack of reluctant laughter.

"There is that," he agreed. "Seriously, boy. How badly *are* you hurt?"

"I haven't damaged any part of my anatomy that I need to secure the precious succession, if that's what you mean," the captain said. "Do you think I didn't know you and your bloody interfering friends at Whitehall would have me on a government transport home to Mother England if I so much as stubbed my toe?"

The earl winced at such plain speaking, but didn't deny it.

The captain had distinguished himself for bravery in the Spanish Peninsula, but he was certain he never would have been transported home for such trifling injuries as a potentially crippling leg wound and a broken head if his father had not been a wealthy nobleman with friends in high places at Whitehall.

"I am going back to the Peninsula, you know," Alexander told Stoneham.

The earl affected not to hear.

"I believe I shall take myself off, my boy, for I can see you are in no mood for visitors." The older man stood and brushed his buff-colored pantaloons with his handkerchief to dislodge an infinitesimal mote of dust. "I shall make arrangements for your removal to the country at once."

The old fox was being evasive, and Alex wasn't about to let him get away with it.

"Cedric," Alex said, laying a hand on his father's arm to stop him. "I mean it."

The earl sat down again.

"Alexander, no one doubts your courage. Your war record will be invaluable when you stand for office, but there is no reason to risk yourself further."

"You never give up, do you?" the captain said. "I have a duty to my commander and my men, so your bloody political ambitions will just have to wait until the French are beaten."

"Nonsense. One captain more or less won't matter to General Wellesley."

"That is beside the point." Alex's head was beginning to throb again. "I refuse to stay safe and snug in London while my men fight without me. As soon as I am well enough to stand up without falling flat on my face, I am going back."

The Earl of Stoneham's dark eyes hardened, but his voice was quite pleasant as he rose.

"Well, Alexander, I don't want to tire you. We will discuss this further tomorrow. Don't worry, my boy, you shall receive the best of care. My man will see about hiring a nursing staff to accompany you to the country. Letitia and I are established at Brighton for the rest of the summer, naturally."

"Naturally," Alex said dryly. Letitia and Cedric could hardly be expected to cut short the pleasure of a summer in Brighton simply because the man they had raised from a boy faced a long, lonely, and painful convalescence.

"We shall visit you briefly in September before we come up to London for the little season," Cedric added, patting Alex on the arm as he left him.

Strange.

Letitia and Cedric's selfish indifference to his feelings and wishes had not bothered Alexander for years, so he was surprised by the wave of sadness that swept over him. He had learned at an early age that while both held him in affection, neither was particularly fond of the company of children. No doubt the liquor was making him maudlin.

Alexander leaned back on his elbows and watched the earl go out the door, determined that he would not play the craven no matter how much pressure his ambitious father applied.

As sobriety returned, the pounding in Alexander's head grew louder and his leg resumed its dull throbbing. Eyes narrowed in pain, he looked across the room to see the pretty girl in yellow writing a letter while the young soldier with the bandage covering his eyes dictated it to her.

She was truly lovely when she smiled, and the captain felt a stab of annoyance as he watched her concentrate on the blinded soldier. Did she and the other fresh-faced, sweet-smelling society ladies not understand that it was cruelty, not kindness, to display their innocent charms to men whose minds and bodies had been broken by horrors that would haunt them to their graves?

But, no. How could they? The little fools knew no more of war than Alexander had known when he boarded the government transport all those months ago, precise to a pin in his crisp new uniform. He had expected to find a glorious adventure, and it had been . . . hell.

And what had the pretty lady offered him, for a body that had been starved and broken? For the nightmares that haunted him?

A plate of gruel.

He glanced at the bedside table and regarded the congealing mass with a shudder of distaste. It appeared to be only slightly less palatable than his own behavior toward the lady. Lord, what had possessed him to force his attentions on an innocent young girl? She *was* lovely, but that was no excuse for his abominable behavior.

You may have been born a gentleman, she had said, *but you certainly do not behave as one.* Alexander gave a mirthless laugh. What a masterpiece of understatement that was!

He glanced again at the gruel. He had eaten worse over the past few months, and he *was* hungry. Pride, however, had stopped him from trying to eat it in front of the girl. It was humiliating enough to return from the war as weak as a cat. It would be infinitely worse to cast up his accounts in the presence of a pretty young lady. Silly perhaps, but there it was. She wasn't looking at him now, however. If only his stomach would stop its infernal churning about, he might be able to force it down.

He almost had resigned himself to eating the unappetizing mess when he remembered that the spoon had been dropped somewhere on the floor. In frustration, he lay back down on the cot and closed his eyes, trying to ignore the throbbing in his head. He flinched when he heard a woman's voice shout in a tone of accusation, *"There* you are, you ungrateful girl!"

Alexander opened his eyes in time to see a plump, fashionably garbed, middle-aged female sweep into the room and confront the girl, who looked up from the letter she was writing with a rebellious expression on her face.

"I should have known you would come here as soon as my back was turned! I forbade you to come here again!" the elder lady said loudly enough for virtually everyone in the ward to hear. "I have been worried *sick* about you!"

"Now, Mama—" the girl began.

"Don't you 'Now, Mama' *me*, missy," the girl's mother cried. "I have brought you all the way to London in this heat to see about hiring a house for your debut next spring and how do you repay me? By running away from the hotel and scaring me half to death!"

"I left you a note, Mama," the young lady said with a sigh. "I *told* you I was going to volunteer at the hospital."

By then, they had been joined by another woman, who was obviously a servant or paid companion. Lowering her voice to a more discreet level, the girl's mother obviously was insisting that she leave with her at once.

Certainly the older woman had the right of it, Alexander thought. This was no place for a girl like her.

It appeared, though, that the girl was putting up a spirited fight. She clearly intended to stay and finish writing the soldier's letter for him. She proceeded to do just that as her mother waited with ill-concealed impatience. When she had finished writing the letter, she put it in her reticule. No doubt she was going to post it for her patient.

In spite of himself, Alexander felt a certain admiration for the young lady's defiance. He always had admired a bit of spirit in a female. And he could sympathize with anyone plagued by an interfering parent.

The matronly woman took the girl's arm and pulled her away from the blind soldier until they were quite close to Alexander's bed. The girl glanced uneasily toward Alexander, who, pretending to be asleep, was watching her through half-closed eyelids.

"Poor man," Vanessa said softly, pulling the stained sheet over Alexander. Was that *pity* Alexander heard in her voice? She seemed to see something on the floor and stooped until she was out of the range of his vision. Then she stood and he could see she had the fallen spoon in her hand. She took a handkerchief from her reticule and carefully wiped it off.

"What are you doing with that filthy thing?" her mother demanded.

"Hush, Mother. You'll awaken him," Vanessa replied, placing the spoon on the tray.

But the older lady was not about to be silenced.

"Vanessa," she hissed. "You should know better than to come to this place alone. What of your reputation? Some of these men are half *naked!*"

Vanessa, Alexander thought. A pretty name, but with no nonsense about it. It suited her.

"Believe me, Mama. My virtue couldn't be safer," Vanessa argued. "Most of these poor men could not get out of bed without help, let alone—"

"Vanessa!" exclaimed her mother, shocked.

"I wasn't going to say it," Vanessa said with a sigh. "Really, Mama, let's not make a piece of work over it. It is all the rage to be patriotic, you know. Besides, London is so thin of company now it is highly unlikely any members of the *haute ton* will see me here."

"Romantic young girls are so susceptible to wounded males," her mother fretted, "and I couldn't *bear* it if you'd run off with someone unsuitable after all our scrimping and scheming to bring you to London so you can make a good marriage. London is full of rich, *titled* old men looking for pretty young wives to spend their money on. Only a fool would settle for a mere scarlet coat."

"Mama, please!" the girl said, looking uncomfortable. "They can *hear* you."

"Gentlemen of fortune, my dear, do not marry young ladies who indulge in odd behavior," the older lady reprimanded her, wrinkling her nose as she indicated their surroundings with a wave of one plump hand. "And spending one's time in a hospital is very odd behavior, indeed, for a lady of sensibility. What are we to do if you *catch* something from one of the poor creatures? All of our hopes will be at an end. Now, do put on your bonnet and come along. Lady Comfrey has invited us to dinner, the sweet, odd creature, and she will number at least three peers among her guests. You must be in your best looks tonight, for all of them are widowers and *rich*, Vanessa! If you can marry one of them, all of our troubles will be over. I am *determined* you shall have a title, my love!"

They had moved away, trailed by the servant, so Alexander missed Vanessa's low-voiced reply to this remark.

So the girl was a fortune hunter, Alexander thought cynically. Lord, there was no escaping them. He could well imagine her reaction if she had recognized him as the future Earl of Stoneham. It would have made no difference that he had the devil's own temper and couldn't recall the last time he had bathed. She and her harpy of a mother would have fawned all over him. It was a dashed bore to be so bloody eligible.

The difference between a fortune hunter and a whore, the earl had always told him, was that the whore was more honest. A man knew exactly what a bird of paradise was offering and how much it was going to cost him. But a fortune hunter would not be satisfied until she had relieved her victim of every last groat.

Alexander was possessed of a deep, abiding sadness as he sank back on the bed and stared at the cracked ceiling.

The girl had seemed so earnest. And her wrists had been so delicate when he had captured them in his hands.

What was it about her that intrigued him? He never had been partial to elegant little brunettes. Statuesque, buxom blondes safely past the first blush of youth were more his style. Yet his mind dwelled on the curve of the girl's rose-hued cheeks, the fringe of dark lashes around those big blue eyes, the sweep of dark, shining hair that contrasted with her smooth, alabaster skin.

And her smile. *Especially* her smile.

She was a fortune hunter, he reminded himself sternly. He *despised* fortune hunters!

Alexander firmly called his thoughts to order.

If he didn't find a way to get around his father's blasted interfering ways, he might be forced to live with the disgrace of having failed to perform his duty to his country for the rest of his life.

This was no time to be daydreaming about dewy-eyed ingenues. His head wound must be more severe than he thought!

His stomach gave a rumble, and he glanced at the plate of gruel. With a grimace, he picked up the spoon and began to eat.

TWO

April 1813
London, England

"Captain Logan is here tonight," Vanessa's vivacious blonde companion said excitedly as the two young ladies sat out the minuet at one side of the ballroom. "They say he was wounded at Salamanca, and that he never smiles. He just stands at the side of the ballroom, 'cynically surveying the company' like Lord Byron."

"I give you fair warning, Diana, if you are going to start misquoting Byron at me, I shall go into strong hysterics," Vanessa said, only half listening. "I have had quite enough of his wretched doggerel inflicted upon me by Mama and my sisters."

"There he is, over by the wall. Lord, isn't he so handsome you could just *die*? Look at those brooding dark eyes! You can tell he's a man who has *suffered*."

Instead of following the direction in which Diana discreetly pointed, Vanessa's eyes scanned the crowd looking for her mother. The Whittaker ladies already had been snubbed by several of their social superiors on this, their first appearance at Almack's. Judging from their chilly reception here, it was unlikely either Vanessa or her mother would be sent vouchers for Almack's again. That was fine with Vanessa, but she had seen the sheen of tears in her mother's eyes before Annabelle excused herself on the pretext of finding a footman to fetch her shawl. For all that the celebrated Marriage Mart was supposed to be the answer to a maiden's prayers, Vanessa would never forgive this great lot of insufferable snobs because they had dared hurt her mother's feelings. Oh, Annabelle would never show it. She had too much pride for that. Pride and desperation. But Vanessa wished every last one of these pompous, over-bred hypocrites straight to . . .

"Van, are you listening to me?" her companion demanded. "Imagine the luck of seeing him here! I wonder if he will dance with anyone."

"Diana Lacey, *do* grow up!" Vanessa said with affectionate scorn, forcing herself to smile at her friend. "Lord Byron is a perfectly ordinary-looking man who puts on airs to make himself interesting. And the more everyone toadeats him, the more insufferable he becomes."

"Not *Byron,* idiot! Captain Logan."

"Don't let your mother hear you sighing over a scarlet coat," Vanessa warned. "You will be fortunate if she doesn't lock you in your room for a week."

"Ah, but this one is different. He is Lord Stoneham's heir, you know. The earl."

"No, I *don't* know," Vanessa said. "Earls are quite above my touch, I'm afraid."

Especially if they still have their own teeth, she added to herself.

Sets were forming for the next dance, and Vanessa tried not to look vexed as she saw her mother bearing down upon her with a middle-aged gentleman in tow. Annabelle's face was triumphant, for her companion was very, very rich and a widower of several years' duration.

Oh, *wonderful,* Vanessa thought. Now she would have to endure Lord Omersley's patting and pinching her all through the next set of country dances. Well, it's why her family scrimped and saved and went into debt to bring her to London, after all, she told herself.

Vanessa forced a smile to her lips and braced herself for the ordeal ahead. Diana gave a little cry of disappointment. "Oh, look. Amabel Warren has got her hooks into Captain Logan now," she wailed. "Her mother will make certain he can't get away from them without promising to take Amabel into supper with him, you just wait and see."

"Well, I wish her joy of him," Vanessa said, her eye on her advancing mother and the elderly *roué* at her side.

Indeed, what were handsome, brooding heirs to earldoms to Vanessa when the most promising of her marital prospects stood before her—bald, bowlegged, and smirking grotesquely with ill-fitting wooden teeth?

Vanessa stood up and gave in gracefully to her fate.

Across the crowded room, Captain Alexander Logan was being held captive by a determined matron intent upon enumerating every one of her daughter's superficial accomplishments as the coquettish miss blushed and disclaimed. He finally managed to extricate himself from the harpy's clutches by the simple expedient of replying to all her raptures with unencouraging monosyllables until she and her simpering daughter had no choice but to abandon him in search of more receptive gentlemen.

Alexander looked around, then lifted his glass in mock salute to his elegant aunt, Lady Letitia, as she performed the minuet with one of her faithful cicebos.

She laughed and blew Alexander a kiss.

He scowled in return.

Alexander's wounds were healed, and it was time he rejoined his regiment in Spain. Instead, he was in London for the social season. Or, he amended, Letitia and Cedric were in London for the social season. Alexander had agreed to accompany them to the City so he could apply to the proper authorities for a return to active duty. Alexander's father still wanted him to sell his commission and embark upon a political career, but Alexander refused to leave the army while Napoleon was still at large.

So what on earth, Alexander asked himself, was he doing in London's most exclusive ballroom, sipping tepid wine

and avoiding the rapt gaze of several dozen simpering females who, with the slightest encouragement, would have
thrown themselves into his unwilling arms?

Perishing of boredom, actually.

They were all the same, these docile, well-bred little
debutantes. No matter how much one snubbed them, the
wretched creatures came back for more abuse. He was
heartily sick of their girlish laughter and inane remarks.
They acted as if he were some sort of hero, the silly chits!
He looked around the reception rooms, disgusted by all
the flirting and chattering going on around him. Did they
not understand what would happen to them all if Napoleon won?

How could they *dance* at a time like this?

He watched absently as the music ended and Lady Letitia's dancing partner relinquished her into the care of her
brother. The earl and his sister, spotting Alexander standing alone at the edge of the ballroom, made their way to
him, no doubt intending to bully him into having a good
time. Letitia had insisted that being around people was
just what he needed to take his mind off the unpleasant-
ness of war.

Just as if it were all over, he thought wryly, now that the
Earl of Stoneham's precious heir was home.

Alexander realized that the war wasn't real to a single
one of these people because the fighting was taking place
on foreign soil. For them, the deprivation of war meant
having to pay exorbitant amounts for smuggled French
brandy. The ladies couldn't wait until all this fuss was over
so they could go shopping once again in Paris.

As Alex continued to watch his father and aunt approach, he made up his mind that he had endured quite
enough of Almack's inferior wine and vapid company for
one night. It was time to make good his escape.

"Oh, darling, I am so sorry," said Letitia in concern
when Alex explained that his leg was bothering him and
he wanted to go home.

Actually, his leg was healed except for an occasional stiffness, but his injury had served him well as an excuse not to take part in any of the so-called amusements of the London Season until now. Alex was not above exaggerating the limp now and again when it suited his purpose.

"Should we go with you?" the earl asked, his voice perfectly bland.

"No, I'll take a hackney," Alex assured him.

He actually had taken a step toward Lady Maria Sefton, the Lady Patroness who so obligingly had sent Letitia a voucher for him, in order to offer his excuses, when the crowd of dancers shifted and he saw the dark-haired young lady from the hospital. In the early months of suffering during his convalescence, her face would occasionally pop into his mind. He saw now that his fevered brain had not exaggerated her beauty.

She was dancing with a man who looked old enough to be her grandfather. The girl's forced smile stiffened when her partner's roaming hand ventured just a trifle too high, as if by accident. She slapped the gentleman's hand away, which might have been taken for coquetry if the expression in the lady's eyes hadn't been so aggrieved.

What was her name? Veronica?

No. That wasn't right.

"That girl in the white dress sashed in green," Alex said to Letitia. "Who is she?"

Letitia brightened instantly and turned around to see which young lady had attracted his notice. Alexander knew his lack of interest in any of the debutantes had begun to make his aunt despair of ever seeing him married. Then she turned back to him, and Alexander could see her eager expression had been replaced by one of disappointment.

"Oh," she said, frowning a little. "That is only Vanessa Whittaker."

Vanessa. Of course.

"Only?" prompted Alexander.

Letitia gave him a straight look.

"No, darling. Not that one," she said bluntly.

"I beg your pardon?"

"Believe me, if she's anything like her mother, she's an absolute pea-goose. I should know. I was at school with Annabelle Whittaker fifteen years ago."

Alex raised his brows at her.

"All right," Letitia admitted in an exasperated tone. *"Twenty* years ago!"

"The girl is a beauty, for all that," Alex observed. "I should think her face and figure would more than make up for the deficiencies of her intellect."

"Alex, you *mustn't!"* Letitia cried. "When I think of all the perfectly unexceptionable girls of birth and fortune I have been at such pains to bring to your notice, I vow I could *shake* you! It's no secret the girl has to marry money. The Whittakers haven't a *sou.* The only reason Miss Whittaker is tolerated at all is because there's goodish blood in her from her father."

"Do I know him?" Alex asked, watching the girl.

"The father? George Whittaker," said the earl. "Not a bad sort. The worst you can say about him is he was fool enough to be caught by a little country nobody like Annabelle in his youth. Dead, isn't he, Letitia?"

"These two years past," his sister confirmed.

Letitia, who had an intelligence network to rival the British Government's, could be depended upon to add her bit.

"Miss Whittaker is the oldest of five daughters, and the only presentable one of the lot from what I'm told. Annabelle is determined that she shall attract a wealthy suitor and save them all from financial ruin, which just *shows* what a ninnyhammer she is," Letitia said. "No man of sense would take the girl with *that* family. With such a shockingly improvident mother-in-law, the poor man would find himself saddled with all their debts and the expense of launching the remaining four daughters into society. Annabelle has great hopes of old Lord Omersley because he seems dotty enough on the girl to marry her in spite of his grown children's opposition. Everyone will say, of course, that Lord Omersley is senile and the girl is a shameless fortune hunter for encouraging him, but it is the best offer she is likely to get."

"Pity," Alexander murmured, his eyes still on the girl.

The earl gave him a shrewd look.

"But you were just leaving, my boy, were you not?" he pointed out.

Alex didn't smile. He hadn't all evening, in fact. But a muscle twitched at the corner of his mouth. The earl had made it abundantly clear with only the tone of his voice that he disapproved of his son's interest in little Vanessa Whittaker. Alex was strongly tempted to stay and renew his acquaintance with the young lady, just to annoy his father. Then he realized that he had no taste for watching her grovel for his favor, like all the others.

"Quite right, Cedric," he said. "I'll bid you both a pleasant evening, then, shall I?"

To his vexation, he saw that he had missed his opportunity for escape because Lady Sefton was engrossed in earnest conversation with a lady and gentleman. His hostess's companions didn't move on until the end of the dance, and Alex had no choice but to stand making conversation with his father and aunt as he idly watched the graceful Vanessa skillfully evade her partner's determined pawing. Poor girl, he thought as the music ended and he watched the old goat lead her up to her mother. Then he brought himself up short. Good lord, was he feeling sorry for a *fortune hunter*?

When the earl pointed out that Lady Sefton was free at last of her companions, Alex sketched a small, mocking bow in his aunt's direction and stepped forward once more to approach his hostess. However, fate intervened in the form of Mrs. Whittaker, who suddenly grasped her daughter by the wrist and towed her toward the earl and his family. Stoneham hastily excused himself, his manner making it clear he had no wish to meet the Whittakers in society.

Alexander, surprised by his father's abruptness, stayed by his aunt's side.

"Oh, *bother,*" Letitia whispered, rolling her eyes for Alexander's benefit.

"Letitia, *darling!*" exclaimed Mrs. Whittaker when she arrived, a little breathless, in front of them.

Alexander's aunt reluctantly made the desired introductions.

"Oh, Lord Blakely," the widow gushed, surprising Alexander with the use of his title. He was accustomed to being addressed by his military rank. "I am delighted to meet you at last. My lord, may I present my daughter, Vanessa?"

"Charmed," he said, giving the elder lady a slight bow and turning to face the girl. Vanessa's eyes widened, and that was how Alexander knew she recognized him from the hospital.

Vanessa replied to his greeting but did not smile.

"Letitia, darling," Mrs. Whittaker said in a stage whisper as she led Alexander's aunt away. "I have heard the most *delicious* rumor, and I knew you would never forgive me if I failed to tell you at once."

It was a clumsy ploy, but it succeeded in leaving Vanessa and Alexander together.

"You must have been in a great deal of pain that day at the hospital," Vanessa said after an awkward silence. "I am glad to see you are recovered from your injuries."

"Thank you. Actually," he said in a tone calculated to depress pretension, "my leg is troubling me. I was about to offer my excuses to Lady Sefton and go home."

The girl raised her chin and gave him a resentful look. She apparently recognized a snub when she heard one.

"How dull," Vanessa said, her big blue eyes alight with defiance. "But naturally you still are inclined to be crotchety and invalidish, and must not be racketing about at all hours like the rest of us." Vanessa shook her head, and the gesture caused her hair, arranged in a profusion of dusky ringlets, to bounce about attractively. "You may imagine my surprise when I realized *you* were the dashing

Captain Alexander Logan all the ladies are talking about. Indeed, I was certain my informant was making a May-game of me."

The kitten definitely had claws and she knew how to use them.

"My *dear* Miss Whittaker," he said in a quelling tone. "I feel sure you are mistaken."

"That is what *I* thought, too," she said, as if sharing a joke. "You'll hardly credit it, but just tonight I heard you compared to Lord Byron."

"You are roasting me," he said. He always had found Byron's behavior perfectly revolting.

Vanessa gave a little shrug, which called Alexander's reluctant attention to her perfect, partially bared shoulders. Her ballgown, though cut well within the bounds of propriety, confirmed his first favorable impression of the young lady's elegant figure.

"Personally, I don't see *any* resemblance between you and Lord Byron," Vanessa assured him. "*He,* you know, is generally perceived to be excessively handsome. Both of you do have a limp, and that probably accounts for it. Although I suppose it probably is unkind of me to say so."

"*Most* unkind," he agreed.

"And like you," she continued, "he goes to balls and stands about looking sulky instead of dancing. *Such* an uncivil man."

She shook those pretty curls again in disapproval.

"Miss Whittaker," Alexander said, trying to sound severe, "I will thank you to remember that I have been wounded in the service of my country. It is most uncharitable of you to subject me to this abuse."

Those blue, almost violet eyes widened artlessly.

"But my lord," she said, looking as innocent as a newborn babe. "I was speaking of *Lord Byron,* of course."

It occurred to Alexander that if the little baggage failed to marry a fortune, she might do very well for herself on the stage.

"My dear young lady, if you have come all the way to

London to catch a title and a fortune, you have a most peculiar way of going about the business."

"Oh, I do assure you, Captain, that if I had any such notion, I never would be so goosish as to waste my time on *you,*" she said, her eyes glittering. "I'm afraid I must concentrate my efforts only on *good* matrimonial prospects."

"Perhaps you are better informed than I, then, because when I left for the Peninsula, Stoneham's fortune hardly was thought to be contemptible."

"Precisely," she said, smiling at him as if he had said something clever. *"Stoneham's* fortune, not yours. Your father appears to be in excellent health. At the risk of being indelicate, Captain Logan, you apparently have recovered from your injuries and no doubt soon will return to war. There is no guarantee that the earl will predecease you. Indeed, he could surprise you yet by marrying and setting up his nursery."

"Stoneham? I wish that I might see it!" Alexander said in genuine amusement at the thought of the hedonistic earl's well-run bachelor household being turned upside down by a brood of lively little Logans.

"Do you, Captain?" Vanessa said, her eyes bright with malice. "I must say that is *excessively* handsome of you. Your father is *such* a distinguished-looking man. It would not be at all surprising if he chose to marry again. My mother always says that only an older man has the patience and wisdom to deal with a skittish young bride."

Alexander was pleasantly occupied in composing a crushing reply to this blatant provocation when Vanessa stepped slightly to the side and directed a flirtatious little wave toward someone who apparently was standing behind him.

"What are you doing now?" he asked.

"Trying to attract Lord Omersley's attention," she replied as her elderly cavalier instantly presented himself in answer to her summons.

"Lord Omersley, I do hope you won't think it forward

of me to remind you, but you *did* invite me to go in with you to supper," she said, casting her eyes down demurely.

"My dear Miss Whittaker," Lord Omersley said as he revealed the full glory of his wooden teeth in a wide grin, "I am delighted, as always, to be of service to you."

The gratified gentleman took Vanessa's hand and directed a look of inquiry at Alex.

"Captain Logan was just leaving," Vanessa said, favoring Alexander with a polite, impersonal smile. "I daresay he is much obliged to you for relieving him of me, because his poor leg is paining him and he must go home to soak it, or something."

Alexander couldn't believe it. The audacious little baggage was *dismissing* him! Since it clearly was out of the question for Alexander to shake the impertinent minx until her teeth rattled, the only course left to him was to sketch a bow in Vanessa's direction, take his leave of his hostess, and get out of Almack's before he made a complete fool of himself.

Vanessa watched the dashing Captain Logan leave the ballroom from the corner of her eye. On some level she knew it was unjust to make him a scapegoat for all the snubs she and her mother had endured this evening, but she had lost all sense of fair play when he made it clear that he expected her to fawn over him like all the other debutantes.

She paid dearly for her moment of triumph by having to endure old Omersley's ponderous compliments throughout supper. But Vanessa considered the satisfaction of giving the arrogant Captain Logan the set-down he so richly deserved more than adequate compensation.

Annabelle Whittaker seemed quite in charity with the world as they left the ball in their rented carriage, and Vanessa had no difficulty at all in reading her mother's thoughts. Never mind that they most probably would not be invited to Almack's again. Lord Omersley had been most marked in his attentions to Vanessa during supper and afterward. Mrs. Whittaker no doubt was indulging herself in a pleasant daydream of Vanessa married to the fabulously wealthy Lord Omersley, and her family free at last from the increasingly strident demands of her creditors.

Vanessa leaned back against the squabs, closed her eyes, and hoped Lord Omersley believed in long engagements.

THREE

"But, darling, it will be good for you to get out of the house."

"The answer is *no*, Letitia," Alexander said as he carved a generous slice of beef from the sirloin in front of him. "I am not going to stand in line on the street for several hours shoulder to shoulder with the nosiest tabbies in London to spend less than ten minutes exchanging polite commonplaces with virtual strangers just so I can fight my way out again to wait for another hour for someone to find the carriage. Of all the silly customs the *ton* indulges in during the Season, a rout is the silliest."

"But, darling, all the world will be there."

"I know," he said when he had finished chewing a bite of his breakfast. "That is precisely why I *won't*. I distinctly remember your stigmatizing the new Lady Mabberley as a 'provincial nobody' and a 'simpering gold digger,' so I cannot imagine why you would want to waste your time going to her reception."

Lady Letitia could have enlightened him, but wisely forbore to do so.

Men were so hopelessly naive about such things.

While the highest sticklers disapproved of the pretentious little nobody fresh from the schoolroom who had contrived to charm the widowed Earl of Mabberley into making her his countess, they could be pardoned for a very natural curiosity to see what atrocities the earl's unworthy bride had perpetrated upon the stately townhouse occupied by the Earls of Mabberley since the early eighteenth century.

For days afterward, Lady Letitia knew, young Lady Mabberley's deplorable taste in furniture and hangings would be ruthlessly dissected in every sitting room of consequence in London. Letitia couldn't *bear* it if she were the only one of her intimates not to have inspected the carnage firsthand.

Besides, it *would* be good for Alexander to mix with good society, she reflected unselfishly. With the exception of last night's appearance at Almack's, Alexander had spent all of his time in London frequenting gambling hells, drinking with low company, and probably wenching as well, for women threw themselves at him in the most shockingly brazen manner. One could hardly suppose Alexander would find a suitable bride while engaging in such pursuits. Therefore, it positively was Letitia's *duty* to persuade him to go to Lady Mabberley's rout. Perhaps if he met some nice young ladies he would stop brooding over Cedric's refusal to let him go back to his horrid old war and enjoy himself. It was unnatural for such a handsome young man to be so serious.

Lady Letitia turned swimming green eyes on her nephew.

"*Must* you turn into a watering pot at this hour?" he snapped, sounding irritable.

Lady Letitia's one talent was the ability to cry at will, and she unscrupulously exploited it, with gratifying results, whenever she wanted to get around her brother or nephew. Since Letitia was capable of sulking for days on end when she didn't get her way, it was wonderfully effective most of the time.

This, unfortunately, was not one of those times.

Dear Alexander's leg must have pained him very much in the night, Letitia thought charitably.

She decided to try another tactic.

"I know you didn't enjoy yourself very much, but I did

so appreciate your accompanying us to Almack's last night," she said.

"I didn't mind," he said.

Letitia gave him a sideways look.

"I am sorry Annabelle Whittaker managed to inveigle you into a conversation with her daughter," she said, trying to sound casual. "Of course, I know you have too much good sense to encourage the girl. It would be excessively unkind to arouse her expectations and those of her mother."

"There you're out, love," he replied with a snort of derisive laughter, "for the fair Vanessa considers me an exceedingly poor marital prospect. She had only to point out that the French might very well put a period to my existence when I return to war, or that Cedric, although he has successfully avoided parson's mousetrap these fifteen years since my mother died, may yet surprise us all by reopening the nursery."

Letitia, who had taken a sip of her coffee, choked. Alexander rose and solicitously patted her on the back until she waved him away.

"I'm all right now, dearest," she said, trying to sound natural while her mind whirled with the implications of Alexander's careless words. It was all very well for Alexander to laugh. *He*, at least, had his career in the army, and he would inherit the earldom regardless of how many other children his father sired.

For the first time in years, the horrible possibility that Cedric might marry and Letitia might become a mere pensioner in his wife's household or, worse still, be forced to live on her own woefully inadequate fortune at one of her brother's minor residences in the country, crossed her mind.

"That scheming little hussy!" Letitia gasped. "She wouldn't *dare* try to get her hooks into Cedric."

"Of *course*, she wouldn't," Alexander said, sounding surprised. "Really, Aunt Letitia. There are times when your mind is entirely too literal."

"Cedric has too much common sense to be taken in by some sly, fortune-hunting little Jezebel," Letitia declared.

"Letitia, please," he said in a sardonic tone. "Can you see *Cedric* harboring a secret ambition to fill this house with the patter of little feet? It won't fadge, my dear."

Letitia closed her eyes and gave an eloquent shudder.

"He *wouldn't,*" she breathed.

"Certainly not," Alexander assured her.

Instead of comforting her, however, this sentiment caused Letitia to become even more alarmed.

Letitia's enthusiasm for attending Lady Mabberley's "at home" suddenly disappeared because, upon reflection, the Earl of Mabberley's foolishness in espousing a chit twenty years his junior was not in the least diverting.

Naturally Alexander, in that irritating way men have, decided to grant Letitia's request the moment she was determined to withdraw it.

"I can see you are determined to go to Lady Mabberley's reception, so I suppose I will have to escort you after all," he said ungraciously. "It will be a dead bore, but people have been *trampled* at these affairs, and you will be safer with a man along."

Letitia, a little stunned by her Pyrrhic victory, could only gape at him with her mouth open.

"Yes. Thank you, dear," she said after a short silence. Alexander nodded and left the room while Letitia's fertile imagination conjured up a terrifying vision of her place at the foot of Stoneham's formal dining room table being usurped by a simpering miss barely out of the schoolroom.

"What is wrong with Letitia?" the earl asked Alexander that night after dinner as the gentlemen enjoyed claret and cigars. Letitia had been uncharacteristically silent during the meal, when ordinarily she would have been chattering about her day's activities.

"It's all my fault, I'm afraid," Alexander said. "Because

of something I said today, the dreadful possibility that you might take a young bride and evict Letitia from her home has taken violent possession of her mind. Do not be surprised if she scratches Vanessa Whittaker's eyes out the next time she sees her."

"My dear boy, perhaps I am being obtuse, but I haven't the slightest idea what you're talking about."

"Letitia thinks Miss Whittaker is about to set her cap at you."

The earl's eyebrows rose.

"Indeed? How gratifying, to be sure. And how did Letitia arrive at this extraordinary conclusion?"

"Miss Whittaker told me she has no intention of setting her cap at *me* because I'm such a poor marital prospect."

The earl's astounded expression caused Alexander to laugh out loud.

"She seemed to think I have far too good an opinion of myself and decided to give me a tremendous set-down. She did this by reminding me that you are in remarkably good health for an older man, and, in the event of my untimely demise, would have no difficulty marrying again and producing a new heir to take my place."

"Did she, indeed? Miss Whittaker appears to be a formidable young lady. It happens, however, that I am not in the least susceptible to the charms of green girls."

"I am relieved to hear you say so. But Miss Whittaker was only trying to annoy me."

The earl suddenly straightened up in his chair and gave a crack of laughter.

"Now I know where I have seen the chit before," he exclaimed. "That day in the hospital—"

"Yes. She brought me food and tried to make me eat it, but I was drunk and took my cursed bad temper out on her. Lord, her eyes are magnificent when she is angry."

The earl gave him a straight look.

"My son, you are not contemplating a flirtation with the girl, are you?" he asked, his expression stern.

"Why do you ask?"

"The betting books at White's are giving six-to-one odds old Omersley comes up to scratch. That possibility is the only thing holding Annabelle Whittaker's creditors at bay. You'll do the girl no good by making her dissatisfied with her lot."

"So Miss Whittaker will be sold to the highest bidder," Alexander mused.

"It is the way of the world," said the earl with a shrug. "She won't be the first girl to solve her family's financial problems with a judicious marriage, and she won't be the last. Vanessa Whittaker is a pretty young female and I wish her well in finding a husband more suited to her age and inclination, so long as it isn't you."

"I thought you were anxious to see me married."

"I am, to a young lady of the proper background. A bride whose mother rents a ramshackle house in Hans Crescent during the season and spends the rest of the year in the country hiding out from her creditors can hardly be an asset to your political career."

"Ah," Alexander said. "And I suppose you have several suitable young ladies in mind for the honor of becoming Viscountess Blakely?"

"Several," the earl agreed. "I presented two of them to you at Almack's, but you weren't paying attention."

"If it gives you any satisfaction, Miss Whittaker already has taken me to task for my boorish behavior in neglecting to dance with all the wallflowers at the ball. She had the effrontery to tell me she'd heard me compared to Lord Byron, but she couldn't see it herself, 'for Lord Byron is generally perceived to be excessively handsome.' "

Alexander gave his father a wry smile, but Stoneham was not amused.

"She's pretty enough," the earl acknowledged. "But that kind of attraction doesn't last, I assure you."

"You forget, I am going back to war," Alexander pointed out. "This is hardly the time for me to be thinking of bridals. Nor have I any intention of making a cake of myself over Miss Whittaker's big blue eyes."

The earl looked about to take exception to Alexander's mention of returning to war, then seemed to think better of it.

"Excellent," Stoneham said, favoring his son with an insincere smile. "Another glass of claret, Alexander?"

The street was clogged with carriages on the day of Lady Mabberley's "at home," and many of the highborn ladies were so impatient to see firsthand what horrors the young countess had wrought that they compromised their dignity so far as to abandon their carriages, take to the streets, and walk to the front door.

Letitia was among them and minced down the street in her thin muslin gown and fashionable slippers with a handsome gentleman on each arm.

"My dear Letitia, how *do* you talk us into these things?" the earl asked in a tone of long-suffering.

She gave him a smug little smile in answer, but it hardened on her lips when she saw that they were about to overtake Annabelle and Vanessa Whittaker.

Alexander stifled a chuckle at Letitia's frown when the earl very kindly addressed a remark to the younger lady. His aunt positively gritted her teeth when Vanessa asked the earl about his famous collection of chess sets from all over the world.

"Papa taught me to play chess when I was very small," Vanessa said. No doubt with visions of coronets dancing in her head, Annabelle Whittaker lost no time in suggesting that perhaps a chess match between her daughter and the earl might be arranged in the near future.

Letitia nudged Alexander and gave him a speaking look, plainly expecting him to disengage his father from Vanessa's clutches.

Since Alex knew Letitia persisted in her ridiculous notion that Vanessa was determined to captivate Stoneham, he stepped between Vanessa and the earl with a word of apology. By now they had entered the hall of the townhouse and stood shoulder to shoulder with Lady Mabberley's other guests like so many pickled fish in a barrel.

"I hope you are enjoying your stay in London, Miss Whittaker," Alexander said to Vanessa.

"Do you?" she replied, looking skeptical. "That is very kind of you, Captain Logan." He noticed that her eyelids looked puffy and she was a little pale. No doubt this was the inevitable result of staying up late at *ton* parties every night.

"Vanessa, *there* you are!" a voice called from behind them. "I am so glad to see you. I wanted to tell you—"

"Just a moment, Diana," Vanessa said. "I think I can just squeeze past . . ."

It wasn't difficult for the slender Vanessa to insinuate herself between the waiting guests and join her friend some distance away.

"Vanessa!" squeaked Mrs. Whittaker in alarm. "Where are you?"

"Over here, Mother," Vanessa's voice answered from somewhere to the left.

She was out of sight, however, and her mother showed every sign of being about to have a fit of the vapors if Vanessa wasn't restored to her at once. The distraught lady hardly could be abandoned at such a moment, so Cedric and Letitia were forced to stand their ground and reassure Annabelle Whittaker that her precious daughter wasn't being torn limb from limb in the crush of bodies.

Alexander reluctantly shouldered his way in the direction from which the troublesome chit's voice had come.

Soon he was separated from his party and had lost his quarry as well.

The sea of visitors threatened to sweep Alexander on up the stairs and into the presence of the host and hostess. He fought against the tide and made for the spot where Vanessa Whittaker had melted into the crowd.

* * *

It is going to be a bad one, Vanessa thought in despair.

She had wedged herself into a corner of the room and was leaning against the wall with her head back and her eyes closed. Every movement made the pounding in her head grow worse. Please God, Diana would find her mother before the pain reduced her to helpless sobs.

"I know just how you feel," a deep, sympathetic male voice said in her ear as the man's large, warm hand touched her arm. "There is something about green and fuchsia stripes that makes one feel quite bilious."

She flinched and opened one eye.

Oh, sweet heaven! Not *him!* Not now!

"I warn you, Captain Logan," she said, closing both eyes again, "that if you don't go away this instant I am likely to be violently sick all over you."

"Well, that is original, at least," he said.

Her eyes flew open just as an off-balance bystander brushed against Captain Logan, almost catapulting him into Vanessa. The captain gallantly stationed himself in front of her and braced his arms against the wall on each side of her shoulders to shield her from the crowd's jostling.

"What is that supposed to mean?" she asked, disconcerted by the closeness of his powerful body. The subtle aroma of bay rum made her head swim.

"I seem to have the most extraordinary effect on females," he explained. "Usually, though, they merely pretend to faint in my arms, which is a great nuisance because of my leg injury—"

"I suppose I cannot stop you from standing there," she said through gritted teeth, "but *must* you be so odious?"

"Have no fear, Miss Whittaker," he replied with maddening cheerfulness. "No one will learn from me that you were perfectly well only a few moments ago. I haven't the least objection to humoring a lovely lady if she takes a notion to relieve the tedium of a dashed boring party with a few harmless theatrics. Is this little performance being

staged for the benefit of any gentleman in particular? Shall
I go away before I spoil sport?"

Vanessa squeezed her eyes tightly shut again as her
breath caught on a little gasp of pain. How could he think
she would employ such vulgar methods to call attention
to herself? But then, what else would a gentleman of Captain Logan's station expect of a shameless fortune hunter?
To her humiliation, she felt a hot tear slide down her
cheek.

"You really are ill," her companion exclaimed, sounding
remorseful.

"How *very* astute of you, Captain," she said without
opening her eyes.

"Forgive me, I thought . . ."

The scent of bay rum grew stronger, and Vanessa could
feel the gentle touch of his fingers on her chin as he
turned her face up to his. His thumb brushed the wetness
at her cheek. She opened her eyes to see him regarding
her with a concerned expression on his face.

Embarrassed, she averted her eyes from his scrutiny in
time to see Diana elbow her way past an affronted gentleman to join them.

"Vanessa," the breathless girl said, "I couldn't find your
mother in this crush—oh, Captain Logan!"

"What is wrong with her?" he asked Diana. He steadied
the blonde girl to keep her from crashing into Vanessa
when an impatient matron barreled past them.

"It is one of her headaches," Diana explained. "She
used to suffer quite dreadfully from them when we were
at school. Oh, Vanessa, is it very bad?"

"No," Vanessa lied.

Captain Logan turned away from them for an instant to
look over the sea of heads from his superior height.

"The outside door is a good twenty feet away from
here," he said, returning his attention to his companions.
"It might as well be twenty miles."

He sighed and slid his arm around Vanessa's waist.

"What are you doing?" she squeaked in surprise.

"Getting you out of here," he said as he bent and slipped his other arm under her knees, then lifted her carefully into his arms.

"Oh, thank heaven," Vanessa said fervently. She closed her eyes and rested her pounding head against his chest. She could hear him talking to Diana.

"Miss, ah—"

"Diana Lacey," her friend supplied.

"Miss Lacey, will you be all right here, or do you want to come with us?"

"It would be a shame not to see the rest of the house now that I'm here, and my mother will have an apoplexy if I leave without telling her," the girl said. "I'll just go and see if I can find Vanessa's mother, shall I, and tell her what happened?"

"Yes, do that," he said. "Tell her I am taking Miss Whittaker home in a hackney. And if Lord Stoneham and Lady Letitia are still with her, would you be so kind as to tell them I will see them at home?"

"Of course, Captain Logan," Diana said.

Vanessa felt her rescuer's muscles flex as he plunged into the crowd, and she clung to him in panic as the jostling hordes nearly tore her from his arms.

"You needn't strangle me," he said mildly. "I promise not to drop you."

"What about your injured leg?" she said, remembering his war wound. "Perhaps you should put me down—"

"Don't be absurd," he snapped as he forged a path to the chaos of the street.

From behind them an awed female voice said, "Ooooh, isn't he dashing?"

When the captain made a rude sound under his breath, Vanessa couldn't suppress a giggle. But it turned into a little sob at the end.

"Steady on, my girl," he said in a bracing tone.

FOUR

Vanessa refused to let Alexander carry her into the shabby house on Hans Crescent after he carefully helped her down from the carriage. But when she walked up the front steps to the entrance, she held her head as if it were made of glass and she feared it might shatter at the slightest vibration.

The plump young lady who opened the door took one look at Vanessa's pale, strained face and held out her arms to enfold her in a maternal embrace.

"Oh, my poor dear," she said sympathetically. "Not another one!"

"Don't fuss, Lydia," Vanessa said in a thread of a voice.

"Who are you?" the girl called Lydia asked bluntly, her eyes narrowing at the sight of Alexander standing behind Vanessa. She wore a cheap, obviously homemade muslin gown, and her light brown hair was dressed very simply. But Alex would have known at once that she was no servant, even if her only claim to beauty hadn't been a pair of remarkable dark blue eyes that were a dead match for Vanessa's.

"Lydia! Captain Logan was kind enough to bring me home from Lady Mabberley's reception. I don't know what happened to Mother. Captain Logan, this is my sister, Lydia—"

"Never mind that," Lydia said, ignoring Alexander. "You shall come and lie down in your room, Vanessa. And

I shall keep the girls from pestering you until you are better."

"It's not so bad," Vanessa protested.

"That's the second one this month," Lydia said. "I *told* Mama she was driving you too hard."

"Perhaps I should send for a doctor," Alexander suggested.

"Good gracious, no!" Lydia exclaimed, shocked. "Mama would eat me alive if I wasted good money on the doctor for one of Vanessa's headaches! Not that the old quack would come, anyway. We haven't paid him yet for Aggie's putrid sore throat."

"Vanny! Vanny!" shouted a high-pitched voice from the other room. It heralded the arrival of a tiny girl of about six years old who pelted into the room and would have thrown herself at Vanessa if Lydia hadn't stopped her.

"Don't, Aggie," Lydia said reprovingly. "Can't you see Vanessa is ill?"

"Oh, I'm sorry," the little girl said. "Does your head hurt again?"

"Vanny!" shouted a slightly older girl from the doorway. "Did you bring us any of those little cakes from the reception?"

"No, Amy-love. I'm sorry," Vanessa said. Her voice ended on an involuntary gasp of pain.

"That's enough!" Lydia snapped. "Both of you, go into the parlor to take tea with Mary Ann and Sally. I shall join you as soon as I have tucked Vanessa into bed."

"Who are you?" Aggie asked Alex curiously.

"Captain Alexander Logan, at your service," he said, bending to take the child's small hand in his. It appeared his aunt was right, and Vanessa was the most "presentable" of her sisters. But there was something very appealing about the child's bright, intelligent eyes and sweet expression. "And you are?"

"Agatha Whittaker, but everyone calls me Aggie."

"And my name is Amy," said the other little girl, making a bid for the stranger's attention.

"It is a pleasure to meet you," he said, shaking Amy's hand as well.

"Are you a guest, Captain Logan?" Aggie asked, her face lighting up. "Because if you are, we can have macaroons!"

Lydia started to protest, but the hopeful looks on her two little sisters' faces apparently caused her to soften.

"Certainly you are welcome to join us for a cup of tea if you wish, Captain," Lydia said. She spoiled the effect of this gracious speech by adding in a disastrously audible undervoice to Vanessa, "It will serve Mama right to have her precious macaroons wasted on a mere scarlet coat."

"Lydia," said Vanessa, sounding embarrassed.

"Come along, love," Lydia said, leading Vanessa away. "Take the captain into the parlor, girls. He hasn't bolted yet, so I suppose he means to stay."

"Yes, Lydia," the children chorused. Each took one of Alexander's hands and ushered him into the shabbily furnished parlor.

There he recognized Sally as the middle-aged servant who had accompanied Vanessa's mother to the hospital when he was just returned from Spain. He was introduced to Mary Ann, a shy adolescent, and seated, at their loud insistence, between the two younger girls.

All the sisters wore similar muslin gowns, inexpertly constructed in various pastel hues, but someone with more taste than skill had tried to brighten the younger girls' dresses with colorful grosgrain ribbons.

From the looks of the table set up in the parlor, slices of plain bread accompanied by a plate of butter comprised the children's afternoon meal when no visitors were expected. When Sally was dispatched to the kitchen to fetch the macaroons, Vanessa's sisters got down to the serious business of entertaining their visitor.

"I like you. Are you going to marry Vanessa?" Aggie asked, interrupting her elder sister's laborious attempt at polite conversation about the likelihood of the fine weather continuing through the week.

"Stoopid!" Amy said with worldly scorn before Alex

could think of a reply to Aggie's artless question. "Mama said Vanessa has to marry that old Lord Omersley or we will have to go back to the country and die old maids."

"*I* am not going to be an old maid!" Aggie said, her eyes glittering with childish defiance. "I am going to wear beautiful dresses made by Madame Celeste and go to parties all the time, just like Vanessa."

"Mama says if Lord Omersley doesn't offer for Vanessa soon, she won't be able to bring any of us back to London to find husbands," Amy pointed out. "I'd rather have a pony, anyway."

"Stop it, both of you," Mary Ann hissed at her sisters. "Will you have milk or sugar in your tea, Captain Logan?" she added to their guest.

"Neither, thank you," Alex said, accepting the cup of plain tea the girl offered.

Sally returned with the macaroons and set them on the table just as Lydia entered the room and seated herself next to Mary Ann. The smaller girls looked at the plate of macaroons hungrily, but didn't reach for it until after Lydia offered the plate to Alex. The girls each took a macaroon when the plate was passed to them, but eyed the remaining treats jealously.

"Have you been to war?" asked Aggie, tugging on Alex's coat for attention.

"Yes," he replied. "I was wounded, so I came back to England on a ship."

"Is it very exciting to go to war?" Amy asked, impressed.

"Very," he said after a slight hesitation.

"Is it true," Aggie asked in a small voice, "that Napoleon eats English children for breakfast?"

"I believe he prefers sweet biscuits with chocolate," Alex replied with a straight face.

"So do I," Aggie said with a sigh, "but Mama makes us have porridge."

"How is Miss Whittaker?" Alexander asked Lydia when the children stopped asking questions long enough for him to get a word in.

"She is resting in a dark room with a vinegar-soaked handkerchief on her forehead," Lydia said. "It's the only thing that helps. I can't understand why Mama did not accompany Vanessa home."

"The reception was such a squeeze that Miss Whittaker was separated from your mother, and she looked so ill I thought it best to bring her home in a hackney at once, leaving word for Mrs. Whittaker."

"It was very kind of you to go to such trouble," Lydia said.

"It was no trouble at all," Alex replied. "It was a *very* boring party, I'm afraid."

Lydia exchanged a look with Mary Ann, and both regarded him through narrowed eyes.

"Perhaps you have heard," Lydia said in a cautious tone, "that Lord Omersley is expected to offer for my sister in the near future."

"I have heard something to that effect, yes," Alex said, equally cautious.

"Do you make a long stay in London, Captain Logan?"

"Only until I receive permission to return to my regiment," he said.

Lydia looked relieved, and the conversation returned to general topics. All but the last macaroon had been eaten by the little girls and Alex was about to take his leave when Vanessa entered the room.

She had exchanged her fashionable muslin gown for one similar to those worn by her sisters. She was smiling, but her expression still was a little strained.

"We saved a macaroon for you, Vanny!" Aggie said.

"Thank you, love," Vanessa said, ruffling her little sister's curls, "but I am not hungry. Perhaps you and Amy would like to share it."

The little girls immediately pounced on the macaroon, broke it in half, and devoured it.

"Are you certain you should be out of bed, Van?" asked Mary Ann in concern.

"I am better now," Vanessa said, her eyes on Alexander.

"I am glad," he said, standing. He shook hands with Lydia, Mary Ann, and, to their obvious delight, the younger girls. "Thank you for allowing me to take tea with you. I enjoyed it very much."

"Will you come again one day?" asked Aggie.

"I should like that," he said, smiling down at her. He turned to shake hands with Vanessa.

"Good day, Miss Whittaker," he said, almost afraid to touch her. She still had that fragile look about her.

"Thank you for seeing me home, Captain Logan," she said softly.

"It was my pleasure."

He left the house, greatly disturbed by the evidence of poverty he saw there. Vanessa, he knew, was a fortune hunter. There was no getting around that. But for the first time it occurred to Alexander that a fortune hunter could be a victim as well as a predator.

The following morning, a dainty bouquet of violets tied with silver ribbons arrived at the Whittaker residence. Vanessa felt a flush stain her cheeks as she buried her nose in the fragrant blossoms. She didn't need to see the carelessly scrawled signature on the card to know who sent them. Lord Omersley's floral tributes invariably consisted of ostentatious bouquets of roses and orchids. Nor would her elderly suitor have bothered to send along a basket of hothouse oranges for her mother and sisters.

Vanessa turned away as her sisters squealed in delight at the extravagant treat. Her mother's raptures made a painful lump rise in her throat.

How kind of Captain Logan.

And how cruel.

FIVE

Alexander was in a fine, flaring temper when he stormed into his father's study and slammed the door behind him.

"Good morning, Alexander," the earl said with a sigh, looking up from his newspaper. "Do sit down and stop glowering at me as if you long to plant me a facer. You won't, you know. Letitia and I may have done an abysmal job of rearing you after your mother died, but even *you* never would be guilty of such a solecism."

Alexander sat down in the armchair on the other side of the desk and stretched his long legs out in front of him. Only the fury in his eyes belied his negligent pose.

Cedric sighed again.

"I suppose this means you have been to the war office and been refused passage on the next government transport," the earl said. "Surely you are not surprised. Did you think I would not learn that you had applied for transportation back to Spain?"

"Do you have *any* idea what a ridiculous position you have put me in?" Alexander demanded. "You reared me to be a *man*, Cedric. Stand aside and let me act as one."

"No!" the earl exploded, pounding the desk with his fist for emphasis. "Do *you* have any idea what it was like for Letitia and me every time the dispatches with the lists of the war dead arrived from the Continent?"

"Oh, yes. The precious succession," Alexander said, his tone cynical. "How *could* I have forgotten?"

"There are more than enough nobodies in England to provide cannon fodder for that bloody Corsican without adding my only son to their number. What is your paltry contribution to the war effort compared with the potential destruction of one of the proudest names in England?"

"And what noble occupation do you suggest I pursue in London," Alexander asked through gritted teeth, "while another man assumes my responsibilities with my regiment? I have done nothing but visit my tailor, drink Blue Ruin, play cards, and defend myself from matchmaking mamas since I came home, and I am heartily sick of it."

"You are *not* going back," Cedric said. "The subject is not open for discussion, Alexander."

"I could take a mistress, I suppose," Alexander said, looking thoughtful. "I haven't done that yet. Someone expensive and shallow probably would suit me best. If I am to follow in your footsteps, it is time I acquired your tastes."

"See here, boy," Stoneham snarled. No one could make the earl lose his temper faster than his own son. "Don't take that tone with me! If you had any sense at all of what you owe your name, you would go to Almack's next week, find yourself a bride, and settle down to the business of setting up your nursery. You would have little trouble walking off with the best of the lot if you took the least trouble to exert yourself."

"Why should I waste my time with Almack's?" Alexander said, his voice dripping with sarcasm. "Just have Letitia invite all the eager debutantes to a ball in this house. I am such a splendid catch that they will beat a path to your door, so dazzled by the prospect of becoming the future Countess of Stoneham that they'll have not the slightest objection to being lined up at midnight in the ballroom so I can take my pick of them. Maybe we should have them come masked. More sporting, don't you think?"

When Cedric didn't answer, Alexander gave his sire a look of disgust and left the room.

The earl sat at his desk and frowned for a moment after Alexander's departure. Then he gave a bark of laughter.

"Capital idea, my son," he said. "That's just what we'll do."

"It will be just like the ball in *Cinderella,*" Diana Lacey exclaimed. Her eyes danced as she shared the latest *on dit* with Vanessa over a strawberry Italian ice at Gunter's. "I wonder if we'll all wear masks, or if Lady Letitia was just funning Mama."

The Earl of Stoneham was hosting a ball at his town-house, ostensibly to celebrate his son's recovery from his battle wounds. But Lady Letitia had whispered in confidence to a dozen of her very closest friends that the real purpose of the ball was to gather all of the *ton's* eligible ladies under one roof so Captain Logan could choose a bride from among them. Predictably enough, the news had spread like wildfire.

"I would have thought that even Captain Logan could not be so lacking in sensibility, but it appears I was mistaken," Vanessa said, stirring the slushy wreckage of her ice with savage little thrusts of her spoon. "Who does he think he is?"

"The Earl of Stoneham's heir, of course," answered Diana, taking the question literally. "*Everyone* will be there. Do you think he really is going to line us up and pick a bride from among us at midnight?"

"Just like a prize bull inspecting a herd of heifers," Vanessa said.

"I thought you liked him," Diana said, sounding surprised. "If he had swept *me* up in his arms and carried me out of Lady Mabberley's townhouse, I would have swooned from sheer ecstasy. Everyone was talking about it the next day."

"It meant nothing," Vanessa said, ignoring the painful lump that threatened to rise in her throat. "Pray don't say anything more about it."

"I won't, if you don't wish it," Diana said. "But I would be terribly envious if you weren't one of my closest friends. Did he kiss you?"

"Certainly not!"

"Oh," said Diana, disappointed. Then she brightened. "I can't decide. Shall I wear my white taffeta with the silver net overskirt to the ball at Stoneham House or the ivory muslin with the blue ribbons?"

"I'm sure I don't care," Vanessa snapped.

How Vanessa's mother had gloated over the cream-colored vellum invitation from Stoneham House! Annabelle refused to listen to Vanessa's impassioned arguments in favor of declining. She never had left off boasting to her acquaintances about the violets and oranges Alexander had sent to the house. Vanessa had been covered with shame the day she and her mother encountered Lady Letitia while shopping on Conduit Street. Annabelle had hinted so broadly for an invitation to the ball that Captain Logan's aunt had been left with no choice but to promise her one.

Vanessa marveled that Diana appeared to be looking forward to the ball with such anticipation. Did she not understand that the arrogant Captain Logan was making a May-game of them all?

It was all she could do to be civil to Diana and the other young ladies they encountered in the shops when they *would* prose on and on about Captain Logan's manly physique, handsome face, and dark, wicked eyes.

Such foolishness! Vanessa couldn't wait to escape from the silly creatures and their irritating chatter. But worse awaited her at home.

"Oh, Vanessa! It would exceed all my hopes to see you become a countess," her mother said with a dreamy glance at the invitation that afternoon when Vanessa returned from her outing with her friend. Annabelle had taken to carrying the thing around with her as if it were some sort of talisman. "*That* would make all those disobliging tradesmen look no-how!"

"You are aiming at the moon, Mother," Vanessa protested.

"Nonsense," Annabelle said with an airy wave of her hand. "He sent you violets just last week. And oranges for the girls. He is ingratiating himself with your family, don't you see?"

Annabelle paused for a moment, then added, "Of course, we shall have to be diplomatic. It wouldn't do to discourage Lord Omersley, for we may yet have need of him."

"Oh, Mother," Vanessa said with a despairing sigh.

"All Captain Logan is likely to offer Vanessa is a slip on the shoulder, Mother," Lydia said from where she was sitting, heretofore unnoticed, reading a book in the window seat of the parlor. She parted the curtains and stepped into the room to face her mother. "He is too handsome. Too rich. Too . . . everything. Why should he *marry* Vanessa? She won't stand the chance of a kitten against a tiger if he decides to amuse himself at her expense."

"Lydia, how dare you!" Annabelle exclaimed, shocked. "Your sister is a lady. And Captain Logan is a gentleman."

"Well, I don't care. Have you seen the way he *looks* at her?"

"I am sure," Annabelle pointed out, "that there is nothing improper in a young man's admiration for a pretty young lady. I was with you that day we encountered Captain Logan in the park, and I saw nothing at all amiss with his behavior."

"Hah! I fancy the big bad wolf had just such a look in his eye before he ate Red Riding Hood's grandmama," Lydia scoffed. "You had better keep Vanessa out of Captain Logan's way if you don't want to see her end up as his *chère amie.*"

"Lydia," Vanessa whispered, feeling her face flame with embarrassment. *"Don't* please!"

"You are simply jealous of your sister's beauty," Annabelle said, turning on Lydia with fire in her eyes.

"That probably is true," said Lydia, outwardly unmoved

by this accusation. "But it is quite beside the point. The Earl of Stoneham would move heaven and earth to prevent his heir from making such a misalliance, and you know it. If anyone gets hurt, it will be Vanessa."

"Jealous and spiteful *and* ungrateful," Annabelle said, thrusting out her lower lip in a pout. "Don't listen to her, Vanessa. Where would we be, I ask you, if I had not hit upon this scheme of coming to London? Still in the country growing potatoes and . . . *cabbages!* I did it for you—*all* of you."

"But it is Vanessa, and not *you,* who will have to marry Lord Omersley," Lydia pointed out. "We could have managed to live frugally for another three years on what this single season in London is costing us. I would have taken a post as governess. Vanessa would have been perfectly content to marry some nice young man of good family from the neighborhood and eventually you would have found husbands for the other girls besides. I'm not saying it would have been easy, but we *could* have gotten by without selling Vanessa to that beastly old man. Now it is too late."

Annabelle's face crumpled.

"All I ever wanted was the best for my girls," she sobbed.

"Mother!" cried Vanessa, putting her arms around her mother's shoulders. "Don't cry. Lydia doesn't mean it."

Vanessa exchanged a helpless look with her sister over their mother's bowed head. Lydia bit her lower lip and fled from the room.

"Don't cry, please," Vanessa said to her mother. "Everything will be all right." She closed her eyes tiredly. "It will have to be," she whispered.

Vanessa knew Lydia was right. Lord Stoneham would have his only son drugged and transported to China before he'd let him marry Vanessa. Lord Omersley was her only choice, and she steeled herself to meet her fate with dignity. The wealth and position Vanessa would know as Lady Omersley meant nothing to her. But when weighed against the possibility of seeing her mother imprisoned in

Fleet Street Prison for failure to pay her debts, or her little sisters thrown on the mercy of the parish, the sacrifice of Vanessa's future happiness seemed the only choice.

At half past ten on the night of the ball at Stoneham House, Vanessa looked down at the torn hem of her favorite blue muslin gown in dismay and, being a well brought up young lady, brushed aside Lord Omersley's apologies for having trod upon it.

"It is quite all right, my lord," she said, grateful, if the truth be told, for an excuse to escape his amorous attentions for a little while. "I shall go repair the damage, if you will excuse me."

Once outside the ballroom, she took a deep breath and looked about her. She wondered how long she could stay away before she was missed. There were too many candles, too many people, too many wilting hothouse flowers blanketing the stale air of the ballroom with their heavy perfume.

But most of all, the ballroom was filled with too many disappointed young ladies smiling and chatting and complimenting one another on their gowns in order to hide the fact that they felt like perfect fools. Captain Logan had demonstrated he was no Prince Charming by failing to show up at his own ball.

Vanessa desperately needed to be alone for a little while and was relieved to find the library deserted. She had repaired her hem with pins from her reticule and was just leaving the room when a hand covered her mouth and a man's arm circled her waist. She struggled, but the man managed to drag her back inside the library. She could hear the door being kicked shut, but she was more angry than frightened.

"Let *go* of me," she said indignantly when the man removed his hand and she whirled to face him, prepared to give him the tongue-lashing he so richly deserved for his outrageous behavior. The words died on her lips when she got a good look at his face.

"It has been a long time, my beautiful Van," her childhood sweetheart said with a disarming smile. His eyes were still as blue as the ocean, and his hair as golden as the sun. He was as handsome as the proverbial Greek god, just as she remembered.

Vanessa scowled at him.

"Not long enough, Gregory. I hear it's *Sir* Gregory now," she said, wresting her arm from his hold and rubbing her flesh as if to remove something unclean from it. "Congratulations," she added in a voice dripping with sarcasm.

Two years ago he had broken her heart, or so she had thought, to marry an heiress whose father's influence was sufficient to earn Gregory a knighthood and advance his career as a diplomat. His engagement was announced an indecently short time after Gregory had come down from university on a family visit and squired Vanessa about the village with every appearance of an infatuated swain. When he had left Yorkshire on that occasion to return to university, he promised Vanessa he would offer for her as soon as he could afford to support a wife. A match between them had been a settled thing between their families for years. At first his letters were frequent and ardent. Then they stopped altogether. The next time she saw Gregory was when he brought his elegant fiancée to Yorkshire to meet his parents.

At the time Vanessa had been certain her life was over, but Vanessa had become quite accustomed to encountering Gregory and his wife, Susan, at parties once she and her family had come to London. While it would be too much to say she was comfortable in Gregory's presence, she could at least meet him in polite company with an outward appearance of civility.

This being confined with him in a private library was another matter entirely, however.

"Don't be angry, Vanessa," Gregory begged, taking her hand. He would have raised it to his lips if she hadn't snatched it away. "I had to speak with you alone and I could think of no other way to arrange it. I followed you when you left the ballroom."

"We have absolutely *nothing* to say to one another," she said coldly. She attempted to walk to the door, but, to her annoyance, he caught her arm and refused to let go.

"Vanessa, my love, you don't know how hard it was for me to give you up once I returned to university and realized that marriage to you would have been the death of my ambitions," he declared. "But you haven't been out of my thoughts for a moment."

"Gregory," she said, shrinking from him. "It is extremely improper for you to say such things."

"No! Vanessa, listen to me. Ours is strictly a marriage of convenience. Susan goes her way and I go . . . mine," he said huskily, pulling Vanessa into his arms.

"Unhand me at *once*, you idiot!" Vanessa demanded as she pushed her hands against his chest and dodged his determined attempt to kiss her.

"Don't be coy, my darling," he said, trying in vain to turn her face up to his. "I know you are as good as promised to Omersley, but I can't bear the thought of his clumsy hands all over you. Come to me instead. We were *meant* to be together."

"Are you *mad*?"

"You don't understand. I am a rich man now. I can afford to buy you all the lovely gowns and jewels your beauty deserves. I know I hurt you when I married Susan, but I would like to make it up to you."

"*Would* you, indeed?" Vanessa said, furious now. She shoved him hard as he made another grab for her. "And *I* would like to box your ears! Now, stop that at once! I refuse to be mauled in this ridiculous fashion."

"I shall set you up in a little house near Brighton for the summer," he vowed, undiscouraged. "You can have your own carriage . . ."

Vanessa was angry enough to do murder.

"God, you inflame me when your eyes shoot fire," he said.

Vanessa slapped his face hard when he reached for her again.

Alexander, who had heard raised voices as he passed the library, decided to investigate when he heard a woman's voice cry out in outrage. He opened the door just in time to see Vanessa slap Sir Gregory Banbridge's smirking face, and Alexander caught Vanessa's shoulders in his hands when she would have run past him and out of the room. He stepped into the library, walking her backward, then reached behind him with one hand to shut the door. With the other hand, he kept a firm hold on Vanessa.

"Please, let me go," she whispered.

Seeing her distress, Alexander faced Sir Gregory with a murderous glare.

"What did you say to her?" he asked with deadly calm.

"See here, Captain Logan. I hardly think that is any business of yours," Sir Gregory said in a tone of hauteur. "This was a private conversation before you barged in."

"I want to know what you said to a well-bred young lady that would cause her to slap your face," Alexander demanded.

"Come now, Captain Logan," Sir Gregory said in a tone of false *bonhomie*. "We are both men of the world. Miss Whittaker and I are friends of long-standing, if you take my meaning. It was a simple disagreement and, I repeat, none of your concern."

Alexander looked at Vanessa, who appeared to be trembling from sheer rage. Cupping her chin, he turned her face up to his.

"What did he say to you, Miss Whittaker?" Alexander asked her.

She turned her face away. Her heightened color told him all he needed to know.

"As bad as all that, is it?" he said softly.

Vanessa made a small, inarticulate sound of embarrassment.

Alexander turned to Sir Gregory, wishing he could tear the bounder limb from limb.

"I would suggest," he said to the diplomat, "that you make some excuse to your wife and remove yourself from this house without delay."

"Ah, I begin to see," Sir Gregory said, sneering. "It appears the innocent girl I knew in Yorkshire is on the hunt for more worthy prey than a mere bureaucrat. Well done, Vanessa."

"Out," Alexander barked.

"He won't marry you, either, you know. Or perhaps you don't care," was Sir Gregory's parting shot at Vanessa. "You would have been better off with me. At least *I* wouldn't have tired of you within a twelvemonth."

Alexander took a threatening step toward him, and the golden-haired young man quit the room with rather more haste than dignity, giving Alexander a wide berth as he went out the door.

"There, now," Alexander said soothingly to Vanessa as he returned his attention to the task of comforting her. He had to remind himself that it would be excessively bad form to force his attentions on the shaken girl after chasing off the cad who had so distressed her. Before he knew what he was doing, he had taken Vanessa in his arms. But after a quick hug, he gave her a brotherly pat on the back and had every intention of releasing her before she could interpret his attempt to console her as an ungentlemanly advance. "He won't trouble you again, at least not this night."

Vanessa looked up, managed to smile, then, to Alexander's astonishment, burst into tears. Alexander held her close and waited for the storm to subside.

"He offered to buy me a house in Brighton," she sobbed, when she could speak. "And a . . . *carriage!* He acted as if I should be *grateful.*"

"It's all right, love," Alexander said, reaching into his

pocket for a clean handkerchief and passing it to her. "Nothing happened, after all."

Vanessa blew her nose and glared at him.

"Nothing *happened*? The man offered to set me up as his mistress!"

"I agree it is very bad," Alexander said, "but you are so beautiful the silly gudgeon probably just lost his head."

"Don't try to humor me, Captain Logan. Gregory has known me for most of my life, and he thinks I am a *whore*. I can well imagine what the rest of London thinks."

"Miss Whittaker—"

"Did you think I would not learn of the bets placed at White's? I suppose the fine gentlemen of the *ton* think a woman willing to marry an elderly peer for the sake of her family's financial security would be willing to do *anything* for money. Gregory was hardly the first to approach me with such an offer. Why do you look so surprised?"

"My poor girl," he said, genuinely sorry. "I had no idea."

"Well, it is no more than I deserve, I suppose," she said. "It is hardly a secret that I came to London to contract an advantageous marriage. Unlike Gregory, however, I intend to be faithful to the person I marry for money."

Her expression was so bleak that Alexander wanted to take her in his arms again. But before he could do so, the earl opened the door, entered the room, and closed the door behind him.

"Ah, Alexander," he said, raising his eyebrows. "Where the devil have you been?"

"You are fortunate to see me at all," Alexander said, his voice cool. "I had determined not to come, but before I hoisted my first bottle of Blue Ruin at the Daffy Club, it occurred to me that Aunt Letitia would suffer far more humiliation than you would if I failed to attend. So, here I am. The prodigal son returned."

"You are impertinent, Alexander," the earl said. "I am certain Miss Whittaker would agree with me that you have neglected our guests most shamefully."

Vanessa looked in dismay from one to the other. She began inching toward the door, obviously bent on escape, but Captain Logan stopped her by catching her hand in his.

"Have I been an arrogant coxcomb again, Miss Whittaker?" Alexander asked, smiling to show her he was teasing.

"Yes, I am afraid so, Captain Logan," she said.

"Well, then, my dear," he said, offering her his arm, "let us go to the ballroom so I may make amends." He turned back to his father with a travesty of courtesy that made the earl visibly grind his teeth. Alexander could well imagine what the earl thought of finding the last young lady on earth he would welcome as a daughter-in-law alone in the library with his son. He almost laughed in his father's affronted face. "Will you join us, Cedric?"

"I suppose so," he snapped, following them.

After Captain Logan had escorted Vanessa back to the ballroom and stood talking with her and her mother for a moment, he behaved charmingly to all the young ladies and danced with as many of them as possible before midnight with every appearance of enjoyment.

"He said it is all a hum," Diana reported as she stopped to chat with Vanessa after her own turn on the floor with Captain Logan.

To each of his partners the earl's son had joked about the ridiculous rumor that he intended to choose one of them as his bride at midnight, intimating that with so many delightful ladies present it would take him long past the witching hour to make such a difficult decision.

The result was that the same young ladies who had been grumbling about his beastly manners earlier in the evening were now convinced he was the most handsome and charming man in London.

Vanessa tortured herself by watching him flirt with all of the other debutantes. Had she once twitted him for standing at the side of the ballroom, refusing to dance?

She was being punished for it now as she watched him squire a succession of radiant young ladies onto the dance floor. Vanessa told herself that she had no earthly reason to be piqued. He had stood up with her for one set of dances. But he relinquished her to Lord Omersley afterward with quite unflattering willingness.

"Are you ready to go, Vanessa?" her mother said, breaking into her thoughts. "It is rather late."

"Yes," Vanessa agreed, accepting the wrap Lord Omersley held out to her. She cast a backward look toward Captain Logan, who was laughing down into the eyes of his partner. "It is."

SIX

On Thursday, two days after the ball at Stoneham House, Lord Omersley gave Annabelle and Vanessa Whittaker the cut direct during the fashionable hour of the promenade in Hyde Park.

Any lingering hope that this public insult could be attributed to a defect in the aging peer's eyesight was laid to rest on Friday, when the Whittaker ladies learned that the betting book at White's was now giving six-to-one odds *against* Lord Omersley's offering for Vanessa before the Season was over.

On Saturday, Diana Lacey sent a note to Vanessa explaining that her mother had forbidden her to visit her friend again for fear of damage by association to Diana's reputation. The missive was blotched with tears.

Determined to present a brave face to the world, the Whittaker ladies put on their finest feathers and went off on Saturday afternoon to call at the homes of several of their acquaintances.

Not one of their so-called friends was at home to visitors.

By Monday morning, several ribald tales about Vanessa's amorous liaisons with various gentlemen were being spread all over London. Vanessa knew at once Sir Gregory Banbridge was behind the gossip, for he had made it clear the night of the ball at Stoneham House that he wasn't about to take her rejection in the manner of a gentleman.

Just after noon, a merchant attempted to storm the

house on Hans Crescent in order to search the ladies' bou-
doirs for several pairs of fashionable slippers for which he
had not yet received payment. Only Lydia's energetic
wielding of a broomstick was effective in convincing the
man to leave.

The post came and went without leaving a single invitation.

The afternoon came and went without the arrival of a
single visitor.

Annabelle Whittaker attempted to buy a pair of gloves
at a fashionable shop and was refused credit.

On Tuesday, the landlord threatened to evict the Whittaker family if the past due rent was not paid at once. Mrs.
Whittaker had been obliged to pay the man a portion of
the rent to get him to go away again, with a promise to
pay the balance of what was owed in the near future.

The necessity of retaining the roof over their heads sadly
depleted their cash reserves, so that by the time Madame
Celeste demanded immediate payment for Vanessa's wardrobe on Wednesday, the Whittaker ladies were in despair.

Alexander was playing cards at White's when Sir Gregory
Banbridge sauntered into the room, hailed several of his
cronies, seated himself at another table, and accepted a
glass of brandy.

"Did you hear the tale Sir Gregory was telling the other
night about the little Whittaker filly?" Alexander's partner
asked.

"Yes," Alex said. His tone was not encouraging.

"It seems he and the fair Vanessa grew up together in
Yorkshire, and—"

"I've heard it," Alex growled, deliberately trumping his
partner's ace.

"Blast it, Logan! What did you do that for?" the man
complained.

Alexander got up and walked to the table where Sir Gregory was making up a very funny story of how as a preco-

cious schoolgirl Vanessa Whittaker seduced him during his
lusty youth in her father's barn.

The captain clapped Sir Gregory on the shoulder just
as the diplomat was lifting his glass of brandy to his lips.
The brandy splashed down the front of his victim's waist-
coat, leaving a dark stain on the light fabric.

"See here! Look what you've done!" Sir Gregory sputtered.

"My apologies," Alex said, taking Sir Gregory by the
elbow and hoisting him to his feet. "I'll have a word with
you, if you don't mind, Banbridge."

"What the devil . . ." Sir Gregory didn't get a chance
to finish his sentence because the captain forcibly was ush-
ering him over to a vacant table.

Thrusting the diplomat into a chair, Alex took the chair
opposite and plunked a deck of cards on the table.

"Cut!" he told Sir Gregory.

"I don't want to play—"

"You'll play," Alex growled, "or I'll plant you a facer
right here in the middle of White's."

Sir Gregory had risen halfway from his chair, but now
he sat down again rather abruptly. Gentlemen at neigh-
boring tables started craning their heads in Alexander and
Sir Gregory's direction. Alexander didn't care.

"What is all this about, Captain Logan?" Sir Gregory
asked, adopting a conciliatory tone.

"The lies you've been spreading all over London about
Miss Whittaker. It is the act of an unprincipled snake to
bandy a lady's name about in public just because she
spurned your advances."

"So? I wasn't the only one who had my hands all over
Vanessa Whittaker that night. I saw the way you were *comforting* her. What makes you so certain my reminiscences
about the chit are lies?"

It would have given Alexander great pleasure to tear the
blackguard's filthy tongue out of his throat. Instead, he
was forced to lower his voice to keep from being overheard.

"Vanessa Whittaker is a lady," Alexander said. "Moreover, the lady has no close male relative to protect her good name. You will stop spreading those ridiculous tales at once."

"Why should I? The girl's reputation *will* go to hell in a handbasket if it becomes known *you* are her champion," Sir Gregory said with an ugly sneer on his face. "I'm afraid you are generally perceived as something of a rake, my friend."

"I am no stranger to violence, Banbridge, which is something that you will learn to your peril if you have the effrontery to insinuate that there is anything at all irregular in my dealings with the lady," Alex said in a voice so soft and menacing that Sir Gregory's face blanched despite his bravado. "If you have any sense of self-preservation at all, you will desist in your attempts to discredit Miss Whittaker. Do I make myself clear?"

"Oh, come now," Sir Gregory said in disbelief. "You cannot be threatening me with physical violence over a penniless little fortune hunter."

"That is precisely what I am doing."

"What if I refuse?" Sir Gregory scoffed with an unsteady laugh. "Are you going to call me out?"

"No. You have proven that you are without honor, so I will not settle my grievance with you as I would with another gentleman. Know that if you do not obey me in this matter, I will stalk you all over London until I find you alone. Then I will beat you to a bloody pulp."

Sir Gregory's eyes widened in disbelief.

"See here, Captain Logan!"

"Unlike you, I have not been schooled in diplomacy, Sir Gregory," Alexander said, leaning closer. "I have been schooled in destruction. It is my profession when I am not cooling my heels in London, and I am good at it."

"You're bluffing."

"Am I? Let us just say that I have skills that are not listed on my official *dossier*, and that you inspire me with a strong desire to demonstrate them."

"You are a madman," Sir Gregory breathed. His horrified expression gave Alexander great satisfaction.

"I think we understand one another. Go back to your friends and remember what I have told you."

Alexander's tone was so threatening that Sir Gregory rose with alacrity and left Vanessa Whittaker's would-be champion to stare into the dregs of his glass.

"What was all that about?"

Alexander looked up to see his father standing by the table.

"Join me, by all means," Alexander said with a mocking gesture toward the chair the diplomat had just vacated. Idly, Alexander began shuffling the cards and dealing.

"Banbridge's friends are in high dudgeon because he won't take up the tale he was telling them about the Whittaker girl before you forced him to have your little conversation," the earl said, taking the cards and peering at his hand. Only by the tightening of his fingers on the cards did he reveal his anger. "Am I to understand you have something to do with the man's sudden discretion?"

"I can't very well permit him to ruin the girl's reputation."

"Why not?"

"The lying scum was slandering Vanessa Whittaker because she refused to become his mistress. He was propositioning her when I heard her shouting at him in the library at Stoneham House on the night of the ball. Naturally I went to investigate. He offered her a love nest in Brighton with her own carriage and she slapped his face for him."

"I can't see why. Sounds like a fair bargain to me," the earl said with a shrug. "Don't turn that murderous glare on me, boy. It may have scared the pantaloons off that man-milliner Banbridge, but it doesn't impress me in the least."

"I will thank you to stop talking about Miss Whittaker as if she were some high-priced bird of paradise."

"Make no mistake, Alexander," Stoneham said with cold

deliberation. "You will drop your interest in Miss Whittaker at once, or I shall take steps to remove you from her orbit. I will forgive my heir almost anything, but a misalliance with a provincial little nobody from the wilds of Yorkshire I never will countenance."

"What will you do? Cut off my allowance? Send me to bed with no supper?" Alexander scoffed.

Stoneham slammed down his cards, stood, and walked away.

Alexander stared at the tabletop in moody silence for a little while. Then, after a moment, he began to smile. His motives had been pure enough when he decided to stop Banbridge from bandying Vanessa's name about. The satisfaction of annoying his father was ample reward for this bit of casual gallantry. If the earl demanded his son's presence in London, Alexander was determined he should take little joy of it.

His good humor quite restored, Alexander was perfectly willing to return to the table where his original three companions were talking quietly after having their game so abruptly interrupted by Alexander's desertion. Alexander picked up his cards, which had been lying facedown on the table where he left them, and looked expectantly at his friends. With good-natured shrugs all around, they picked up their own cards and resumed their play. After a moment, one of Alexander's companions said he couldn't help noticing that Alexander and Sir Gregory had been having an argument, and he wondered if Alexander would care to enlighten them.

Alexander made light of the whole affair, saying it was a simple misunderstanding.

As far as Alexander was concerned, he had done all that could reasonably be expected for Vanessa Whittaker. With luck, a new scandal would soon emerge to divert the *ton*, and all the gossip about Vanessa would die down. Then Vanessa could resume her husband-hunting plans. The next time Alexander saw her, she probably would be a fashionable matron with a doting elderly husband and a handful of pretty youngsters.

Alexander took a sip of excellent claret, and it tasted like vinegar in his mouth.

The landlord, odious little man, had returned. This time he insisted he was not about to be fobbed off, and he had been insensitive enough to make his demands in front of the children.

"Mama, will we have to leave London?" asked Amy, worried.

Annabelle gave a helpless little shrug of her shoulders.

"But Captain Logan will not know where to find us!" exclaimed Aggie. For days after Alexander's visit she had made Vanessa extremely uncomfortable by asking her repeatedly when their magnificent visitor would come again.

"What's this about, miss?" the landlord said sternly. "You are as bad as your mother, filling a man's ears with nonsense about all the grand folk she's been rubbing elbows with. Captain Logan, indeed! As if the son of an earl wouldn't have better things to do than to hobnob with the likes of you in Hans Crescent."

"How dare you!" exclaimed Lydia.

"Well, if you are going to encourage the brat to tell lies—"

"It is *not* a lie!" Amy cried. "Captain Logan *did* come to visit us, and we gave him tea and macaroons. He sent us oranges the next day, and they were ever so sweet."

"And he sent flowers to Vanessa!" Aggie said, thrusting her lower lip out in a pout.

"Amy! Aggie, love," Vanessa protested. "That will do." She bent down beside the girls and tried to quiet them.

"So Captain Logan sent you flowers, did he?" he asked, looking at Vanessa with a speculative look on his face. She peered up at him through narrowed eyes. "Happens I know something of this Captain Logan. If he's such a good friend of yours, he wouldn't mind making you a small loan.

His father is as rich as Golden Ball, they say. Maybe I'll drop by Stoneham House and have a word with your young man, miss."

"No!" Vanessa protested. "Please, you must not!"

Her mother's expression, to Vanessa's despair, was that of a lady who had been visited by a Clever Idea. This invariably was a portent of disaster in their household.

"It is true that Captain Logan has always been very friendly to our family," the elder lady said. "His aunt and I were great friends when we were at school together. He would no doubt take it amiss if you persist in making a nuisance of yourself here."

The man's open scorn made Vanessa itch to slap his sneering face.

"Is that so?" the landlord said. "Bein' as how you're such good friends and all with this Captain Logan, I'll just pay him a visit and see if it makes any difference to him whether you lose the roof over your heads."

"No!" Vanessa protested in horror as he turned on his heel and marched out the door.

She would have started after him if her mother hadn't caught her arm.

"He is only bluffing, darling," Annabelle said with a crafty little smile on her face that struck terror in Vanessa's heart. "If he does have the impudence to call at Stoneham House, I promise you the earl's butler will send the repulsive little mushroom about his business in a trice."

She gave a sigh of satisfaction.

"Isn't it wonderful?" Annabelle boasted to her daughters. "Due to my presence of mind in claiming friendship with the Earl of Stoneham's sister and son, he left without collecting the rest of the rent!"

"What is this about, Alexander?" The Earl of Stoneham demanded when a message was conveyed to him by his impassive butler that a person wished to be admitted into the presence of Captain Logan to discuss a matter of some urgency regarding a young lady.

"I have no idea," Alexander replied, folding the paper he had been reading and laying it on the table between them. "Does the person have the appearance of an irate father, perhaps, or a member of the legal profession?" he asked the butler.

"As to that, I could not say, my lord," the butler said with a sniff of self-importance. "But I *would* venture to say the person is neither a member of the gentry nor of the professional class. He appears to be occupied in trade."

"How alarming. Shall we have him in, Cedric?"

When his father returned no answer, Alexander nodded at the butler, who returned a short time later with a floridly dressed man of vulgar appearance. The man annoyed both gentlemen by bowing several times, crumpling his hat in his hands, and staring about at his surroundings as if to memorize them, no doubt so he could recount their splendor to his family and acquaintances at a later date.

"I assume you have a purpose in calling, Mr., ah, Bindle?" Alexander suggested coolly.

Recalled to his errand, the man favored both Alexander and the earl with an oily smile.

"That's the right of it, Captain Logan," he said. "But, begging your pardon, it would best be discussed private-like, if you take my meaning."

"Yes. I believe you said there is a lady's good name involved. If you would not mind?" Alexander suggested to his father. When the earl scowled at him, Alexander added, "Rest easy, Cedric. To my knowledge, I have not committed any sort of indiscretion that is likely to result either in a bolt to Gretna Green, or in a trip to the cents per cent."

The earl gave his son a withering look and left the room.

"Now," said Alexander, turning to the landlord, whom he had not invited to sit down. "Perhaps you will state the nature of your business. Who is the lady concerned in this matter?"

"The Whittaker family is renting a house from me in

Hans Crescent," the landlord said, watching Alexander carefully for some reaction.

"And?" Alexander prompted.

"The ladies owe me two months' rent."

"I see. And what do you imagine this has to do with me?"

"Bein' as how the young miss said you were a great friend of theirs—"

"Indeed?" Alexander asked, his eyebrows raised.

"Well, she said you visited them at their house and sent flowers. And oranges, or some such. I wondered if the girl was making up a tale. Her mother is always carrying on about her great friend Lady This and Countess That until it could make your head spin, and that's a fact. Are you saying that you are not acquainted with the Whittaker females? I thought as much!"

"No, actually I did visit the Whittaker *ladies,*" Alexander said slowly. "And you will permit me to say that whatever you are charging them to occupy that dilapidated residence probably is far more than the privilege is worth. Did Miss Whittaker actually suggest that you apply to me for the balance of their rent?"

The man reddened, and gave Alexander a belligerent look before he carefully schooled his features into their former ingratiating expression.

"Well, not exactly," the man admitted.

Not exactly.

Alexander had thought it was impossible for a man as cynical as himself to be disillusioned about anyone, but now he found he was mistaken. It appeared that "the young miss" was every bit as opportunistic as his father had warned.

He was about to send the landlord about his business when a perfectly brilliant thought occurred to him. The earl had made it clear that the one transgression he would not forgive his son would be a misalliance with Vanessa Whittaker. Was it not possible that Stoneham would send his son packing to the ends of the earth—or, more specifically, back to his regiment—if he thought that Alexander was about to form a romantic liaison with the lady?

Alexander regarded the tradesman with narrowed eyes.

"We have before us a matter of some delicacy, my good man," Alexander said, motioning the landlord to a chair. "I want it to be understood that my dealings with Miss Whittaker are honorable ones, and to speak of our transaction outside this room will incur my severest displeasure."

"Transaction, your lordship?" the little man said hopefully.

"Yes," Alexander said, taking a pen to write a draft on his bank.

The landlord left a happy man, with a payment not only for the Whittakers' back rent, but also for several months' advance rent in his pocket.

Alexander's bid for freedom from his father had begun.

The next move in the game came the following day, when Alexander rose uncharacteristically early and visited a certain fashionable shop.

Alexander had remembered little Aggie Whittaker's artless confidence that Madame Celeste was the creator of Miss Whittaker's charming gowns, and he was willing to wager his next quarter day's allowance that not one of them had been paid for.

On the pretext of selecting a present for his Aunt Letitia's birthday, he drew the modiste into conversation and was not surprised when Miss Whittaker's name discreetly was dropped into the conversation by the shrewd businesswoman. It seemed the landlord was not the only one of the Whittakers' creditors whom "the young miss" had told about his supposed interest in her.

So far, Alexander thought with satisfaction, all was going according to plan.

As with the landlord, Alexander made it plain that his intentions toward the fair Miss Whittaker were honorable ones, and that he willingly would discharge the young lady's obligations in exchange for Madame Celeste's solemn promise that neither the young lady herself nor, indeed, anyone else, would learn the identity of her benefactor. Of course, Alexander had observed that there were several ladies in the establishment, and if they accidentally overheard portions of the low-voiced conversation, well, it couldn't be helped.

"Mrs. Whittaker mentioned that you were a friend of the family's when she was in the shop yesterday," Madame Celeste admitted. "I thought she—that is, I had no idea—but I will send a note around to her house at once to make certain there was no misunderstanding about the bills I submitted to her for payment."

"Very good," Alexander said, smiling. "I know I can depend upon your discretion."

Madame Celeste beamed.

Alexander then purchased an expensive shawl and a pair of gloves for his aunt, confident that by nightfall all of London would know that the Earl of Stoneham's heir had fallen hopelessly under the spell of Vanessa Whittaker's exquisite blue eyes.

Ordinarily it was against Alexander's principles to impose on a lady to achieve his own ends. But by attempting to use *him* to fob off her creditors, Vanessa had vanquished the last of his scruples.

All is fair in love and war, he reminded himself.

And this, most definitely, is war.

All of England appeared to think after the victory at Salamanca and the French Army's retreat into Russia that Napoleon was virtually defeated, but this confidence was as illusory as it was dangerous. While the Corsican commanded an army, he was a threat to England and the world.

Alexander vowed that his military service would not end with his being carried bloody and helpless from the battlefield. He was determined to return, in time-honored military tradition, to fight another day. If that meant he had to make Vanessa Whittaker his pawn, so be it.

The calculating little fortune hunter was going to help him get back to his regiment. When next he saw her, he planned to make it plain to the young lady that she had no choice in the matter.

Vanessa's eyes widened in horror when the dressmaker's servant delivered a lovely ballgown and an exquisite opera cloak of blue velvet lined in cream-colored satin.

"Mother!" Vanessa cried when Mrs. Whittaker had smoothed out the rich folds of the cloak and placed it around Vanessa's stiff shoulders. "What have you done?"

"I have bought you the prettiest gown and cape in London, or at least *you* thought so when you went for the fittings," Mrs. Whittaker said, looking smug. "*Some* daughters would be grateful."

"It is beautiful, Mother, but how are we to pay for it? Oh, we must send it back at once!" Vanessa looked down at the box in which the gown had come. "Madame Celeste's clerk must have made a mistake in sending it to us," she said. "It would be out of the question for me to keep it."

"Nonsense, darling," Mrs. Whittaker said with an airy gesture of dismissal. "Madame sent a note of apology around this morning, saying that she was sorry for the misunderstanding about our bills, and that she stood ready to supply us with anything we require for the rest of our stay in London. So, naturally I sent a note right back, reminding her that she still had this gown and cloak in her workroom, and she sent it around immediately."

Mrs. Whittaker flashed Vanessa a smile of triumph, plainly expecting her daughter to be impressed by her cleverness.

"But, why should she do that?" Vanessa asked in confusion. "Mother, I have more than enough dresses we cannot afford already. We have to send it back."

"Absolutely not! I won't permit you to wear one of your old gowns to Lady Huntington's ball on Friday. If you appear one more time in public wearing your blue muslin, I shall die of embarrassment. The thing is in tatters."

"I mended the tear quite carefully, I promise you, so it hardly shows at all. And I have not worn the white gown with the green sash above three times, not that it matters. Have you forgotten that we have not been invited to Lady Huntington's ball?"

"Ah, but we have. Lady Huntington sent a servant over with an invitation this morning. It seems ours was overlooked when her man took the rest of them to the post, and she wrote the prettiest note begging us to attend."

Instead of being relieved that she and her mother appeared once again to be accepted into society, Vanessa found her mind possessed of an exceedingly unwelcome suspicion.

Ever since the younger Whittaker girls had mentioned Alexander's name to that odious little landlord, Mama had implied, ever so casually, to the subsequent tradesmen who called at their home that the son of the wealthy and influential Earl of Stoneham was quite one of the Whittakers' closest friends. From there it was a simple matter to let slip that Captain Logan's interest in the family had to do with his admiration for the eldest daughter of the house.

Amazingly, Mrs. Whittaker's little fiction was being accepted about town.

How else could one explain why the landlord had sent men to repair the section of the roof that leaked, or why Lydia had encountered no resistance at all from the butcher when she ordered a leg of lamb billed to the family's account? It had been the first time since before the ball at Stoneham House that the butcher had allowed them credit.

That afternoon several ladies came to call after being decidedly cool toward the Whittakers for a week, and a few of them rather too casually dropped Captain Logan's name into the conversation. When this happened, everyone in the room watched Vanessa closely for her reaction.

Vanessa's dreadful suspicion was confirmed later in the day when Diana Lacey and her mother joined the chatting ladies in the parlor. Only a few days ago, Diana had been forbidden to visit the Whittakers. Now, it seemed, her mother was anxious to encourage the friendship between the two young ladies.

Vanessa whisked Diana off to her room on the pretext of showing her the new gown and cloak.

"Thank heaven you invited me upstairs. I couldn't have contained myself another moment," Diana declared when they were alone. "Vanessa, you sly thing! And you pretended there was nothing between you! You must tell me *everything!*"

"Perhaps you should tell me."

"Now, don't try to tell me it isn't true. Everyone in town is saying that Captain Logan is desperately in love with you, and he means to offer for you before he returns to war. They say he and Sir Gregory Banbridge had an argument at White's, and afterward Sir Gregory suddenly left town. Captain Logan must have threatened to call him out because of all those horrid things he was saying about you."

"That is utter nonsense, Diana," Vanessa said, pacing back and forth across the tiny room in agitation. "They must have been arguing over something else. It cannot have been me. I cannot imagine who could have started such a silly rumor."

In her heart, though, she was afraid she knew. After inventing a Canterbury Tale about her daughter's supposed romance with the heir to an earldom, why should Mrs. Whittaker balk at starting the rumor of an imaginary confrontation between the dashing Captain Logan and the dastardly Sir Gregory? Vanessa could just see her mother making a dramatic story of it. There was nothing Annabelle enjoyed more than being the center of attention.

A veritable avalanche of invitations fell upon the ladies

in Hans Crescent over the next few days. Vanessa's heart sank as her mother, now with unlimited credit at all the shops, gleefully embarked upon a new frenzy of spending.

Vanessa grimly attired herself in her new gown on the evening of Lady Huntington's ball. Captain Logan would be certain to attend, and Vanessa would need all the false courage she could get in order to face him.

Alexander set his empty wineglass on a roving servant's tray and watched with a cynical eye as every person in Lady Huntington's ballroom fell silent and stared with anticipation at Vanessa Whittaker when she appeared at the head of the stairs.

The young lady was a vision with her dark curls dressed high on the top of her head and her lovely form displayed to advantage in a rose pink muslin gown with a low-cut, V-shaped bodice and tiny puffed sleeves that left most of her shoulders bare.

But Alexander didn't delude himself that her striking brunette beauty was what held the rapt attention of all Lady Huntington's guests.

They were waiting with bated breath for Alexander to make a cake of himself over the girl in public, and he was, for once, perfectly willing to oblige them.

SEVEN

Vanessa took a deep breath and descended the staircase in Lady Huntington's mansion, uncomfortably aware of the seventy pairs of eyes riveted upon her. Incredibly, her mother smiled down into the sea of upturned faces for all the world as if she had nothing to hide.

"Look, there is Captain Logan," Annabelle whispered.

Vanessa took a deep breath. Of course she had seen him the moment she looked down into the ballroom.

He was smiling, but even from that distance Vanessa could see the cynical expression in those piercing dark eyes. His formal dress uniform made him look formidable. She had to force herself not to turn tail and run when he approached the foot of the stair.

The crowd of people instinctively parted to clear a path between them. Captain Logan had been looking straight up at Vanessa, but now he cocked his head a little, as if in amusement.

Vanessa concentrated on keeping her shoulders back, her spine straight, and her chin up as she walked down the stairs. She forced her gloved fingers to relax on the polished handrail and willed her stiff lips to turn up at the corners. With luck she would not trip on the hem of her gown in her nervousness and land in an ignominious heap at his feet. At least, she prayed, let her face her disgrace with some dignity.

Captain Logan must have heard the rumors. How could

he avoid it when their supposed romance was the talk of London? Vanessa felt her face go hot with embarrassment. He was going to expose her mother's lie before the very highest sticklers in London. She just knew it!

To her surprise, the captain stepped forward to take her hand and bring it to his lips as soon as she reached the bottom of the stair.

"Good evening, Miss Whittaker," he said. His voice was perfectly pleasant, but she distrusted the mocking expression in his eyes. The back of Vanessa's hand tingled where he had kissed it through her glove. Politely, he turned to her mother. "And Mrs. Whittaker. How delightful to see you again." Annabelle blushed with pleasure.

At least he wasn't going to denounce them in the middle of the ballroom floor, Vanessa thought with some relief.

Not yet.

"Here is our hostess to greet you, my dear," Captain Logan added as Lady Huntington came up to them. Vanessa had no idea what to make of it. "I shall come to claim you for the first waltz. And I shall take you into supper, if I may."

"Yes. Of course," Vanessa said, her voice sounding strained to her own ears.

"Darlings, I am so glad you could come," said Lady Huntington, kissing both Vanessa and her mother on the cheek. This affectionate gesture from one of London's most prominent hostesses startled Vanessa, for the woman hardly had known they were alive before rumor connected Vanessa with the Earl of Stoneham's son.

Once the ball officially was opened, Vanessa's hand was solicited for every dance. Never in her life had she been so popular. Were these the same people who had snubbed Vanessa and her mother at Almack's?

The other gentlemen apparently had decided she must be a diamond of the first water simply because Captain Logan supposedly was in love with her. Or perhaps they thought it was safe to flirt with her because a lady who had managed to attract such an eligible *parti* as the future Earl of Stoneham would be unlikely to set her cap at a lesser man.

From her place on the ballroom floor she could feel Captain Logan's gaze upon her. He was standing at the side of the ballroom watching her every move as she was handed from one partner to another. She couldn't resist stealing nervous little peeks at him. Every time she did, he was *smiling* at her, exactly as if she were a delicious bit of pastry he intended to take a bite of before long. It was positively unnerving! She replied to each of her partners' remarks quite at random and hoped she wasn't making too great a fool of herself.

Her partner for the country dance had gone to fetch her a glass of lemonade when Captain Logan stepped smoothly to her side.

"I must speak with you privately," he said in an undervoice.

Before she could reply, her former partner returned with the lemonade and the two gentlemen made polite conversation while she sipped it. The young man tactfully withdrew after a moment or two, leaving her in Captain Logan's company.

"Your cheeks are quite flushed," he said, taking her elbow and guiding her from the room. "I trust I can escort you to the terrace for a breath of air without causing too much damage to your reputation."

Vanessa gave a guilty start. Was he being sarcastic? She glanced quickly at his face, but his expression was impassive.

When they reached the darkness of the terrace, Vanessa took a deep breath and faced him. Her back was at a pillar and Captain Logan loomed over her. The clean, masculine fragrance of bay rum she always associated with him mingled with the flower scents of Lady Huntington's garden.

"I know what you are going to say," she began, "and I can explain. My mother was *desperate* or she never would have . . ."

She broke off in confusion. His dark eyes were mysterious in the moonlight. His face was much too close.

"Your mother?" he prompted, lightly tracing the curve of her cheek with his hand. She closed her eyes as his fingers skimmed lower, following the contour of her neck to her collarbone. His voice was soft. "My dear, I did not bring you out onto the terrace in the moonlight to discuss your mother."

"Please don't toy with me," she said, pushing his hand away to stop further exploration of her sensitive skin. She couldn't *think* when he did things like that! "If you are going to ring a peal over me, I wish you would get on with it!"

"Now why would I want to ring a peal over you, I wonder?" he asked, standing even closer.

"I mean the rumors, as if you didn't know! After Gregory was spreading all those horrid stories about me, my mother spread the news around town that you and I—that we—in short, that there is some sort of an understanding between us. Lydia and I tried to reason with her, but—"

"And you would have me believe your *mother* started these rumors? Try again, Miss Whittaker. You will find me much more comfortable to deal with if you tell the truth."

He looked so stern that Vanessa quailed.

"W—what do you mean?" she asked.

"I had it from your landlord that 'the young miss' herself told him about the flowers I had sent to your home. The old scoundrel had the effrontery to call on me at Stoneham House and suggest that I might like to pay the balance of your rent in order to spare your family embarrassment."

Remembering that dreadful day when her little sisters innocently had boasted of Captain Logan's visit to their house, Vanessa was ready to sink.

"And you assumed I would be so vulgar and so encroaching as to—" She felt her cheeks grow hot with fury.

"You chose the words, not I," Alexander said. "Rather let us say it was enterprising of you to take advantage of the situation. I would think better of you if you would own up to your actions instead of seeking to blame your *mother* for them."

"Why, you—"

"Temper, temper, Vanessa."

"I did not give you leave to call me by my Christian name, sir!"

He caught her by the wrists and hauled her against his chest.

"You have given me the right to take any liberties I choose, my sweet." His face was very close to hers, and his tone was threatening. Her breasts were flattened against his hard body, and heat suffused her skin. "Be grateful that, at least for now, I am willing to be satisfied with the use of your Christian name."

"Captain Logan, please," she said, looking up into his implacable face. "I am not what you think me. It was my little sister's innocent remark that gave the landlord the idea to—"

"Now you will blame your indiscretion on a child. Really, Vanessa, there is no need to defend yourself. Did I not say I commend your resourcefulness? In fact, you are going to use your impressive talent for theatrics in order to extricate me from a certain difficulty."

"I don't know what you mean," she said, trying to shrink away from him. He released her wrists, but slipped one strong arm around her waist to keep her from escaping.

"Now, now," he said, cupping her face in his free hand. "No need to be shy. We are about to become very good friends." His thumb stroked her cheekbone in a way that made her shiver. "Indeed, I thoroughly expect to enjoy this." His trailed his fingers down the side of her face and pulled the puffed sleeve of her dress aside so he could caress her bare shoulder.

"No," she breathed, averting her face. She should have struggled, but her suddenly lethargic limbs refused to obey her. His gentle, almost reverent touch on her skin was awakening unfamiliar sensations in her body that left her confused and wanting more.

"Oh, *yes*, my dear." That low, deceptively gentle voice continued, "When your landlord applied to me for the balance of your rent, I paid him. In fact, I paid your rent through the end of the season. I settled Madame Celeste's bills as well and instructed her to apply to me for payment on all future ones. However, if I should indicate publicly that the rumors of our romantic involvement were not true, say, by giving you the cut direct in public or by showing interest in a different young lady, I'm afraid your mother's remaining creditors will descend upon her like a plague of locusts."

"Why are you doing this to me?" she asked in despair. "I don't understand any of this." His fingers traced a languorous path from the hollow of her throat to a point just above the cleft in her breasts.

"I was discreet, I assure you," he said. "All the gossips in London believe my intentions toward you are honorable. And they will continue to do so as long as you cooperate."

"You are quite mad. Please, Captain Logan, I . . ." Vanessa closed her eyes. Mercifully, he had stopped exploring her heated skin with his touch. But she was strangely languid, and she felt the strong arm he had put around her waist accept more of her weight.

His voice seemed to be coming from far away. She tried to focus her mind on what he was saying. Their bodies were so close that Vanessa could feel the sounds vibrate in his chest.

"I am prepared to offer you additional relief from your family's financial difficulties if we can come to a mutually satisfactory agreement."

The words were like a glass of icy water thrown against her face. Her eyes flew open. Strength flowed back into her limbs. Her will was hers again. She strained against his arm and stared up into his face with narrowed eyes.

Vanessa could think of only one kind of "mutually satisfactory agreement" a man of Captain Logan's fortune and breeding would be likely to seek with a young lady in her circumstances. Although she had received several offers of this nature since her arrival in London, this one hurt the most.

She had made a complete fool of herself by submitting to his intimate caresses. And this fresh humiliation had come of it.

"You are as bad as Gregory, you despicable hypocrite! How *could* you suggest such a thing?" Vanessa demanded, drawing her hand back as if she would slap him. Instead, she allowed it to drop to her side and tried to slip out from between his body and the pillar at her back. He caught her wrist when she would have fled.

Then he had the gall to *laugh* at her.

She would never forgive him for this insult. *Never!*

"Let go of me this instant, or I shall scream!"

"Vanessa, I am not offering to set you up as my mistress."

The words were quiet. She looked up into his face and saw he was perfectly serious.

"You're not?" she asked in surprise. He let go of her wrist. She peered up at him in suspicion, poised for escape.

"No. Of course not. I want to go back to my regiment, but my father has arranged with his bloody influential friends to keep me cooling my heels in London until the war is over. It is of vital importance to him that I find a suitable bride to serve as my political hostess and settle down to the serious business of producing heirs to his precious title."

"I fail to see how I can help you," she said.

Captain Logan hesitated.

"You are the last young lady in London my father would wish for me to marry. Cedric was furious when he found out I confronted Banbridge at White's over those disgusting lies he was spreading about you."

"Do you mean to tell me that was *true?*" Vanessa couldn't

believe it. "I thought it was another of my mother's inventions. Why should you do that for me?"

"It occurred to me that Banbridge thought he could get away with ruining your reputation without fear of reprisal because you have no close male relatives to defend your honor. It was the act of a coward, and I never could abide a coward. I told him if he didn't retract his lies, I would be forced to resort to physical violence."

"You *didn't*," she said, awed.

"I'm afraid I did. My father caught wind of the affair and made it plain that he would not tolerate a misalliance between myself and you. Of course, at that time I had not thought of coercing you into helping me annoy Cedric to the point where he would be glad to send me into the deadly embrace of the enemy. But since *you* have no qualms about bandying my name about to serve *your* ends, *I* need have no compunction in compelling you to serve *mine*. I plan to convince my father that I am on the point of offering for you. I then will make a bargain with him: I will agree to stop courting you on the condition that he stops blocking my attempt to return to war. You can then cry off, and we both will be free. Since our engagement will not have been announced in the papers, there will be no harm done."

"You and your father must despise us very much if the mere thought of an alliance with my family would make him willing to risk your life," she said. She had thought she was immune to all types of snobbery, but she had been mistaken.

"It is hardly a question of despising you—" he said, sounding impatient.

"Don't bother to deny it. I have become quite accustomed to gratuitous insults, I assure you. We fortune hunters cannot afford to be overly sensitive," Vanessa said, looking him straight in the eye. She was not about to let him see that he had hurt her. "What is it, precisely, that you require of me, Captain Logan?"

"I am suggesting nothing improper. All I want is to be

permitted to visit you at your home with your mother and sisters present, to take you driving in the park, to squire you to balls, that sort of thing. I am perfectly aware that while I am making a fool of myself over you, I may scare away any serious suitors you might have. Regrettable, but I see no way around it."

"I don't think we need worry about that," she said. "Gentlemen were hardly tripping over one another to pay their addresses to me *before* Gregory set out to ruin my reputation."

"Their loss, my sweet," he said softly.

Captain Logan gave her that devastating smile of his and took both of her hands in his. How could he *charm* her at a time like this?

But just the same, she found herself being charmed.

"What do you say?" he asked. "Do we have a bargain?"

"It appears I have no choice," she said, feeling helpless.

"You needn't look so Friday-faced, Vanessa. Think of it as your patriotic duty."

"Of course," she said waspishly. "We both know that England has no chance against Napoleon unless you return to war to lend General Wellesley your support. How worried the poor man must be that you won't arrive in time."

"Oh, very good," he said, giving her a look of approval. "I believe I am going to find our courtship quite entertaining."

"Don't depend upon it," she snapped.

The abominable man seemed to find her defiance amusing.

"You really are quite beautiful when you are angry, Vanessa."

"Do I appear to be *stupid*, Captain Logan?"

"Not at all. To return to our bargain. I shall give you two thousand pounds apart from what I have spent on your rent and on Madame Celeste's bills." His fingers lightly skimmed her bare shoulder where it met the fabric of her gown. "If this charming creation is an indication of how your mother has been spending my money, I whole-heartedly approve. The lady has no talent for economy, but her taste is impeccable."

"No!" Vanessa felt her face go hot again with embarrassment. She yanked her sleeve up from where he had pushed it off her shoulder and glared at him. He laughed softly and withdrew his hand. "It is bad enough you have paid our bills, but to accept outright payment—"

"What a very strange fortune hunter you are," he said, giving her a quizzical look. "You *can* accept payment, and you shall. This will be a straight business transaction."

"No, I—"

"*Think*, Vanessa. You could settle your family's bills and repair to Brighton for the summer where you will have another chance to attract a rich suitor. We both know why your mother brought you to London for the Season. I can make it possible for you to take care of your family in the only honorable way for a young lady of your station."

"Are you mocking me?" she asked.

"Strangely, no," he said, looming over her again. "Vanessa, two thousand pounds is nothing to me. I have a handsome independence left to me from my maternal grandfather quite apart from the allowance my father makes me. But two thousand pounds would make a big difference to you, would it not?"

"It would," she admitted, swallowing hard. "But why should you care? I already am at your mercy."

"Let us just say I am strangely reluctant to see you sell yourself too cheaply to another such dotard as Omersley out of desperation. Do you accept my offer or not?"

She bowed her head.

"It appears I have no choice," she said softly. "I accept."

"Shall we seal our bargain with a kiss?" The handsome officer raised her face to his with one warm, lazy finger under her chin. The timbre of his voice made her knees go weak with anticipation. He was very, very good at this, she thought in despair. Lydia had been right. Vanessa wouldn't have the chance of a kitten against a tiger if he chose to amuse himself at her expense.

Captain Logan gave her a smile that was almost tender. "There is no need to look so frightened, my dear," he whispered. "This won't prove fatal, I promise you."

His lips were surprisingly gentle. The kiss, though brief, left her in shambles.

"There," he said, stepping back and taking her arm. Apparently the kiss that rocked her to her soul didn't affect *him* in the least, she thought, feeling disgruntled. "Let us go inside and give the old tabbies something to talk about."

"Certainly," she replied in what she hoped was a brittle, sophisticated tone. "One must do one's poor best for Mother England."

Alexander and Vanessa returned to the ballroom just in time for the promised waltz, so he swept her into his arms and whirled her out onto the floor. She was as light as a feather in his arms. From the corner of his eye, he saw Vanessa's mother give them both an ecstatic little smile. It clearly was Annabelle Whittaker's moment of triumph.

"Darling," Alexander told her, "no one will believe we are in love if you don't relax a bit."

"I shall have not a shred of reputation left if you insist upon holding me so closely," she whispered back.

She was so soft and fragrant and beautiful. Just to tease her a little, Alexander tightened his hold around her waist until their bodies were almost touching, and he was pleasantly engulfed in the scent of orange blossom. To cross that invisible line and actually cause her breasts to brush, even briefly, against his chest would be to ruin her utterly in the eyes of the high sticklers watching them, and both of them knew it. No danger of that, however. Alexander knew just how far he could go before a young lady's family had just cause to demand that he make an honest woman of her.

He had tested these limits often during his wild youth.

Alexander was jerked out of his thoughts by a sharp pain in his upper arm.

"You little vixen! You *pinched* me!" he said in disbelief. London's most eligible bachelor was accustomed to a bit more respect from his dancing partners.

Vanessa gave him an adoring look for the benefit of their audience.

"And I shall do so again if you do not relax your hold a little," she said sweetly.

He shook his head.

"You are a cruel woman, my lovely Vanessa," he said, reluctantly loosening his grip on her waist so she could step back a little.

"And don't you forget it," she snapped.

She looked irritated when he laughed, but, truly, he couldn't help it.

When the waltz was over, Alexander brought Vanessa another glass of lemonade and stationed himself near the chairs where she and her mother were sitting.

"Must you glare at them so?" Vanessa complained as a young man started to approach her but thought better of it when he encountered the look in Alexander's eye. "I have known poor Robert Langtry all my life, and you are scaring him half to death."

"Definitely, I must," he replied, bending his head close to hers so he could whisper into her ear. Such a pretty, delicate little ear. He kept thinking of that moment in the garden when he had crushed her slender body to his and she had melted in his arms. Alexander's intent had been to humiliate Vanessa, to show her that he was in command. Instead, the natural sensuality of her response to his caresses almost had caused him to lose control. The shy, innocent kiss she gave him to seal their bargain made it obvious that she hadn't had much experience with kissing or, indeed, any other kind of lovemaking. He had wanted to drag her into the shrubbery with him and remedy this situation immediately. "I am a jealous swain, remember?"

he said, thinking it was too close to the truth for his comfort. "And you, my sweet, could contrive to look a trifle more smitten."

Vanessa turned those big blue eyes on him and simpered. Then she fluttered her long, dark lashes at him. Her look was such a comical parody of a coy maiden flirting with an eligible marital prospect that it nearly undid him.

"Oh, love," he said, laughing so loudly that people were craning their necks to hear their conversation. He lowered his voice. "Surely you can do better than that. Didn't they teach you *anything* at that school in Bath?"

"How ungallant of you, sir! Perhaps I should practice on poor Mr. Langtry. He is certain to be more appreciative of my efforts."

"If you do, it will have to be pistols at dawn. *Such* a bore."

"Don't be ridiculous!"

"True. If I am going to waste a perfectly good bullet, I had rather it be on Banbridge. Speak of the devil . . ."

Vanessa followed the direction of Alexander's nod and her eyes widened. Alexander gave her hand a reassuring squeeze as Sir Gregory and Lady Banbridge reached the bottom of the staircase.

"Don't look so frightened, Vanessa," Alexander whispered. "He will be perfectly civil while everyone is watching, I promise you. Chin up. There's a good girl. Have you a saddle horse stabled in London?"

"A saddle horse?" she repeated, looking at him as if he had taken leave of his senses. "Whatever would I do with a saddle horse?"

"Meet me in the park of a morning, of course. If we are seen riding together, it will make an excellent impression on the early risers and sportsmen." And allow him greater freedom to be alone with Vanessa. Alexander was playing with fire, and he knew it. But he couldn't help himself.

"I don't ride."

"Nonsense. *Everybody* rides," he said, taken aback.

"I don't ride," she repeated. "When I was young, I was afraid of horses. By the time I was older, my father already had been obliged to sell off his stable."

"I see. Well, then. It behooves me as your most ardent suitor to see to this neglected aspect of your education. I shall bring a gentle horse from my father's stable to Hans Crescent one day, and we shall begin."

"Alexander," she said, turning to face him. It was the first time she ever had used his Christian name and it sounded delightful on her lips. "Not only do I not have a horse, but I do not possess a riding habit."

"Well, *that* can be remedied at all events. Order one from Madame Celeste. Order several."

"I thank you just the same, but I really have no desire to learn how to ride a horse."

"My darling Vanessa, neither my father nor my Aunt Letitia would believe for an instant that I seriously could be interested in a young lady who does not ride. And for our scheme to be successful, they must believe me to be very seriously interested, indeed."

When Vanessa didn't answer him, he looked to see what had captured her attention. He saw Sir Gregory was heading their way with his wife on his arm, and he had stopped to address a remark to Mrs. Whittaker. Vanessa's mother blushed and looked embarrassed.

Alexander gave a theatrical sigh and put his hand on Vanessa's shoulder.

"I shall have to put a bullet through the bounder after all," he said in a tone of mock regret.

Sir Gregory came to a stop before them after his wife went on to chat with another lady.

"Good evening, Miss Whittaker. Captain Logan," he said. The sneer that twisted his face boded ill for Alexander's contention that the diplomat would not dare make a scene at so public an occasion.

"Back in town so soon, Banbridge?" Alexander drawled. "Pity. You would have found the air of the country much more beneficial to your continued good health, I promise you."

"Your concern is quite touching," Sir Gregory said. "Would you care to dance, Vanessa?"

"Yes, but not with you," she said coolly. "And I will thank you to address me as Miss Whittaker."

"If you think his intentions toward you are honorable, you are a bigger fool than I took you for."

"Have you no sense of self-preservation, Banbridge?" Alexander asked, standing behind Vanessa's chair and putting his hands on her shoulders. Lord, he would love to plant the man a facer. But he could hardly do so in Lady Huntington's ballroom.

"Perhaps you should return to your *wife,* Sir Gregory," Vanessa suggested.

"I can't stand by and watch him ruin you," Gregory said, giving Alexander a look of pure hatred. "I *love* you, damn it."

"The thought of you posing as the guardian of the young lady's virtue rather boggles the mind, Banbridge, after the little scene I interrupted in my father's library," Alexander said. He forced his lips into the semblance of a pleasant smile for the benefit of their audience when what he truly wished to do was crush the villain's windpipe. He felt Vanessa's shoulders quiver under his hands. "Why don't you take yourself off before I ask you to name your friends?"

"For two gentlemen so intent upon preserving my reputation, you are making rather a botch of things," Vanessa remarked. Alexander felt a surge of admiration for her prosaic tone. "Sir Gregory, do go away. We have absolutely nothing to say to one another."

Then she looked up at Alexander and gave him such a tender look that it nearly staggered him. He had to remind himself that she merely was playing the part he had assigned to her. And being paid quite handsomely for it.

Vanquished for the present, Sir Gregory moved off to join his wife.

Alexander felt Vanessa's eyes on him and looked down into her lovely, vulnerable face.

"Shall we go in to supper, my dear?" Alexander said, offering his arm. She rose from her chair and took it.

"Certainly, Alexander," she said. "Suddenly I am quite famished."

EIGHT

The next day Alexander sent Vanessa a small bouquet of violets tied with long, curling silver ribbons, and a poem.

Vanessa turned the posy with its elegant silver holder in her fingers and strongly considered boxing her devoted swain's ears the next time she saw him.

Why could he not have sent a flashy bouquet of roses instead? A vulgar display of hothouse flowers would have been a blatant attempt to signal his interest, and she could have accepted them with no loss of composure. But this little nosegay of violets was too personal, the gift of a lover, not a casual admirer. And it was the second time he had chosen them for her.

Violets reminded him of the color of her eyes, his poem said. It was quite possibly the most dreadful doggerel Vanessa ever had read, but Vanessa found it all the more endearing because of it. She could imagine his wicked dark eyes sparkling with mischief as he concentrated his efforts on making as wretched a job of this sentimental bit of trash as he possibly could. The excruciatingly awful rhymes mockingly extolled her patience, her kindness, her modesty, and her sweet, shy, and submissive demeanor. Her eyes were soft, simmering pools of delight. He wanted to cover her dainty feet with kisses and suck her earlobes.

The odious beast!

If it wasn't just like the unprincipled Captain Logan to

break down all of her defenses by acting the part of a buffoon. How could he do this to her?

Vanessa knew she would keep the silly poem forever, even though it was written to give credence to the myth that he was an ardent suitor. No doubt Alexander expected her to flaunt this trophy before all of her female acquaintances.

Well, she wouldn't! She knew she was a fool, but his poem was too precious to share with anyone. When she was old and gray, she would read it over and over. Perhaps she would have convinced herself that the incompetently expressed sentiments were real by the time she was grown quite senile.

"It is the privilege of a devoted admirer to send any number of silly verses in praise of his beloved's beauty," the card accompanying the bouquet read. "I hope you will tolerate this poor attempt with your usual graciousness, my sweet Vanessa."

Without thinking, she hid the poem behind her back when her mother entered the room.

"Who are they from, my love, as if I didn't know?" Annabelle asked with an arch smile.

Annabelle was the last person on earth Vanessa could trust with the knowledge that Captain Logan's supposed courtship was a mere sham. Much as she loved her, Vanessa had no illusions that her mother was clever enough to avoid giving the game away inadvertently. And she knew that Annabelle was entirely capable of inventing some elaborate scheme calculated to entrap Captain Logan into marriage with her daughter. This must be avoided at all costs.

Vanessa reluctantly handed Annabelle the card.

"Oh, my love!" Annabelle declared. "It is beyond my fondest hopes. Where is this poem the card refers to?"

"It is merely a bouquet of flowers, Mother. The sort of thing a gentleman might send to anyone," Vanessa said, striving for an indifferent tone. "As for the poem, I have mislaid it somewhere."

"Too personal to show your mother, is it?" Annabelle said with a knowing smile. "Sly puss! You shall be a viscountess before the Season is over. You must change immediately into your new pomona green day gown. You will want to look your best when he calls this afternoon."

"Mother!" Vanessa said in despair.

"Come along, darling," Annabelle said, maddeningly confident. "You must trust your mother. Remember how upset you were when I had the clever scheme of telling those impertinent tradesmen that you were in a fair way of being engaged to Captain Logan? You can see how well it answered, for he couldn't take his eyes off you all last night. The rumors must have put the idea into his head. If he does not call on us this afternoon, then I know nothing of smitten young men."

By two that afternoon, the parlor was full of visitors. To Annabelle's obvious delight, some of them were from among the ranks of the very *haute ton*. Others, Vanessa thought, were simply nosy parkers waiting to see if Captain Logan would make an appearance. Vanessa sat stiffly on the edge of her chair, nervously pleating the fabric of her new gown in her fingers. Everyone was staring at her. She wished he would come so they would be satisfied and go away again.

Diana sat down in the chair placed next to Vanessa.

"I am so happy for you," Diana said, squeezing Vanessa's hand. "If you don't ask me to be one of your bridesmaids, I shall never forgive you."

"Don't be an idiot," Vanessa said in an undervoice. Diana only laughed.

Just then, the butler showed Captain Logan into the room, and he stood in the doorway for a moment, smiling graciously at everyone. The very picture of an eager suitor, he bowed over Annabelle's hand and headed straight for Vanessa's side. By then some of the early arrivals had begun taking their leave, no doubt determined to be the first to bring the tidings of Vanessa's surprising conquest to other ears.

"Good afternoon, Miss Whittaker," Alexander said with his usual assurance when Diana made a show of rising so he could take her place beside Vanessa. "Leaving so soon, Miss Lacey?" he asked.

"Yes, Mama wanted to make several other calls today," Diana answered. "Vanessa," she added, turning to her friend with a significant look. "We must have a long talk very soon. Shall we go to the library tomorrow?"

"I am afraid Miss Whittaker already is engaged to go riding with me tomorrow," Alexander said blandly.

Diana gave Vanessa a smug smile and went on to take her leave of Mrs. Whittaker.

Vanessa gave Alexander a reproachful look.

"I have told you, Captain Logan, that I have no wish to learn how to ride a horse."

"It is all arranged, my dear," he said, looking amused. He lowered his voice. "Most fortunately, Madame Celeste has several riding habits in her shop that can be altered quickly to fit your measurements. Her clerk will deliver them to you later this afternoon so you may make your choice. In fact, they probably will be waiting for you by the time we return from our excursion to the park."

"What excursion to the park? I can hardly leave our guests—"

"To be perfectly precise, my dear, they are not *your* guests but your mother's, and she will be occupied in entertaining them for the rest of the afternoon. It is a beautiful day, and my father's open carriage is outside. Shall we invite your sisters along for company? The carriage is big enough to accommodate all of us."

"How very kind of you," she exclaimed. "My sisters would enjoy it of all things! The poor things have been cooped up in the house almost the entire time we have been in London. I don't know how I can thank you enough for such consideration!"

He looked slightly taken aback.

"Not at all. It would be a great pleasure," he said after a short silence. "Perhaps you would like to ask them to accompany us while I visit with your mother's guests for a little while."

Vanessa felt like a perfect fool. How could she have forgotten, even for a moment, that this was all a carefully calculated performance to lend credibility to their supposed romantic involvement? Embarrassed, she nodded in agreement and left the room to do his bidding.

It didn't occur to her to refuse. Her sisters would enjoy riding in an earl's carriage very much, and she had no desire to deprive them of this unexpected treat. In truth, she was too much of a coward to want to be alone with Alexander just now. His violets and his poem had left her feeling much too vulnerable. And her skin tingled every time she thought of the way he had touched her last night.

As she dealt with her little sisters' raptures and went to her room to change into her carriage dress, she forced herself to harden her heart against Alexander's charm.

Vanessa might be his pawn, but she refused to be his victim.

"Oooh! Captain Logan, may we feed the ducks?"

"Certainly you may, Miss Agatha," Alexander said, dropping a few pennies in the child's hands to pay for the stale bread being sold by peddlers near the pond. He gave some coins to Amy as well.

The little girls and Mary Ann hurried away, leaving Alexander with Vanessa and Lydia, who doggedly refused to leave her elder sister's side. Alexander eyed the plump, determined girl with some amusement and tried an experimental smile to break down her reserve. Not one crack appeared in the facade of the young lady's disapproving face.

"Wouldn't you like to go along to make sure the children don't fall into the pond, Miss Lydia?" Alexander said pointedly.

"No," was Lydia's uncompromising answer. "Mary Ann will take care of them."

Alexander rolled his eyes and Vanessa tried unsuccessfully to stifle a giggle. Alexander gave her a look of deep reproach.

"My good girl," Alexander said, returning his attention to Lydia. "It is perfectly proper for me to converse alone with your sister in the park with all these witnesses present."

"Certainly it is, sir, so long as I am with you both," the girl agreed.

"As you say," he said, giving in with good grace. "Should you like to have a peppermint stick?" he added, spying a peddler passing by with some of the candies in his hand.

"No, thank you, sir," Lydia said stiffly.

Alexander shook his head, signaled the peddler, and purchased a handful of the peppermint sticks.

"Be reasonable, Miss Lydia," he said, presenting the younger lady with one. "You will hardly have compromised your virtue or your sister's by accepting a peppermint stick from an unmarried gentleman."

With a reluctant smile, Lydia accepted the treat and took an experimental lick.

"Thank you, sir," she said.

Vanessa was astounded. If Alexander could charm so determined a dragon as Lydia, she herself was lost.

To her horror, she heard a child's scream and a splash from the direction of the pond. Alexander took off at a run and after a startled second, Vanessa and Lydia picked up their skirts and ran after him. Little Amy, soaked to the skin, was sitting on the ground next to the water with Mary Ann and Aggie hovering near her. Thankfully, the water had not been deep where she fell in, and she had been able to walk to shore.

"She fell in," Aggie said tearfully.

"It's all my fault," Lydia cried, "for not going with them!"

"Nonsense," Alexander said, quickly stripping off his coat and bundling the shivering little girl up in it. He bent down and picked her up, holding her close. Amy's teeth were chattering. "Come along," he said over his shoulder to the others as he carried Amy toward the carriage. He cradled the whimpering child in his arms and whispered reassurances to her as the rest of the Whittaker girls caught up with him and scrambled into the back of the carriage. Alexander handed Amy into Vanessa's waiting arms. Then he drove the carriage straight to Stoneham House at a dangerous pace, heedless of the curses of other drivers.

Once there, he alighted quickly and held out his arms for Amy. Without hesitation, Vanessa handed the child over to him. He then ran up the stairs of Stoneham House and was admitted by the butler.

"Send someone immediately for the doctor," he called out as he ran past the butler. "When the young ladies come in, tell them I am taking their sister to the blue room and have someone show them the way. Meanwhile, have one of the maids come up and start a fire in the room."

"A fire, sir?" asked the startled butler.

"Just do as I say, and be quick about it!" Alexander barked.

Then he rushed up the stairs, taking them two at a time, without waiting for a response.

When he reached the top of the flight he heard a flurry of footsteps behind him. By the time he had seated Amy on the bed of the blue room and stripped his damp coat off of her, Vanessa and Lydia had burst through the doorway.

"Here," he said, stepping back. "Get those wet clothes off her."

Before he had finished his sentence, Vanessa and Lydia had pushed him out of the way and seized their little sister, who had begun crying again.

The maid ran into the room and began busying herself at the fireplace. Mary Ann and Aggie came through the doorway. Mary Ann rushed to help her older sisters with Amy, and Aggie, looking lost, stood by the door. Her little face was pinched with distress and tears were rolling down her cheeks.

Alexander, after glancing at the bed to see Vanessa, Lydia, and Mary Ann fussing over Amy, bent down in front of Aggie and wiped away her tears with his handkerchief. Then he opened his arms to her.

"It's all my fault," the little girl sobbed, throwing her thin arms around his neck. "It was my idea to feed the ducks. I spoiled everything."

"No, sweetheart," Alexander said. He was unaccustomed to being around children. If asked, he could have said quite truthfully that he had no interest in these small, noisy, demanding little creatures his married acquaintances set such store by. But something about Vanessa's little sisters aroused feelings of protectiveness he didn't know he had. He held Aggie for a moment, then stood and took her hand. "It was an accident. If anyone is to blame, it is I. Come with me, and we will find something warm for your sister to put on."

They hadn't gone far when the Earl of Stoneham accosted them.

"What is the meaning of this, Alexander?" the earl demanded wrathfully. "The whole house is in an uproar!"

"One of the Whittaker children fell in the pond at the park. I brought her here because Stoneham House was closer than their own house in Hans Crescent," Alexander said, tightening his grip on Aggie's hand and brushing by his father. "If you'll excuse us, I have to find something warm for a little girl to wear."

He went to Letitia's room where he surprised his aunt in the act of writing a letter.

"What is it, dearest?" she asked, standing up from her pretty little gilt-trimmed desk.

"I need something warm for a little girl," he said.

"How little?" she asked suspiciously.

"A bit larger than Miss Agatha here."

Letitia looked at Aggie with narrowed eyes.

"Letitia, this is Aggie Whittaker. Her sister fell in the pond at the park," Alexander explained, exasperated by his aunt's apparent stupefaction. "Are you going to help us or not?"

"Of course I will help. My cashmere bedjacket should serve the purpose," Letitia said. "Now all we have to do is find it." She pulled on the bell rope and her dresser appeared immediately at her summons.

"Here it is, Madam," the dresser said, producing it from a wardrobe drawer after Letitia had explained the problem. "It rather smells of camphor, having been put away for the winter, but—"

"It will do quite well," Alexander said, snatching the costly trifle from the woman. He gave his aunt a look of pure gratitude. "Thank you, Aunt Letitia."

Then he took Aggie's hand and went back to the blue room. By then the sisters had dried Amy off briskly with the thick white towel that had been folded by the basin and pitcher in a corner of the room. Alexander tossed the bedjacket to Lydia and suggested that Mary Ann accompany himself and Aggie to the parlor. Once there, he invited them to sit on the sofa and left them to go out into the hall again.

"Ah, there you are," he said when he found the butler. "Has the doctor been sent for?"

"Certainly, my lord," the butler said, looking offended.

"Good. Have one of the maids bring refreshments to us in the parlor. And send someone to Hans Crescent to escort Mrs. Whittaker here."

"Yes, my lord," the butler said.

"Good man," Alexander said, returning at once to the parlor where he applied himself to the task of soothing the apprehensions of the young ladies.

He had just succeeded in calming them down when Mrs. Whittaker arrived and threw them into a fresh state of agitation.

"Oh, my poor little lamb!" the lady cried. "Where is she?"

"Here, ma'am," Alexander said, taking her arm and escorting her to the blue room. The doctor, surprised in the act of listening to Amy's chest with one of his instruments, looked aghast when Mrs. Whittaker launched herself upon him and began pelting him with questions about her daughter's condition.

"Look, Mama!" Amy said quite cheerfully. "Captain Logan's aunt lent me this pretty, soft robe to wear. Was that not kind of her?" Amy touched the rolled-up sleeve of the blue cashmere jacket reverently.

"My precious baby!" Mrs. Whittaker cried hysterically. "Oh, my poor little one! You could have been drowned."

Amy promptly burst into tears, and Vanessa bent over the child to calm her.

"Mother, the doctor does not think she will become ill because of Captain Logan's quick thinking in bringing her here before she could take a chill," Vanessa said.

She gave Alexander such a look brimful of gratitude that he forgot for a moment that he wasn't really in love with her.

"It was nothing," he murmured.

"Oh, how can I ever thank you!" Mrs. Whittaker cried. The doctor cleared his throat.

"Miss Amy must rest now," he said pointedly. "If you will pardon my saying so, all of this excitement is very bad for her. I will not have my patient agitated."

"Yes, yes," Mrs. Whittaker agreed at once. "All of you must be quiet and let poor Amy rest. There, there, darling. Don't cry. Mama is with you now."

Alexander accompanied the doctor to the door and thanked him for coming so quickly.

Then he returned to the parlor to find that Vanessa and Lydia had joined the younger girls.

Vanessa stood at once and came toward him when he paused at the threshold.

"You were wonderful, Alexander. I don't know how we can thank you," she said.

"No thanks are necessary," he said, clasping her outstretched hand in his for a moment. "It is what anyone would have done."

He deliberately turned away from her and addressed the younger girls.

"Is there any tea left?" he asked.

"Yes, Captain Logan," said Mary Ann shyly, lifting the pot. "Shall I pour for you?"

"Please," he replied, seating himself on the sofa between the two younger girls. "Let us ring for some more cakes. And we shall have some tea and cakes sent up to your mother and sister in the blue room."

"Alexander, darling," Letitia said from the doorway. "Is the child all right?"

"The doctor thinks there is no harm done," he said, pleased that she would ask. "Do join us."

"Thank you," she said, taking a chair near Vanessa.

"I was just about to ring for more tea and cakes," Alexander told her. "And I thought perhaps some could be sent upstairs to Mrs. Whittaker and Miss Amy."

"Oh, of course. I shall take care of it, if you will excuse me for a moment," Letitia said, mindful of her role as hostess. She was as good as her word, because shortly after she returned to the room, a maid came in bearing not only more tea and cakes, but some more substantial fare as well.

"You will all stay to dine, of course," Letitia said. "And this evening, if Mrs. Whittaker thinks it is wise, we will bundle little Amy up quite warmly and send her home in the traveling coach. It is large enough to accommodate all of you and permit the child to lie down as well."

Alexander looked sharply at his aunt. Her message was perfectly clear to him, if not to their guests. By offering the traveling coach, Letitia was ensuring that the nobodies from the wilds of Yorkshire would be out of Stoneham House by nightfall. He considered it churlish of her not to offer them accommodations for the night.

"I don't know how we can repay such kindness," Vanessa said earnestly to Letitia.

Letitia gave Vanessa a sweet, false smile and patted her hand.

"Think nothing of it, my dear," she said. Her tone was perfectly civil, but her eyes were cold. "It is my pleasure."

"How could you fill my house with those encroaching, shabby genteel . . ."

Words failed the earl as he faced his unrepentant son over port in the dining room. All the young ladies, even little Aggie, had risen at Letitia's signal to retire to the parlor. Cedric did not approve of children at the table, but that was one of his minor grievances at the moment. At least he had been spared the sight of Annabelle Whittaker's simpering face over his dinner. Her meal and Amy's had been sent up to the blue room on a tray.

"The child was soaking wet," Alexander said. "I could not permit her to contract an inflammation of the lung when it was within my power to prevent it."

"I don't see why not. The brat is not your responsibility."

"She was in my company when the accident occurred. I could hardly leave her and her sisters in the park to fend for themselves."

"Yes, tell me more about *that*, if you please. It isn't quite in your style to be escorting a nursery party around the park of an afternoon. I told you I would not permit you to trifle with the likes of Miss Whittaker, and I meant it."

"I am of legal age, Cedric. I don't need your approval to see whichever young lady I please," Alexander said.

"You will be sorry if you don't obey me in this matter, Alexander."

Alexander's brows rose.

"What an unnatural parent you are," he observed. "When I was haunting the gin parlors of London, gambling and drinking and whoring, you had no fault to find with the way I spent my leisure time. But when I take an interest in a perfectly respectable young lady, you fairly shout the house down with disapproval."

The earl's fist hit the top of the linen-covered table, making the crystal glasses rattle.

"I won't be trifled with, damn you. If you must amuse yourself, do it with married ladies who know the way the game is played or with whores. You are no callow youth to be ensnared in the toils of an ambitious little slut barely escaped from the schoolroom."

Alexander shot to his feet.

"I will not permit you to call Miss Whittaker names in my presence," he said. "She is a guest under your own roof. You have a lot of gall lecturing *me* on propriety."

"She is no guest of mine. *I* didn't invite her. I would not be surprised if that mother of hers didn't put one of her girls up to pushing the brat into the lake in order to worm her way into Stoneham House. Annabelle Whittaker is probably furious that the child isn't seriously ill. She probably planned to foist the brat and the rest of her daughters on us for weeks and weeks until the child was out of danger."

"What a stupid thing to stay! I won't stay for another minute and listen to such drivel. I am going to join the ladies."

"Alexander, come back here! I am not finished speaking with you."

"Well, I am finished *listening* to you," Alexander growled as he stalked from the room.

He had to stand outside the parlor door for a minute or so until he managed to gain control of his temper.

Then he came to his senses.

What was wrong with him? He should be pleased with Cedric's contempt for the Whittaker family. The way the earl had insulted Vanessa's breeding and morals should have been music to Alexander's ears. After all, Alexander intended to take advantage of that contempt in order to extricate himself from his father's machinations. His plan was proceeding nicely.

So why was he so angry? He felt as if someone actually had insulted the woman he loved.

Which, of course, was utterly ridiculous.

Alexander did not love Vanessa.

It was all a sham, he reminded himself sternly.

A pretense.

A lie.

He forced a smile to his lips and went into the parlor where he planned to sit down next to Vanessa and devote all of his attention to entertaining her. Not because he loved her. But because it was part of the plan.

NINE

Alexander drove Vanessa to the park in his curricle on the day appointed for her riding lesson, having instructed one of the grooms from his father's stable to meet them there with a gentle mare for Vanessa and a stallion for him. He hadn't thought it wise to expose Vanessa to London traffic—or, indeed, London traffic to Vanessa—her first day on horseback.

He eyed the chestnut stallion with resignation. It was a perfectly respectable horse, well bred and well trained. The Earl of Stoneham would tolerate no inferior horseflesh in his stables. But it wasn't Midnight, his own favorite mount. Alexander had broken Midnight to bridle himself, and the high-spirited stallion was unreliable with other riders. Alexander, therefore, couldn't very well expect the groom to bring him. After Midnight, unfortunately, horses such as this aristocratic resident of his father's stable made for an unexciting ride.

And was Vanessa grateful for Alexander's noble self-sacrifice?

Not in the least.

"I don't want to do this," she said, backing away when Alexander led the gentle mare up to her.

Even the arrival of an exquisite blue riding habit from Madame Celeste's shop had failed to inspire Vanessa with any enthusiasm for the sport, so Alexander was prepared for an argument.

"Come now, Vanessa," Alexander said in a bracing tone, reaching out to capture her hand in a firm grip. "Don't be a coward. Most children sit a horse by the time they are ten years old, if not before." He tried to guide her fingertips up to make contact with the horse's head, but Vanessa obstinately curled her hand into a fist to avoid petting the creature.

"I don't care that most people learned to ride when they were children of ten. I didn't, and I fail to see why I should learn now," she said.

"Stop it, Vanessa. You can't seriously be afraid of this horse. It is so gentle a baby could ride it."

"Afraid? Of course I am not afraid! What a ridiculous idea!" When the mare turned its head in her direction, Vanessa gasped and took another step backward.

"My mistake," he said dryly, retaining his hold on her hand. "If you are not afraid, what possible objection can you have to learning how to ride?"

"I just don't want to," she insisted. For all her protestations, her voice was higher than usual. "Please, Alexander. It can't be *that* important."

Alexander hardened his heart against Vanessa's look of entreaty and wished she didn't look so beautiful in the sapphire blue riding habit Madame Celeste had made for her. It was fortunate that Vanessa was frowning. If she smiled at him, he might lose his head altogether and promise her anything.

"My dear girl, I thought we had been over this ground before," he said with a long-suffering sigh. "Teaching you how to ride will give me any number of excuses to see you alone in public without damaging your reputation. When Cedric learns of this—"

"I know," Vanessa interrupted, giving him a look of pure loathing. "He will agree to *anything* to keep his precious heir from falling into the clutches of the wicked fortune hunter. It is a wonder he doesn't keep you under lock and key to preserve you from such a hideous fate."

Alexander gave her a look of exasperation, but he couldn't quite stop his lips from turning up at the corners.

"You are only pretending to be insulted, Vanessa, to distract me from the issue." Her guilty look confirmed his statement. "You have made it abundantly clear that you don't care in the least what Cedric thinks of you or your family. Nor can I think of one good reason why you should. Now stop prevaricating and get on the bloody horse."

"I don't like horses," she complained.

Alexander stared at her in disbelief at this heresy. No English lady with any pretense to gentility would *dare* admit she didn't like horses. It simply wasn't done.

"Nonsense," he said.

"I don't think I will like sitting so far above the ground," she argued, pulling her hand out of his. "And they *smell.*"

"My father keeps a first-rate stable, Vanessa," he said, trying to sound severe. "It is one of the few things about him I find worthy of admiration. I can assure you that *none* of his horses smell. They wouldn't dare."

Vanessa put her hands on her hips and shook her head at him.

"*All* horses smell. They are *animals.* One has to feed them and muck out their stables, and they're so everlastingly stupid that they can't even give birth without help, and, in short, having them is a great deal of botheration and expense. My mother is always complaining because we can't afford to keep a carriage and horses of our own in London and, for the life of me, I can't imagine why."

"Vanessa," he said warningly, "you are trying my patience."

"Alexander—"

"You agreed to help me rejoin my regiment—"

"I can still do that without learning how to ride."

Alexander realized it was time for extreme measures. He would have to tell her the truth.

"All right," he admitted. "I want you to learn how to ride because our supposed courtship is going to be intolerable for me unless you do."

"How vastly flattering," she said, raising one brow. "I have a wonderful idea. Why don't you ask the *horse* to pose as the future mother of your children. I am sure you would be very happy together!"

"I knew you would take it like this," he said with a sigh. "Have some pity on me, Vanessa. I am spending every afternoon sitting in your mother's parlor being stared at and giggled over by her friends, and every evening dancing attendance on you at balls. I have given up gambling and drinking entirely in order to convince my father that I am reforming my rakish ways and seriously contemplating matrimony. To put it mildly, this is hardly what I am accustomed to in the way of entertainment. If you learn how to ride, at least I will have some excuse to enjoy the fine weather while it lasts. Do you not occasionally wish we could have a sensible conversation instead of having to play to an audience?"

Vanessa bit her lip. Indecision was written all over her lovely face.

"I will hold the horse's bridle for the entire time," Alexander promised, seeing that she was weakening. "To begin with, all you have to do is sit on the horse while I lead you around in a circle."

"I probably will fall off!"

"If you do, I shall catch you. Come along, Vanessa. Don't be tiresome."

He made an impatient gesture indicating she was to come forward to face him, and when she didn't comply he reached for her hand.

"Alexander, no!" she cried, stepping backward.

"This is nonsense," he said, frustrated. "I know you were afraid of horses as a child, but there is no reason to be afraid of them now. I will help you overcome your fear, if only you will cooperate."

"I beg your pardon," she said, looking mortified. "I am making a complete fool of myself, but I can't seem to help it."

"Surely you know you can trust me to keep you safe."

As soon as the words were out of his mouth Alexander wished he could take them back. What an idiot he was. The way he had bullied and manipulated Vanessa into co-operating with his plan, he probably was the last man on earth she trusted.

She tilted her head up a little and looked at him.

"Yes," she said, sounding surprised. "I believe I do. Isn't that curious?"

The look of dismay on her face was so adorable that Alexander laughed. When he gestured for her to come forward again, she did so without hesitation. Without knowing quite how it happened, he found her in his arms.

Alexander lost all interest in the riding lesson.

Staring into Vanessa's eyes, holding her narrow waist between his hands, he couldn't resist kissing her. And, wonder of all wonders, she kissed him back. Not very expertly, to be sure, but the sweetness of her response made up for it. When he drew back to look at her, she raised one gloved hand to her swollen lips. Her eyes had gone all soft and smoky.

I am *not* in love with Vanessa Whittaker, Alexander told himself, feeling a little desperate. He *refused* to be in love with her.

Alexander very badly wanted to kiss Vanessa again, but he forced himself, instead, to allow his hands to drop to his sides.

"Time for your lesson, Vanessa," he told her in the same uncompromising tone of voice he used on raw recruits under his command. "You said you trusted me. Prove it. Up you go."

"I *knew* I would regret admitting that," she said ruefully.

Trying not to smile, he bent and cupped his hands.

"Put your foot in my hands, and your hand on my shoulder, and when I straighten up, seat yourself in the saddle. Are you ready?"

"Yes," she said, looking as if she were about to make the acquaintance of her executioner.

She was trembling.

"None of that, my girl," he said, trying to sound stern. "It won't be so bad. You'll see. Up you go."

It took two tries. The first time the horse moved, so Vanessa screamed and pushed herself away from the saddle instead of sitting on it. Alexander had to catch her or let her fall to the ground. The second time she managed to sit on the sidesaddle, but she looked so uncomfortable that Alexander forgot himself and put a hand on her knee to reassure her that she was safe.

"Captain Logan!" she exclaimed, looking scandalized.

"I beg your pardon," he said, hastily withdrawing his hand. "You hook your right leg around—" He started to reach for her leg in order to help her guide it into the proper position.

"I know where it goes, Alexander," she said, slapping his hand away. "I have seen *other* ladies on sidesaddles. I just haven't been on one personally until now."

He watched her carefully to make sure her position was correct. When he was satisfied, he took the bridle.

"Here we go, now. If you feel yourself sliding, cry out and I'll catch you."

Alexander felt like a perfect fool, walking slowly around the little clearing with a neophyte equestrienne clinging like a burr to the pommel of the mare's saddle. Several of his acquaintances on their morning rides passed by on the path and, seeing him thus engaged, stared at him in utter disbelief. A few laughed. Alexander reflected that perhaps it was fortunate he didn't intend to frequent his club for a long while. No doubt he would be teased mercilessly about being tied to Vanessa Whittaker's apron strings.

The things he did for Mother England!

However, it was hard to feel resentful when he glanced back at Vanessa and she rewarded him with a tentative smile.

"I suppose it isn't so bad," Vanessa said, holding onto the pommel as she was jounced in the saddle.

She seemed more resigned than afraid, which Alexander considered progress. When the mare stepped into a rabbit hole and stumbled, she even managed to hold onto the pommel and avoid sliding off the horse's back.

"That's my girl," Alexander said. He already had started toward her with his arms extended to catch her. When he saw she had managed to retain her seat, he caught up the bridle again and continued walking. "Someday you will thank me for this," he said, looking back at her over his shoulder.

She gave him a look of deep reproach.

"Hardly," she said, with a touch of her old spirit.

They managed to make several full circles without mishap by the time Alexander decided his dignity had been abused enough for one day. He reached up and caught Vanessa at her waist. Looking relieved, she put her hands on his shoulders and allowed him to help her to the ground.

"There. Are you all right?" he asked, retaining his hold on her for longer than was necessary. He noticed she still had her hands on his shoulders, clutching at the fabric of his coat.

"Yes," she said, casting her eyes down.

"Good. Now we will give the tabbies something to gossip about over their knitting."

"All right," she said, sounding a little breathless. She turned her face up to his and closed her eyes. It was apparent that she thought he meant to kiss her for the benefit of the other visitors to the park, and it took all of his self-control not to oblige her.

Stolen kisses were all very well in their place, but he had something a bit more flamboyant in mind. Alexander allowed himself a moment of pure pleasure in anticipation of Vanessa's probable reaction to his next move. He would be fortunate if she didn't murder him outright for this.

Alexander called to the groom who had brought the horses. He had chosen the man carefully because he was a young fellow, and the biggest gossip in the stables. Word soon would be all over Stoneham House that Alexander had taken one of the mares from the stables to teach Miss Whittaker how to ride.

Cedric and Letitia would be livid.

"Take the curricle and the mare back to Stoneham House," he said to the groom. "*Directly* to Stoneham House," he added sternly when the young man's eyes lit with anticipation. "Miss Whittaker and I will ride double on the stallion to Hans Crescent."

He was not looking at Vanessa, but he could feel the smoldering look she directed at his back through several layers of clothing.

"I have changed my mind. I don't trust you at all, Captain Logan," Vanessa said for Alexander's ears alone as the groom tied the mare's reins to the carriage frame. "You are a rogue and an unprincipled scoundrel."

"That sums it up quite nicely. Cheer up, Vanessa. Think what a romantic picture you will make, riding before me on this noble steed." His mocking tone had been calculated to annoy her, and it succeeded admirably.

"You are a cruel, insensitive beast," she said, her eyes brilliant with blue fire.

"Undoubtedly. It isn't far. You will be perfectly safe, I assure you."

Alexander took Vanessa by the waist and lifted her to sit sideways on the stallion's saddle. Then he seated himself behind her. The horse pranced a little and, to Alexander's delight, Vanessa gave a startled cry and wrapped both arms tightly around his waist, pressing the side of her face against his chest.

Her eyes were still closed when he tipped her chin up with his finger and kissed her soft, sweet lips.

"Don't be alarmed," Alexander said when she opened her eyes and looked searchingly into his face. He wasn't sure whether he was trying to remind Vanessa or himself that their supposed romance was only a temporary arrangement. "Just a bit of practice. You are quite getting the hang of this."

To Alexander's relief, his mocking tone succeeded in taking that vulnerable look off her face.

"I hate you," she whispered vehemently.

"I know, darling," he replied as he guided the horse down the path and nodded to another lady and gentleman on horseback, both of whom stared at them. "I hate you, too. Stop squirming like a ten-year-old and smile at the nice, nosy people."

Vanessa's feelings for Captain Logan were so disturbing that on the following day she deliberately went on a shopping excursion with Diana Lacey to avoid his inevitable afternoon call.

Unfortunately, she found herself scrutinizing every gentleman that approached in the hope of seeing him. This simply would not do. Even the good-humored Diana was becoming quite impatient with Vanessa's preoccupation.

When Vanessa returned home, she heard her younger sisters' laughter coming from the parlor. She smiled, glad that they were finding something to amuse themselves. To her astonishment, she entered the room to find Alexander occupied in playing cards with Amy, Aggie, and Mary Ann.

"Alexander!" she exclaimed, annoyed by the way her heart fluttered in her breast at the sight of him.

Looking guilty, Alexander rose to his feet.

"Good afternoon, Vanessa," he replied with something less than his usual self-possession.

Vanessa's eyes narrowed in suspicion. Mary Ann blushed scarlet and looked exactly as if she expected to receive a severe scold.

"Vanny, Captain Logan is teaching us how to gamble!" Aggie said excitedly just as Vanessa realized from the look of cards on the table that it had been no nursery game they were playing.

"Is he, indeed?" Vanessa pointed an accusing finger at the sheepish-looking officer, who had been shaking his head, to no avail, at the little girls to silence them. "Alexander, this time you have gone too far! How dare you try to corrupt my sisters?"

"Now, Vanessa—" he began.

"Mary Ann, I am disappointed in you," Vanessa interrupted, turning her wrath on her teenage sister. "Amy and Aggie are too young to know better, but surely you—"

"This is entirely my fault," Alexander interrupted. "If you are going to give anyone a bear garden jaw, let it be me."

Vanessa put her hands on her hips.

"And I will thank you not to use such vulgar expressions in front of the children," she snapped. "You have taught them quite enough bad habits for one day." She turned her attention to her sisters. "Where are Mother and Lydia?" she asked Mary Ann.

"Sally fell down the back stairs, and Mama and Lydia are in her room with her. Captain Logan had come to call just after it happened, and he went for the doctor because, of course, we have no manservant since Mama had to dismiss Rodgers. The children were upset because the doctor would not permit them to be in Sally's room while he was examining her ankle, so Captain Logan stayed here with us until after the doctor left."

"Why didn't you say so?" Vanessa asked, alarmed. "Is Sally all right?"

"The doctor said she is very fortunate, for her ankle was only sprained a little," said Mary Ann. "She has to stay off of it for a few days. The children were very upset, and—"

"Thank heavens her injury is no worse," Vanessa said, feeling like a villainess. "I am sorry I shouted at you, Mary Ann."

"It's all right—" Mary Ann started to reply.

"You shouted at Captain Logan, too, and he is a *guest!*" Amy interrupted, her little face indignant on behalf of her hero.

"You must beg Captain Logan's pardon, Vanny," Aggie insisted, equally outraged, "or we shall tell Mama."

"Yes," Vanessa said, biting her lip. "I do apologize, Captain Logan." Her tone was hardly gracious, but she couldn't help it.

"Accepted." It was obvious that he was trying to keep from laughing at her discomfiture. Vanessa cheerfully could have boxed his ears.

"Girls, I would like to speak with Captain Logan in private, if you don't mind."

"Lydia would have a fit if I left you alone with a man," Mary Ann said, shocked.

"Captain Logan occasionally exercises poor judgment," Vanessa said, "but he is a gentleman, nonetheless. I will be perfectly safe in his company, I assure you. Run along, now."

"No. If we go, you will shout at Captain Logan. And he never will call on us again," Aggie cried.

Vanessa gave Aggie an incredulous look, and the child raised her chin belligerently. It seemed to Vanessa that her younger sisters' manners had deteriorated dramatically since Alexander had become a frequent visitor to their home.

"Please, Aggie," Vanessa said, indicating the door.

The three younger Whittaker girls reluctantly trooped to the doorway. Amy and Aggie looked back at Captain Logan with worried expressions on their faces. The dreadful man had the audacity to give them an exaggerated wink from one of those wicked eyes. Reassured, the girls giggled and went on out of the room.

Alexander was still smiling when he turned his attention to Vanessa.

"You wished to speak with me, my dear?" he asked, walking purposefully to her and putting his arms around her waist. To her consternation, he looked as if he were going to kiss her. "Dare I hope you've missed me?"

"Alexander," she snapped, drawing back to avoid his lips. "Stop that at once!"

"I am a gentleman," he reminded her in a teasing voice. "You are perfectly safe with me. Have I told you how very beautiful you are when you are angry?"

She put her hands against his chest and gave him a shove with all her strength behind it.

"Alexander, stop trying to make me laugh!"

He gave a long-suffering sigh and held his hands out to indicate he was harmless.

"What have I done to annoy you now, my love? I had persuaded myself that I was being the very model of a perfect suitor, sending flowers to my beloved, teaching her how to ride, staring at her like a dolt at balls, being kind to her mother and sisters—"

"Being kind! Is it kind to give them a taste for gaming?"

"We weren't playing for stakes," he said. "They taught me one of their nursery games. Then they said it was my turn to teach them a game, and this was the simplest one I knew. You are entirely too sensible to be angry with me because I have taught your sisters a harmless game of cards. Tell me what is bothering you."

"This is all so complicated." She began pacing the floor in agitation, and Alexander propped himself against the mantle to watch her. He had the gall to look amused, the irritating man! "When this began, I thought about how awkward it would be for me when our false betrothal was ended, but it didn't occur to me that my sisters would be hurt. Alexander, they have grown very fond of you."

He raised one eyebrow.

"This may be a surprise to you, Vanessa, but females, as a rule, are inclined to be fond of me."

"You don't understand. They talk about you all the time. Whenever we propose to set foot outside the house they ask if we will meet you at our destination, or if you are going with us. And if the answer is no, they worry that you will call while we are out and may be offended that no one was here to receive you. I can't bear to see their affections trifled with."

Alexander strode forward and captured her shoulders, putting an end to her restless movements.

"Precisely what are you accusing me of?" he asked.

"Surely you don't think it is any part of my intention to hurt your sisters. If so, you do me a grave injustice."

"I know that," she said impatiently. "It's just we, that is, my sisters—"

She averted her face.

"What?" he asked, taking her face in his hands and forcing her to look at him.

"My sisters will miss you when you . . . leave," she said in a thread of a voice.

"Will *you* miss me, Vanessa?" he asked.

"That is neither here nor there. We were speaking of my sisters," she said, horrified to hear her voice quaver.

He gave her a thoughtful look.

"Yes, so we were. Pray continue."

"Toward the end of his life my father cared for little except gaming, and the younger girls have no pleasant memory of him. They never have known the affection of a father and, Alexander, I'm very much afraid that they—in short, they have quite innocently come to regard you, if not precisely as a father, as a doting elder brother."

Alexander looked absolutely appalled.

"Vanessa, you must be mistaken!" he said. His chagrin was almost comical. She might have laughed if she hadn't been so concerned on behalf of her sisters. "Surely there is some gentleman in your family who has been kind to the poor little things?"

"The so-called *gentlemen* in my father's family, my uncles and cousins, completely lost interest in us when my father committed the solecism of letting the fortune he inherited from *his* father run through his fingers. For all they cared, the lot of us could have been thrown on the parish. Certainly they never went out of their way to be kind to any of us."

"What about your mother's family?"

"They came *en masse* to the funeral expecting to sponge off the wealthy widow," she said bitterly. "We have heard nothing from them since they realized that we were in need of financial assistance ourselves, and they might reasonably be expected to contribute toward our upkeep. The younger girls have known nothing but the company of women from birth, so it is not surprising that they have formed an attachment for you."

"I had no idea," he said. "But I fail to understand why you are so concerned. I watch my language carefully when I am with them, I assure you, and I will promise not to teach them any more card games, if you insist."

"Alexander, are you completely dense?" She started pacing again. "No doubt you have been kind to them simply to lend credence to the pretense that you wish to marry me, but . . ."

Alexander's expression of good humor quite vanished at this remark.

"You have a high opinion of me, don't you, my sweet?" he asked, looking so affronted that Vanessa took an involuntary step backward. "Is it so surprising that I might pay attention to three fatherless children unless I have ulterior motives?"

"You must admit that gentlemen rarely become fond of lively little girls unless they are very pretty. The neighborhood boys used to refer to Mary Ann, Amy, and Aggie as the three little pigs. It made me furious, but Mama always said beauty in a female is very important to gentlemen, and they aren't likely to take notice of a plain young lady unless, of course, she has a fortune."

"Your mother was mistaken," Alexander said.

"Perhaps. But in my limited experience with gentlemen I would have to say my mother's opinion seems to be more the rule than the exception. Aggie and Amy and Mary Ann will be so disappointed when our arrangement is at an end. Lydia even has started looking upon you with a more kindly eye."

Alexander lifted one eyebrow.

"That is surprising. The girl terrifies me. I had quite a good opinion of myself until I met Lydia."

"What nonsense. As if any mere female could shake your

odious self-consequence. Mama thinks you are Prince Charming personified."

"Yes, but she had a similar high opinion of Lord Omersley, so I will not let it go to my head. Seriously, I find Aggie and Amy vastly entertaining. They are such sweet, affectionate little things. And Mary Ann, for all her shyness, has a good head on her shoulders. I can see why a man might want children of his own."

"Alexander? Are you feeling quite the thing?" Vanessa asked, feigning concern.

He smiled at her.

"I must be getting sentimental in my old age. Vanessa, I promise you that when all of this is at an end your sisters will not be harmed. I will even write to them, if I can."

He put his hands on Vanessa's shoulders and looked down into her eyes.

"Now tell me what is really bothering you."

Vanessa looked away, and she could feel her face flush scarlet. Like her sisters, she was becoming entirely too attached to Alexander, but she could hardly tell him that!

"I don't know what you mean," she lied.

"No?" His tone was skeptical. "Then you won't mind if we discuss the next stage of our plan. Cedric, I am delighted to report, is beginning to be worried. It shouldn't be long at all now before he gives in and allows me to be recalled to my regiment."

"That is good news," she said, feeling far from glad to hear Alexander might soon be leaving for war.

"Yes, and not a moment too soon," he said, "for the word from Eastern Europe is grim. Vanessa, the times call for drastic measures."

"What drastic measures?"

"I am going to propose to you at Lady Ernestine's ball."

"Impossible!" Vanessa exclaimed. "It is too soon! We have not known one another long enough. No one will believe it!"

Alexander pulled her into his arms so quickly that she

stumbled against him and had to hold onto his shoulders for support.

"We will make them believe," he said softly as his dark eyes burned into hers.

TEN

After he had relinquished his hat to the Whittakers' maid, Alexander's attention was arrested by the sound of a giggle coming from some point above him.

"Captain Logan," said Amy in a stage whisper.

Alexander saw the little girl peeping from between the banisters. He grinned and beckoned to her to come down. She looked from side to side and stopped within a few steps of him so she could jump into his arms. He caught the child against his chest and she wrapped her arms around his neck.

"I am supposed to be in bed," she confided, wiggling her chubby little toes against his knee.

"You, my little hoyden, are ruining the fit of my new coat," he said, enormously pleased by her affectionate greeting. "And, I strongly suspect, have rumpled my cravat as well. Vanessa and your mother will most likely refuse to be seen in public with me."

"I'm sorry, Captain Logan," she said, giggling.

"Alexander," he said. "I have told you that you may call me Alexander, Amy."

"I forgot," she said, giving him a shy look from beneath her stubby, sand-colored lashes. "You aren't wearing your uniform tonight. You look different."

"I know," he said. "Do you think Vanessa will be disappointed?"

Amy looked him up and down solemnly. The dark coat

of formal dress was unfamiliar garb for him, and he felt a
little self-conscious under her scrutiny. Perhaps he had
been foolish in giving into vanity and having it made. It
served him right that Amy probably had destroyed its perfection. But she was so warm and sweet and soft that he
didn't much care.

"Well?" he prompted.

"I think she'll like it," was the child's verdict.

"Thank you, sweetheart," he said, smiling at her.

The child blushed prettily and Alexander reached up
to touch her soft cheek. Her dark hair was braided, and
she was wearing a white nightgown soft from many wash-
ings. Alexander had a sudden vision of what Vanessa must
have looked like at that age. He gave Amy a hug, loving
the feel of her little arms around his neck.

"You are most welcome, Alexander," Amy said shyly.

Alexander put her down so her bare feet would touch
the floor and patted her on the head. Amy darted back
up the stairs, giggling. Alexander straightened to see Vanessa standing at top of the stairs, solemnly watching him.
He wondered how long she had been standing there.

Vanessa bent to listen to something Amy said, laughed,
and sent the child on her way with a light pat on her little
bottom. Then Vanessa smiled at Alexander and continued
down the stairs.

"Mama will be down in a moment," Vanessa told him
apologetically when she reached him. Her smile faded.
"Why are you looking at me like that?" she asked, and
Alexander realized he had been staring. He took her
gloved hand and turned it over, kissing her wrist.

"You look exquisite," he said.

Vanessa rolled her eyes.

"I *should* look exquisite," she said. "When you see what
this gown cost, you probably will expire on the spot."

"Whatever I paid, it was worth it," Alexander said gallantly, and he meant it. The gown was an ethereal creation
of white gauze over satin with a low neckline and puffed
sleeves slashed and threaded with violet ribbon. More vio-

let ribbon encircled the high waistline just under Vanessa's full breasts. She was an angel come to earth. No wonder he had been caught staring like a mooncalf.

Vanessa gave Alexander a quizzical smile that acknowledged the compliment, but made it clear that she didn't believe a word of it. It occurred to Alexander that for all her beauty, Vanessa wasn't in the least conceited about her looks.

Alexander handed her a square-shaped box.

"More flowers?" Vanessa exclaimed. "As you can see, I am wearing the ones you sent this afternoon."

"I noticed," he said. The little nosegay of violets was secured at her waist. Vanessa had chosen the gown to please him. He knew it as surely as he knew his own name, and he couldn't stop what he suspected was a very silly grin from spreading over his face. "These are for your hair."

The box contained a cluster of fragrant white rosebuds with stems resting in a tiny glass vial of water. The vial was secured to a clip so it could be placed in a lady's coiffure.

"How lovely! I've never seen anything like it," Vanessa exclaimed, stepping to a mirror on the wall to pin the flowers in her hair.

"No, don't," Alexander said, coming up behind her and admiring their reflected images in the mirror. He closed his hand over hers, then removed the ornament from her fingers. "Permit me."

Vanessa looked surprised, then relaxed and lowered her hand to her side. "So this is what we look like together," she mused as she watched his reflection in the mirror.

"We are accounted to be an uncommonly handsome couple," he said, holding the ornament against her hair. "How about there?"

"Yes," she said, sounding a little breathless. "It would look well there."

One of her soft, shining curls caressed Alexander's finger as he secured the roses above her left temple.

When he was done, Vanessa surprised him very much

by turning to face him and standing on tiptoe to kiss his cheek.

"What was that for?" he asked, pleased. In the time he had known Vanessa, she never had touched him voluntarily. She seemed willing, at times, to accept his kisses—even to enjoy them—but never, until now, had she initiated any affection between them.

"Your other presents were for show," she said, her eyes solemn, "but this was different, was it not?"

Alexander was taken aback. It was different. He had seen the elegant little hair ornament when he ordered the violets, and at once he had imagined how pretty it would look among the dark masses of Vanessa's beautiful hair. Somehow she had known that this was a genuine gift, not a prop to lend credence to the pretense of a liaison between them.

That sweet, sincere kiss on the cheek inflamed him more than all the practiced seductions of his past flirts. He mustn't let Vanessa find out how she affected him. He didn't know which of them would be the more embarrassed.

The Earl of Stoneham afforded his fellow guests at Lady Ernestine's ball a great deal of entertainment by glowering at his heir for the first half of the evening.

"I think this is going to work," Alexander said to Vanessa as he brought her a glass of lemonade. He smiled down into her eyes with the most tender expression on his face. Vanessa had to hold the lemonade with both hands to keep from dropping it.

Vanessa reminded herself, quite firmly, that Alexander probably had a reputation all along the Spanish coast for more conquests than that hateful Corsican. Otherwise, she might be in some danger of succumbing to his charm.

And that, she knew, would be to make an utter fool of herself.

She fluttered her eyelashes at him for the earl's benefit.

"He looks as if he would dearly love to murder one of us," Vanessa murmured, referring to the earl.

"Yes," Alexander agreed. "Or send one of us to the continent to serve as target practice for the bloody French."

"Don't say that!" Vanessa cried out before she thought. Several persons nearby turned to look at her.

"Very good, my dear," Alexander whispered. "One would think you genuinely cared."

She almost replied that, *of course,* she cared! But she stopped herself in time. After all, the whole idea behind this silly farce was to get him shipped out posthaste to battle.

"I think it is time for us to go out onto the terrace for a breath of air," he said. "That should set old Cedric's hackles up properly."

Vanessa stole a glance at the earl, and the look of pure venom he directed at his son almost made her recoil. But the arrangement she had with Alexander was going to save her family from disaster, so she lifted her chin, smiled at Alexander, and took his arm when he offered it.

Lady Ernestine's garden was illuminated with pretty lanterns, but the terrace itself was shrouded in darkness. Vanessa could see the glimmer of jewels as other ladies strolled along the stone floor of the terrace with their escorts. Alexander took her to a dark corner and put his arms around her.

"How fortunate that your gown can be seen in the dark," he said, looming over her in that irritating way he had. It made her senses spin. She told herself, firmly, that she didn't like the helpless way it made her feel when his strong, muscular body was so close to hers. "The tattlemongers will waste no time telling Cedric that his son and heir is trifling with the little fortune hunter in the moonlight."

She felt his fingers touch her face and tilt it up. His dark head bent and his lips were growing closer.

"Why do you call your father by his Christian name?" she blurted out.

Alexander straightened, and she could see the flash of his white teeth in the darkness.

"Shy, Vanessa?" he asked. She could hear the mocking smile in his voice. Without being able to see it, she knew one of his eyebrows was raised in that maddeningly arrogant way of his.

"No. Of course not," she said, standing her ground. "I just wondered."

"It hardly seems appropriate to discuss my father at a time like this."

"On the contrary, my *dear* Alexander, it seems entirely appropriate since this little performance is being staged for his benefit."

"*Touché,* my sweet. Cedric was, and is, a vain man who resented being reminded of his paternal responsibilities once he was freed of his marriage by my mother's death. He disliked being called 'Father' by a half-grown adolescent because it reminded him of his age, so I was instructed to address him as 'sir,' even when we were alone. I obeyed until I was too old to be caned, then I started calling him Cedric. Don't bother to point out how disrespectful it sounds, love. He actually prefers it because it allows him to pretend he isn't old enough to have fathered a man of my age."

"Your father should be ashamed of himself," Vanessa said, indignant on behalf of that confused, motherless boy being told to address his only living parent as "sir." Vanessa fancied she could hear that little boy's hurt behind the lazy, sardonic drawl in which Alexander related the story.

"Do stop looking at me as if I were a child of ten, barefooted and begging crusts of bread in the street," Alexander said harshly. "Let us talk of more pleasant things. Would you prefer diamonds or sapphires?"

Vanessa blinked at him in surprise. "Diamonds or sapphires?" she repeated.

"For your betrothal gift."

"Oh, that. It doesn't matter," she said.

"Are my ears deceiving me? I have yet to meet a lady indifferent on the subject of jewelry."

"It isn't a real betrothal gift. What do I care what you bring me? I'll only have to give it back when all is at an end."

Alexander suddenly swept her into his arms and kissed her so passionately that her knees were trembling by the time he released her. She heard a smothered giggle from behind her, and the sound of footsteps retreating. If she had forgotten their reason for being on the terrace, Alexander, apparently, had not.

"Sorry, my dear," Alexander said, as if in apology for the interruption. His tone was so matter-of-fact that Vanessa could have boxed his ears. "I heard someone coming and it seemed too good an opportunity to miss. You were saying?"

Vanessa firmly removed his hands from her waist and forced her voice to be as dispassionate as his.

"I have changed my mind," she said. "I want both."

"Both?"

"Diamonds *and* sapphires. I am a fortune hunter, after all, and the earl will expect me to have very expensive tastes."

Alexander threw back his head and laughed.

"Good point. Nothing remains but to seal the bargain," Alexander said, taking her in his arms and kissing her again. "There. Since you have no official male guardian, and since your mother is unlikely to object to the match, I think we may consider ourselves unofficially engaged to be married. Your mother may expect my call tomorrow afternoon."

She didn't say anything.

"Vanessa, is something wrong?" he asked, apparently sensing her discomfort. "Would tomorrow be inconvenient?"

"No. Not at all," she said, her imagination conjuring up her mother's probable reaction to a proposal of marriage from Captain Logan. No doubt Annabelle would celebrate her daughter's good fortune with a fresh frenzy of spending, and Vanessa's little sisters would be thrilled by the prospect of having Alexander as a brother. Her family's disappointment when the match came to nothing would be heartbreaking.

Alexander cupped Vanessa's face in his hands and forced her to look at him.

"Something is bothering you," he said. "This is neither the time nor the place to discuss it, but we shall talk it all out tomorrow, I promise you."

He kissed her on the forehead and took her arm to escort her back to the ballroom. Once inside, Vanessa encountered such a look of venom from the earl that her steps faltered and Alexander had to steady her.

Alexander's father hated her. Not just the idea of his son marrying someone unsuitable, but *her*. Personally.

"Courage, my love," Alexander whispered. "He is too mindful of his own consequence to start a row in the middle of a ballroom."

"What will he do to you?"

Alexander stopped and smiled down at her.

"Don't look so concerned, Vanessa. I'll grant you he looks formidable. But short of disinheriting me—and he will hardly do that since I am his only heir—there is nothing he *can* do."

Except send you off to war to be killed, Vanessa thought.

"Smile, darling," Alexander said, "and try to remember you have made me the happiest of men."

Vanessa and Alexander whispered together during supper, and on the few occasions they were separated by the width of the room, they exchanged languishing glances.

The earl looked as if he might suffer an apoplexy when Vanessa and Alexander went down to the dance for the third time—signaling before the *ton* that Alexander's intentions were serious—and Lady Letitia, meeting Vanessa once in the withdrawing room, gave the younger lady a look of such wounded reproach that Vanessa was ready to sink.

Only Alexander's firm hand under her elbow gave Vanessa the courage to get through the evening.

"Well, I think that went rather well," Alexander whispered to Vanessa in the carriage after first looking at the seat opposite to make sure Annabelle was asleep. The elder lady's gentle snores reassured him. "You were perfect," he added, turning her gloved hand over and kissing the palm. "An inspired performance, as usual, my love."

Vanessa snatched her hand away.

"The audience has gone home, Captain Logan. There is no need to continue the play."

Her voice sounded childish and petulant to her own ears, but she didn't care. Alexander responded by taking her in his arms.

"Think of it," he whispered as his lips descended upon hers, "as rehearsal."

ELEVEN

On the following morning, Alexander paid a visit to London's most prestigious jewelers, Rundell and Bridges. There he saw a pair of delicate sapphire and diamond earrings set in silver filigree that might have been made for Vanessa. In fact, they were the only things in the store worthy of her.

He forced himself to turn his back on the display case where they resided. He was not buying Vanessa a gift, but a prop to lend authority to her performance as a gold-digging fortune hunter, and nothing would do except the most ostentatious piece of jewelry he could find. Alexander imagined the earl might have an apoplexy when Vanessa started flaunting her trophy around town.

At first Alexander despaired of finding what he wanted. Rundell and Bridges enjoyed a clientele composed of the most refined families in England, and everything on display was of the highest quality and in excellent taste. But while looking in one of the cases, he was distracted by a flash of light and glanced up to see a clerk examining a necklace with a loupe. The flash of light was the reflection of a very large diamond in the glass, and Alexander knew his search was over.

"I should like to see that necklace, if you please," he said to the startled clerk.

"*This*, sir?" the man asked in a tone of strong disapproval as he surrendered the bauble. "We purchased it as one of a group from the estate of a recently deceased, er, ahem, lady and planned to break up the piece to make several smaller ones. The design is not quite what one would wish, but the stones are of excellent quality. We can reset them in a different mounting, if you like, or in several mountings, for there are enough stones here to make several pieces of jewelry."

"No. I want it just the way it is," Alexander said, turning it over in his hands.

Alexander lingered over the transaction long enough to make certain all the early shoppers visiting the store got a good look at him. He waited while the clerk wrapped the package, then put his treasure in his breast pocket. Alexander regretted that etiquette decreed it still too early for a gentleman to pay a call on a respectable young lady. He couldn't wait to see Vanessa's face when she opened the box. He gave a regretful glance at the dainty sapphire and diamond earrings that had caught his eye when he first entered the store, then, on impulse, he bought them as well.

It was customary to give one's mistress a farewell gift when the relationship was dissolved. Why not one's former fiancée? Alexander liked the thought of giving Vanessa the earrings when he returned to war as a keepsake in addition to the two thousand pounds he had promised. If their ruse worked, she would deserve them. She could keep the necklace as well, he decided in a sentimental burst of generosity. If the two thousand pounds was not enough to pacify her mother's creditors, she could pawn the thing.

Alexander left the store and signaled a waiting hackney. He considered returning to Stoneham House, but he had no desire to face his father. After a slight hesitation, he directed the driver to drop him at his club. It seemed as good a place as any to pass the time until he could call on Vanessa. Alexander had not visited his club in a long time, and he was hailed as one newly risen from the dead by his cronies.

It was with great satisfaction that he noted the betting

book at White's was giving fifteen-to-one odds in favor of his offering for Vanessa before the Season was over. He hoped someone had shown the pertinent entry to his father.

Alexander had expected to enjoy returning to the masculine world of cards and good brandy, but to his surprise he felt oddly disoriented. His acquaintances' talk of sporting events, superior horseflesh, and the physical charms of various opera dancers bored him. He marveled that these so-called educated gentlemen could think of nothing better to occupy their minds when their privileged world was in danger of being swallowed by Napoleon.

Alexander's tedium was relieved when Sir Gregory Banbridge strolled into the cardroom. The diplomat's affable smile froze on his face when he saw Alexander sitting at one of the tables. All conversation was silenced as Sir Gregory advanced.

"Tired of your little ladybird so soon, Captain Logan?" the blond man said, sneering. "I should have thought Vanessa would prove more entertaining."

Alexander stood up so fast he almost upset the table, and he had Sir Gregory by the throat before the man could get away.

"Steady, old man," said one of Alexander's scandalized friends, taking him by the arm. "Can't do this sort of thing here. Isn't at all the thing."

Gritting his teeth, Alexander forced his fingers to relax. Sir Gregory straightened his cravat and glowered at him.

"Care to name your friends?" Alexander drawled, deliberately keeping his voice low so others in the room couldn't hear him. "Lord, how I'd love to smash your face."

Sir Gregory turned pale. Clearly he had thought he was safe in antagonizing his nemesis before so many witnesses. Alexander's lip curled in contempt at the man's cowardice. He found it difficult to believe that the intelligent and high-spirited Vanessa, even at a young age, could have fancied herself in love with this pathetic excuse for a man.

"Just a joke," Sir Gregory sputtered. "No harm meant."

Alexander made a move toward him, but his friend tightened his grip on his arm. "Let it go, man!" he whispered. "The fellow isn't worth it."

Instead of making a lunge for Sir Gregory, Alexander took a deep, calming breath. What in the bloody hell was wrong with him? All the man had to do was mention Vanessa's name in a disparaging manner and Alexander wanted to do permanent damage to the bounder's pretty face. Perhaps he would be doing him a favor. A broken nose might give it character.

However, mauling Sir Gregory would have the undesirable effect of feeding Vanessa alive to the gossips, so he desisted.

"Get out of here, Banbridge," Alexander said, "before I change my mind."

The words were barely out of Alexander's mouth before Sir Gregory had fled to the safety of the street.

"So, are you going to offer for Miss Whittaker?" Alexander's friend asked after Sir Gregory was gone. "I rather wish you would. I have a monkey riding on the wager."

"It would be presumptuous of me to tell you my intentions before I have offered for the lady," Alexander said. "What if she won't have me?"

"Hah! She'll snap you up so fast your head will spin," Alexander's friend said. "She seems to be a sensible girl, even if her mother hasn't two thoughts to rub together in her head. With all that nasty talk that was making the rounds, the girl knows she can't afford to be choosy."

"Now, Harry. I'd hate to have to ask you to name *your* friends," Alexander said. He deliberately kept his tone light, but this reference to the way Sir Gregory tried unsuccessfully to ruin Vanessa made Alexander want to go out on the street, locate Banbridge, and plant the cad a facer after all.

Some of this must have shown in his expression because his companion gave him a penetrating look.

"So that's the way of it, is it?" his friend said, quirking one eyebrow up. "You've made me a very happy man, old boy, because it looks like the wager is going to pay off handsomely."

"Then the least you can do is indulge me in a hand of cards and a glass of brandy."

"Right-O," Harry said enthusiastically.

"After Alexander marries Vanessa, will he live with us in the country?" Aggie asked, her bright eyes hopeful. "Maybe, since he is going to be our brother, he will teach us how to ride the way he taught Vanessa."

"It is most improper for you to refer to Captain Logan by his Christian name, Agatha dear," Mrs. Whittaker pointed out. "Although I know all of us quite consider him part of the family already."

"But he told us to call him Alexander," Amy protested. "He *likes* us to call him that."

Mrs. Whittaker smiled and gave a satisfied little nod in Vanessa's direction.

"I wish he would hurry," Amy complained. "After he asks Vanessa to marry him, may we have tea and macaroons, Mama?"

Ever since one of their neighbors had brought them the news that Captain Logan had been seen at Rundell and Bridges making a purchase that morning, the Whittaker ladies had been in a state of near hysterical anticipation. Vanessa had been whisked away to her room, where her mother and sisters gave her a great deal of contradictory advice on which gown to wear and how to have her hair dressed when Captain Logan came to make his offer. The little girls had bounced upon the bed excitedly, interspersing their own opinions, until Lydia had called them to order.

"Calm down, girls. It may all come to nothing, after all. Captain Logan might even have been buying a present for his aunt or a timepiece for himself," Lydia pointed out.

"Why do you always have to try and spoil everything?" Aggie asked, making a face at Lydia.

"Because I don't want you to be too disappointed if he

doesn't offer for Vanessa. *Someone* in this family has to show some sense," Lydia said as she tucked one of Aggie's curls back into the bandeau that held it back from the child's face.

"I notice *you* are wearing your nicest dress," Mary Ann pointed out.

"Yes, and Lydia looks very well in it, too," Vanessa interjected when Lydia blushed. She was almost tempted to tell them the truth, just to end the suspense. She caught herself in time, however. She had gone too far now to let anything jeopardize the bargain she had made with Alexander. Success would mean some measure of temporary security for them all. Vanessa didn't dare confide in anyone for fear of botching the opportunity. "Don't worry, Lydia. Everything will be all right. Here, help me do my hair. I would not say so for fear of hurting her feelings, but Sally never does it half so well as you do."

Except for Vanessa, all the ladies were nearly witless with anxiety by the time Alexander arrived.

"Darling, I wish you would change out of that yellow gown," Mrs. Whittaker fussed, regarding the pretty jonquil muslin gown Vanessa was wearing with disapproval. It was the same one Vanessa had worn to Chelsea Hospital on the day she met Alexander, but Mrs. Whittaker, of course, did not remember that. "Perhaps you should have worn the pomona green instead, but you wore that Tuesday, and so it might be too soon for him to see you in it again."

It was the fourth time that Mrs. Whittaker had suggested that Vanessa go upstairs and change into another gown.

The ever-practical Lydia patted her mother on the hand. *"Enough,* Mama," she pointed out with unanswerable logic. "If he is truly coming to offer for her, he already has made up his mind and the gown will not matter."

Just then, the Whittakers' remaining maid bustled into the room, obviously reveling in the importance of her role in the little drama.

"Ma'am," the maid said in a hushed tone usually reserved for the presence of Royalty or of Death, "Captain

Logan would like to speak with you on a private matter of some importance, if it is quite convenient.''

Mrs. Whittaker gave Lydia a triumphant look and told the maid she would be delighted to see Captain Logan. When the maid left the room, Mrs. Whittaker shooed all of her daughters out of the parlor over the little girls' noisy protests and received Vanessa's supposed suitor alone.

Five minutes later, the maid informed Vanessa and her sisters, who had been waiting in Vanessa's room for just such a summons, that Mrs. Whittaker required Vanessa's presence in the parlor immediately.

When the little girls would have followed, Lydia and Mary Ann exchanged looks. Each captured a squirming child in her arms.

"Go, Vanessa," Lydia said over Aggie's head as the furious little girl tried unsuccessfully to break loose. "We will hold them back as long as we can, but I would advise you to accept him quickly before these little hoydens pester him with questions and cause him to change his mind.''

Vanessa's heart was thudding as she stepped into the parlor, for all the world as if she really were a nervous prospective bride. Alexander gave her a sheepish little smile. Her mother was shedding happy tears.

"Oh, my dears. I am so happy! To think of my little girl being done so much honor," Mrs. Whittaker said, sniffing so much that her words were barely intelligible. Alexander handed Annabelle his own white handkerchief.

"Thank you, my dear boy," Mrs. Whittaker said, adding coyly, "I will leave you lovebirds alone now, for I know you have much to talk about.''

After the elder lady left the room, Vanessa and Alexander merely stared at one another, neither apparently knowing how to begin.

"Mother is going to be so disappointed when it all comes to nothing," Vanessa said at last.

"I know," Alexander said. "I sincerely regret that.''

"Well, I suppose it can't be helped so we may as well get the thing over with. I believe you were about to beg me to make you the happiest of men." She tried to keep her tone light, but her face was hot with embarrassment. To her annoyance, the incorrigible Alexander had the gall to look amused.

"Yes, I believe I was." Devilish was the only way to describe the laughter in his eyes. "Vanessa, my angel, my darling, my own true love, will you marry me?"

Vanessa tilted her head, as if considering his offer.

"Aren't you forgetting something?" she asked.

"Am I? I never have proposed marriage to a lady before, so it is entirely possible that I have left something out. If so, I pray you will enlighten me."

"Is the gentleman not supposed to propose marriage on bended knee?"

"If that will please you, my sweet, I certainly will try," he replied. "However, I was wounded in battle, and my poor leg goes a little stiff on me now and again."

Vanessa rolled her eyes. "Oh, dear, how could I have forgotten? In that case, I accept."

Alexander kissed her hand. "There," he said, looking relieved. "We are engaged."

"Good," said Vanessa, equally glad to have the business over with. "I shall call the girls. You must know one of the neighbors saw you at the jewelers' this morning and told Mama, so she immediately assumed you were buying a betrothal gift and told the girls that you would be coming to make me an offer this afternoon. Mama wanted me to change my gown, and the girls kept jumping up and down on the bed . . ."

Vanessa broke off in consternation. She was babbling, and she couldn't seem to help herself. Alexander, the provoking man, just stood there listening to her with an incredulous look on his face. "They have been in a state of high excitement all day," Vanessa went on, "and Mama told them they could have tea and macaroons to celebrate . . ."

Alexander ended her rambling by putting one hand over her lips, then pulling her into his embrace.

"Have *you* not forgotten something, my sweet?" he asked.

Vanessa nodded, feeling shy, and closed her eyes, tilting her face up to be kissed. At the first touch of his lips, she wound her arms around his neck. He crushed her to his chest and pressed tender kisses along her jawline, her cheek, and her closed eyes.

"That was very nice," he said, continuing to hold her in a loose embrace when he was through. "However, I was referring to this." He reached behind her to pick up a rather large box from the low table behind her. He had to bend her backward to do it, and she was conscious of being supported in one of his strong arms while he looked down into her face with a teasing expression in his eyes. Alexander could easily have kissed her, but he didn't. He merely retrieved the box and released her when he had returned her to an upright position. Vanessa hastily withdrew her arms from around his neck and put them behind her back.

"Oh," she said, embarrassed. Heavens! She practically had attacked him like a brazen hussy! What must he think of her?

"I can't accuse you of being mercenary, at all events," he said. "Open it."

Vanessa took the silver foil-wrapped package and went to sit on the sofa. Alexander sat down beside her and rested his arm across her shoulders. It was a very loverlike pose, and Vanessa's throat suddenly felt constricted.

"Before you open it, I think I should explain—" he began.

"Yes, I know," she said, carefully removing the paper. Whoever had wrapped the package used a great deal more ribbon than was necessary. Vanessa unwound the pretty ribbon and smoothed it, thinking that there was enough length to make each of her two younger sisters a hair ribbon. "You will want it back when our engagement is at an end. I had expected that."

"I didn't mean . . ."

By that time Vanessa had opened the box and drawn out the necklace. She was speechless with astonishment at first, then she burst into laughter.

Alexander looked chagrined, but she honestly could not help her mirth.

The central stone had to be at least four karats. The little blue and red chips that surrounded the big white gem in a sort of sunburst design managed to transform a gem that was merely too large into something truly garish. The links in the chain were punctuated with small, muddy yellow stones that appeared to be rather inferior topazes.

"This is the most vulgar thing I have ever seen in my life," she said, awed. "It is *perfect*. When your father and your aunt see it, they will be convinced I am the most calculating fortune hunter on earth."

"I must say I am glad you are taking it this way," Alexander said, visibly relieved, "but you always were a sensible lady. I thought exactly the same thing when I saw it, but afterward I wondered if you would be insulted when I gave it to you."

"Why, because it is paste? Actually, it is a relief because I had terrible qualms of conscience at the thought of your buying an expensive item of jewelry for me as a betrothal gift. I would have worried about losing it. The *ton* will assume the thing is genuine, of course, and that you are besotted enough to indulge my vulgar tastes."

"Yes, that was clever of me, wasn't it?" Alexander said after a short silence.

"Very." Vanessa held the stone up to the light, fascinated. "The way the thing sparkles, one would swear it was real! It can't be paste. The other stones look remarkably genuine as well, but the big one is dazzling. Is it a sort of crystal?"

"Sort of," he said. "Now that we have observed all the formalities, it is time to share our joy with the rest of your family. Your mother's cook, as I recall, makes delicious macaroons."

Vanessa gave him a grateful look.

"The girls would like it of all things, Alexander. They wanted to know if you would come live with us in the country. Apparently they think that now I have found a husband, there is no longer any reason for us to remain in London."

"Indeed?" he asked, one eyebrow raised.

"Yes. Aggie hopes you will teach them how to ride, the way you taught me."

"My star pupil," Alexander said fondly. "We will have you rushing your fences next."

"Not likely," Vanessa said, rolling her eyes.

The afternoon passed very merrily, Annabelle's cook having done justice to the occasion with an elaborate array of refreshments.

"Darling," Annabelle said to Vanessa when Alexander had gone. "I am so very proud of you! A viscountess! We must arrange the fittings for your trousseau at once! St. Paul's! You *must* be married at St. Paul's!"

"It is too soon to begin the fittings," Vanessa said in alarm, thinking of the exorbitant cost of wedding finery.

"Nonsense," Annabelle scoffed. "It would be wise to retain Madame Celeste's services far in advance, for there is a great deal of work to be done. To do justice to St. Paul's, you should have at least a dozen bridesmaids."

"But surely Vanessa will be married from our house in the country, Mama," Lydia said, surprised. "A London wedding would be very dear. However are we to afford it?"

"Everyone of consequence," Annabelle said smugly, "is married at St. Paul's. And after Vanessa marries the Earl of Stoneham's heir, *nothing* will be too good for her. Or for us."

Vanessa bit her lip. She should have foreseen this. Her mother was determined to spend a fortune on a wedding that would never take place.

And, short of giving the game away, there was nothing Vanessa could do to stop her.

TWELVE

The next few weeks passed with dizzying swiftness for Vanessa. It seemed all of London was anxious to fete the newly engaged couple with balls, dinner parties, afternoon receptions, riding parties, and lazy afternoon excursions by boat down the Thames.

In the teeth of all this frivolity, the Earl of Stoneham treated his son's fiancée and her family with cold politeness in public and with thinly veiled contempt in private. Lady Letitia was slightly more friendly to Vanessa, but hardly welcoming. So Vanessa was somewhat surprised when her mother came into the room where she was resting one afternoon to tell her that Lady Letitia had arrived and wanted to speak with Vanessa on a matter of some importance.

Vanessa was exhausted. She had been arising early every morning to go riding with Alexander after staying out very late every evening at balls. In the afternoons, she had parties and visitors to occupy her time. She tried to deny herself to Lady Letitia, but quickly rose from her bed when told that her visitor insisted the matter was urgent and that she must speak with Vanessa alone.

"Lady Letitia," she said breathlessly when she arrived in the parlor. "What is wrong? Has something happened to Alexander?"

"He never will marry you, you know," Letitia said in a pseudo-sympathetic tone by way of greeting.

Vanessa eyed Alexander's aunt with resentment.

"Do you think not?" Vanessa said with lifted eyebrows. "Why do you say that?"

"Oh, come now, my dear," Letitia said with a little trill of laughter. "You must know that there is not a romantic bone in Alexander's body."

"I am afraid I know nothing of the sort." Vanessa's head was pounding.

"Don't be a little fool! He is trifling with you. He wants you in his bed, and when he gets what he wants, he will discard you like he has all the others. Why do you think he has not sent a notice of your engagement to the newspapers?"

"Has Alexander been betrothed to a great many young ladies, then, and discarded them all?" Vanessa asked. "If so, I have not heard of it."

"Certainly not. You simply have been a more difficult conquest than most. It is the thrill of the chase, you see."

"Then I shall have to see that the chase isn't over until the ring is on my finger, won't I?" Vanessa's voice was cold, but she was seething inside. How could she have thought Lady Letitia elegant and charming? She was an adder, and Vanessa had a sudden picture of a small, confused, motherless boy being raised by this poisonous woman.

"Don't think you will find it pleasant to marry into our family," Letitia said, her eyes snapping. "I can assure you that you will not find it pleasant at all."

"Not find it pleasant to marry the heir to an earldom and have all his lovely money to spend?" Vanessa said, deliberately lifting one eyebrow in that odious manner she quite deplored when Alexander employed it. "Oh, I think I shall manage to amuse myself quite tolerably. Perhaps I shall redecorate Stoneham House when my husband inherits the title. I always fancied a whole house done in"— Vanessa paused while she tried to think of a very vulgar color—"scarlet."

"You shameless little hussy!" Letitia breathed. "You would not dare!"

"No need to be alarmed," Vanessa said with a smile as false and sweet as Letitia's own. *"You* shall not be there to see it. By the time the workmen are finished with the transformation I shall make sure you are installed quite cozily in the dower house, wherever that might be. Or perhaps you will predecease your brother, so you needn't worry."

Letitia's famous gardenia-petal skin was becoming quite mottled with rage.

"No one in the family will accept you. Don't expect *me* to include you in the circle of my intimates. You shall be quite shunned by society if I wish it so."

"Do you think I care for that? I shall have plenty of company when I have all of *my* family installed at Stoneham House."

Vanessa stood and offered her hand to Lady Letitia.

"Now you must excuse me. You interrupted my little afternoon sleep, and I do need to be in my best looks tonight. Dear Alexander is escorting me to a ball. I imagine I need stand on no ceremony with you and can safely leave you to see yourself out. I quite consider you one of the family."

Vanessa yawned in Letitia's face as the elder lady stood and regarded her with a look of pure hatred.

"Do call again sometime, *Auntie,"* Vanessa said, turning her back on her uninvited guest. "I have so enjoyed our little chat."

"You think you have won," Letitia sputtered, "but you will be sorry you crossed me! If you do manage to marry Alexander, I shall see you take no joy of it!"

That evening Vanessa dressed with special care in the most daring of her new gowns—a deep blue satin creation that clung lovingly to every curve—and the effect of the low-cut neckline with the diamond necklace was quite startling. By the time Vanessa had dampened her petticoats, the gown left nothing to the imagination. These were extreme measures, but Vanessa was determined to make sure that neither the Earl of Stoneham nor his spiteful cat of a sister could miss her declaration of war.

"Vanessa," gasped the scandalized Mrs. Whittaker when her daughter entered the drawing room. The last time she had seen the gown in Madame Celeste's salon, it had been a demure ballgown entirely appropriate for a well-bred young lady in her first season. That was before Vanessa had taken it back to Madame Celeste for drastic alterations. "You look quite—quite—"

"Magnificent," Alexander said, his eyes fastened on Vanessa's bosom. "My dear, I congratulate you. Nothing could show off your, ah, jewels to better advantage."

"Thank you, darling," she said, drawing on her gloves. "Do not let Sally wait up for me, Mama. We shall be very late. Shall we go, Alexander?"

"At once," he said, looking amused as he presented his arm to her. "I understand," he continued after they were settled in the carriage, "that my aunt paid you a visit today. I collect by your appearance that she was rather clumsy in making her disapproval of our engagement known. Permit me to say that if displaying your . . . charms in this manner is your method of retaliation, I heartily approve. Is that *rouge* on your face?"

"Yes," Vanessa said in a tone that dared him to object.

"I rather thought so. I predict it will be a very interesting evening."

"I think it is appalling that your aunt thinks she can meddle in your affairs. You are a grown man, after all."

"You weren't the only sufferer. While you were enduring my aunt's visit, Cedric was lecturing me on the duty I owed my name in his study, and a most unpleasant interview it was." Alexander laid his hand over Vanessa's. "I, of course, was obdurate in my insistence that I would marry you and no other. He is almost ready to crack, Vanessa. Our plan is succeeding beyond my wildest hopes. Cedric and Letitia both will be at the ball tonight, and I am depending on you to give a performance that will strike terror in their hearts."

"I can hardly wait," Vanessa said, eager for battle.

*   *   *

Alexander could only admire the way Vanessa flaunted the diamond necklace before the other debutantes, giving every appearance of a young lady in high croak.

But while everyone else was fooled, Alexander could see the strain behind her smiling countenance.

"I do not believe you have seen dear Alexander's betrothal gift to me," Vanessa said quite loudly, addressing this remark to Lady Letitia. Alexander's aunt deliberately had snubbed Vanessa when they came face to face, but Vanessa, to Alexander's amusement, had caught Lady Letitia's arm and all but forced her to take notice of her.

"Is it not lovely?" Vanessa had asked, all but sticking her bosoms in the lady's affronted face.

"Yes, it is quite *large,*" Letitia said, her eyes blazing with malice. "In fact, one could say it would be a more appropriate gift for a gentleman's *chère amie* than for his betrothed bride."

"Indeed, am I not to be envied? Few gentlemen are as generous with their wives as they are with their mistresses. But then, a spinster such as yourself, Lady Letitia, can hardly speak with any authority on the subject. My darling Alexander," Vanessa added, directing a languishing glance at her devoted cavalier, "can deny me nothing."

Alexander, catching the look, smiled and kissed his fingers to her.

"More to the point," Letitia tittered, "do you deny *him* nothing?"

"No, nothing at all, "Vanessa assured her blandly. "Dearest," she added, rudely talking to Alexander across Letitia, "I am quite parched. Do escort me to one of those chairs and fetch me a glass of lemonade."

"Your wish is my command, my love," he said, offering his arm. When they were out of the fuming Letitia's earshot he added under his voice, "Are you all right, Vanessa?"

"Perfectly," she replied. "Why do you ask?"

"You have the headache again, do you not?"

"I am afraid so," she admitted, allowing her shoulders to sag a little. "I am trying my best to hide it, but it hurts so badly."

"Why did you not tell me? I would never have forced you to accompany me tonight if I had known."

"Did you not make it clear," she said, sitting down with every appearance of relief, "that it was very important for me to attend this ball tonight and flaunt our relationship before the *ton*? How could I fail you now when your father is on the point of withdrawing his objections to allowing you to return to war? What is the agony of having one's brain pounded to bits by the hammers of a thousand little gremlins residing in one's head when one has such a noble cause to uphold? Do not concern yourself. I shall be better in a moment."

Alexander fetched the lemonade. Vanessa drank it down without comment and leaned back against the wall.

"We are going home," he said in concern when she seemed no better. "Immediately."

"No," she said. There was pain behind her beautiful eyes, but she had managed to force a brittle smile to her lips. "I won't allow your odious aunt the satisfaction of oversetting me."

"Whatever did she say to you this afternoon?" he asked, frowning.

"Nothing I did not expect." Vanessa gave a little gasp of pain and closed her eyes again.

"That settles it," Alexander said, taking her hand and helping her to her feet.

"I am better now," she argued. "There is no reason to cut short the evening."

"Liar. Wait here." He stood and started to walk away.

"Alexander—"

"I will be right back," he said, giving her shoulder a comforting pat. After a whispered conference with his hostess, he returned to Vanessa and led her to their hostess. The lady, to Vanessa's surprise, guided them upstairs, summoning a maid they encountered in the hall to accompany them.

"Here you are, then, Miss Whittaker," that good lady said, showing them to a comfortable bedroom. "Lie down and rest, for there is nothing worse for a headache than the jarring of a carriage ride." She gave Alexander an arch smile. "I will leave you in your young man's capable hands, my dear."

The maidservant set a lighted candle on the table, bobbed a curtsy, and showed herself out.

"You must think me a paltry creature, indeed," Vanessa said, giving Alexander a wry, but pained, look.

"Hush, love," Alexander said soothingly as he helped her sit on the bed.

"Alexander," she squeaked when he began removing her slippers. "There is no need—"

"Do not be alarmed, my dear," he said, putting the slippers on the floor and taking her shoulders to lower her to the bed. "I am not going to remove anything else." She started to protest, but then gave a sigh of relief and lay back against the pillows. "That's better," Alexander said. He covered her lovely body up to her neck with the sheet he found folded at the foot of the bed in order to protect her modesty. That gown really did leave little to the imagination. Although he hoped he was a gentleman, Alexander was only human. A rap sounded at the door and a maid entered with a basin and a bottle.

"Ah, thank you," he said, smiling at the maid and relieving her of the basin and bottle of vinegar.

"Shall I stay with the young lady, sir?" the girl asked.

"No. I do not wish to impose upon her ladyship's staff when I am persuaded you must all be occupied in serving the guests," Alexander said. He couldn't bear the thought of abandoning Vanessa to a stranger while she was ill. "I shall take care of my fiancée. You may go."

The girl looked doubtful, but obeyed.

Vanessa's pain-glazed eyes opened at the first touch of

the vinegar-soaked cloth on her brow, but then she gave a sigh of relief and relaxed.

"Alexander," she whispered.

"Yes, my dear?"

"I am sorry I spoiled everything."

"Nonsense. My aunt is seriously alarmed, and after your conduct tonight my father is ready to row me and all my gear across the channel himself to prevent our marriage, I promise you. I am much obliged to you."

Vanessa's lips twitched.

"I was utterly shameless, wasn't I?"

"You were magnificent," he said, raising her hand to his lips and kissing it. "Lie still, now. I am going to blow out the candle so you can rest your eyes."

"Thank you, Alexander," she whispered.

"My pleasure," he said, locating a straight-backed chair and sitting in it, prepared to stand vigil all night if he must. Before long, a young maidservant tiptoed into the room and offered to sit with Vanessa so he could return to the party. But by then Vanessa was recovered enough to eat some of the supper that had been laid out for the pleasure of the guests. When the supper was over, they watched the dancing for a little while, then took their leave as unobtrusively as possible.

Alexander, after thanking their hostess for her kind offices, tenderly helped Vanessa into his carriage and held her in his arms while she rested against his shoulder all the way to Hans Crescent.

Because he drove about the city quite aimlessly for hours after escorting Vanessa home, it was past three o'clock in the morning when Alexander returned to Stoneham House. The earl was waiting up for him.

"You have been in many ways a most unsatisfactory son," Cedric told his heir without preamble, "but you never have given me cause to think you a fool before now."

"Indeed?" Alexander said, forcing a smile to his lips as

he poured himself a glass of brandy and seated himself in the chair before his father's desk. "You refer, I collect, to my approaching nuptials?"

"Can you not see the little hussy is after your money and a coronet, you young idiot?"

Alexander forced his stiff shoulders to relax.

"Is that not what all of them want?" he answered mildly, taking a sip of his drink.

"I tell you, I won't have it!" Cedric thundered.

"I am very much afraid you will have to. I am of age, you know. Vanessa's birth is unexceptional, if her fortune is not. I want her, Cedric. And I mean to have her."

"Then make her your mistress, damn it! Pay her for her favors. Considering what that necklace must have cost you, the little slut owes you a tumble or two."

Alexander shot to his feet.

"Cedric, hear me now," he said through gritted teeth. "Vanessa Whittaker is a virtuous young lady, and I hold her in the highest esteem. No matter how much I want her, I never would insult her by offering to take her under my protection. If you try to stop us from marrying, we will elope to Gretna Green."

"Hear *me*, Alexander!" the earl shouted. "If you persist in your courtship of Vanessa Whittaker, you risk becoming estranged from your family."

Alexander gave a crack of laughter and swallowed the rest of his drink straight down, slamming the crystal on the mahogany surface of his father's desk and shattering it.

"Have we ever been anything else?" he asked bleakly as he turned his back on his father's angry face and left the room to make his way to his lonely bed.

"What is it?" Vanessa asked, her smile of welcome dying on her face when she saw Alexander's bleak expression.

"Nothing, my sweet," he whispered, seating himself beside her on the sofa and taking her hand in his to press a kiss to its palm. The room was crowded with guests listening to a humorous anecdote being told by Diana Lacey's mother. "Shall we take a turn in your mother's garden?"

"My mother does not have a garden, but we may go outside and observe the weeds growing behind the house, if you like," she whispered back, sensing that Alexander had something of importance to disclose to her in private.

But when they were alone he simply sat down on a crumbling stone bench and pulled her down on his lap.

"Alexander!" she exclaimed, scandalized. "What if someone should see us?" But he looked so serious that she wound her arms around his neck and allowed him to hold her close.

"Are you quite recovered from your headache?" he asked, straightening after a moment and framing her face with his hands. She blushed under his scrutiny.

"Of course, I am," she said. "Alexander, you are frightening me. What has happened?"

"Nothing very dreadful," he said. His smile looked forced. "Cedric and I had a blazing row last night over our supposed engagement. It was to be expected, after all."

"What did that horrid old man say to you?" Vanessa demanded, bristling in Alexander's defense.

Alexander gave her a smile of such sweetness that Vanessa's heart melted.

"Nothing I haven't heard all my life, sweetheart, so don't trouble yourself on my account," he said, holding her close again. After another moment he kissed her lightly on the lips and stood, catching her around the waist to prevent her from being tumbled off his lap and onto the ground.

"If you aren't going to tell me what he said, why did you bring me out here?" she asked, puzzled.

"For comfort, love. Simply for comfort," he said, taking her hand and raising it to his lips. "Thank you."

He escorted her back to her mother's parlor and, within a few minutes, took his leave of his hostess.

"What was all that about?" Lydia whispered when Vanessa returned to the parlor and seated herself beside her sister. "He didn't say above a dozen words the entire time he was here."

"I have no idea," Vanessa replied.

That evening Alexander sent a message to his solicitor that he would be much obliged to that worthy gentleman if he would call at Stoneham House between the hours of nine and eleven o'clock the following morning for the purpose of receiving Alexander's instructions in the drawing up of his last will and testament.

THIRTEEN

Alexander was on the point of leaving Stoneham House for Hans Crescent early one afternoon when a uniformed military aide arrived with an official communication for him.

There was only one thing it could be.

Alexander took the letter to the library and read it quickly. He had expected the tidings it brought to give him more satisfaction. Now he would be permitted to serve his country, and his honor would be preserved. Instead, his predominant emotion was regret because there wasn't time to visit Vanessa before he left for the continent.

Perhaps it was just as well.

Alexander didn't know how long he could have continued seeing Vanessa every day on terms of such intimacy without losing his head. Despite the fact that their relationship was based on pretense, he was more comfortable with her than with anyone else in his world.

He was writing a hasty letter of farewell to her when the earl entered the room.

"I suppose I have you to thank for this," Alexander said, standing and showing the official communication to the earl. "I am to report for active duty within the hour after reading this letter. A government transport is leaving from the docks today, and I have to be on it."

"Damn it, boy," said the earl after he had read it. "I didn't want to do this. You forced my hand. When I learned about that blasted will, I knew you were serious about marrying the little minx. That property has been in your mother's family for generations."

"I am the last of my mother's family, Cedric, and I have a perfect right to leave it however I choose. At least I will go to war with a lighter heart knowing that if something happens to me, Vanessa and her family will be provided for," Alexander said.

"Hah! Do you think she will wear the willow for you? She will no doubt have some other fool in thrall before your ship lands on the continent!"

"You don't know her at all," Alexander said. "Vanessa has more integrity than anyone else I know."

Although Cedric didn't know it, Vanessa would be perfectly within her rights to marry another man in Alexander's absence. However, Alexander was certain that Vanessa would wait until the mountains crumbled for a man she truly did love. He wished with all his heart that he could be that man.

"Integrity! That would be laughable if it weren't so pathetic!"

"And speaking of integrity, Cedric," Alexander said pointedly, "I wish I had time to have a discussion with my solicitor about the propriety of his sharing a confidential matter such as my will with a third party."

"A third party! I am your *father!* And he is *my* solicitor as well."

"I want your promise that you won't contest the provisions of my will if I don't return alive from the war. It's important to me, Cedric."

"You are of legal age, and there is nothing I can do to put the will aside," the earl said.

"Oh, you would try, I imagine."

"Of course, I would try. It galls me to think that little fortune hunter will have it."

"Perhaps she won't," Alexander said. "There is every reason to suppose I might survive the war. Indeed, I imagine you wouldn't have withdrawn your objections to my returning to Spain if you didn't think it likely I would come back alive."

"Of course I know you are likely to come back! What kind of a father do you think I am?" To Alexander's surprise, Cedric actually sounded hurt. "You will never know what this decision cost me. Someday you will thank me for this, you mark my words. Fighting the French is likely to take a long time, and I would be willing to wager my chestnut bay that Vanessa Whittaker finds herself another victim before you are three months gone."

"What a cynical old man you have become!"

The earl actually flinched.

"You are a romantic young fool, Alexander. With your intelligence and my influence, you could have had a brilliant political career. Now you are throwing it away for a woman!"

"*I* am throwing it away for my country," Alexander said quietly. "*You* have thrown it away for the woman."

The London docks were teeming with soldiers awaiting transport to Spain, but Alexander rarely had felt so alone.

All around him the other soldiers' wives, sweethearts, parents, and children were bidding their tearful goodbyes. Cedric had accompanied Alexander to the docks, but the earl was on the point of leaving after having shaken his son's hand. Letitia, of course, had not come, for no lady of her sensibility could be expected to tolerate the vulgar jostling one would be likely to encounter in this place. Alexander had said his formal farewells at Stoneham House. Letitia and Cedric had expressed their hope that Alexander would return to them in good health and spirits. He had expressed the hope that they would enjoy tolerable weather in Brighton, where they were soon to repair for the summer.

It was no more than Alexander expected, after all. He believed that both Cedric and Letitia harbored considerable affection for him. But in their family, excessive displays of emotion were considered undignified. Neither the

Earl of Stoneham nor his sister would have dreamed of making spectacles of themselves in public merely because their last living relative, and the only hope for the survival of their house, was about to leave for death or glory.

Strange.

Before Alexander had become an intimate of Vanessa's family circle, he hadn't thought he was missing anything. He had been amazed the first time he escorted Vanessa and her mother to a ball and saw the way the younger children lined up to receive their mother's and Vanessa's fond kisses and hugs. He had become accustomed to the easy affection that existed among the mother and daughters, for it seemed to spill over onto him. He would miss cuddling the little girls in his lap and taking them for rides in the park in his father's carriage.

He would miss Vanessa's kisses.

Lord, how he would miss Vanessa's kisses!

"Alexander!"

Alexander turned, blinked, and could do nothing to restrain the silly grin he knew was spreading across his face.

Vanessa's disheveled hair was falling half down her back, and her white muslin dress was sadly rumpled. She looked as if she had run all the way from Hans Crescent. Her eyes were red and swollen from crying.

Alexander never had seen such a wonderful sight.

He caught her in a fervent embrace when she ran straight into his arms. The footman he had dispatched to her home with his hastily written letter stood off to the side, his expression wooden. Alexander exchanged a fleeting look with his father over Vanessa's head. Cedric clenched his jaw, motioned to the footman to follow him, and walked toward the water to give the couple privacy. He had that much decency, at least.

Vanessa lifted her face to Alexander's, and her hair fell like a dark curtain over his arm. Alexander kissed her soft lips and tasted the salt of her tears on his tongue.

"If this is being staged for my father's benefit, I don't want to know," he said as Vanessa began covering his jaw with soft, ardent little kisses. He closed his eyes in pure ecstasy.

"God, you are beautiful," Alexander whispered. "Every time I see you, I am amazed by how beautiful you are."

"And you are an insensitive beast," she said between kisses. "How *dare* you think you could just send me a letter with a bank draft for two thousand pounds in it and leave the country without seeing me?"

"You had fulfilled your part of the bargain. I love your hair down like this. If we didn't have an audience, I would be sorely tempted to—"

"Alexander! You have not listened to a word I've said! Don't you understand that I am *very* angry with you?" Her words ended on a little sob.

"If this is anger," he said, cupping her face in his hands and kissing her eyelids, "give me more."

"Don't be absurd," she said, giving an involuntary little chuckle.

"That's better. Listen, Vanessa. This is important. I've left you my estate in my will—"

"You've done *what*? Alexander, how *could* you?"

"We've no time for the vapors, love. If you learn that I am dead, you must go at once to my solicitor. Don't let Cedric and Letitia bully you into giving up your claim. The estate came to me from my mother's family. I am the last of their blood, so you won't be cutting out any rightful heirs for it."

Vanessa put her hand over his mouth and looked up into his face.

"I won't listen to you!" she cried.

He took her hand away from his lips and held it against his chest.

"You must. There isn't much time. My solicitor is also my father's solicitor. I thought the man could be trusted, but he told my father about the will."

"And your father immediately had you recalled to war," she said bitterly. "That horrid old man! He would rather see you *dead* than married to me!"

"I am rather experienced at soldiering, love," Alexander said, smiling. "My chances of returning are quite good. If you will recall, the whole point of our little charade was to have me recalled to Spain."

"I don't want to read in the newspapers about your leading any reckless charges into enemy lines," she said sternly.

He threw his head back and laughed. "You have been reading those thrilling accounts of battle the war office issues to the newspapers. Pure propaganda, most of them. I hope I am not precisely a coward, but I am not a fool, either."

"That's all very well," she argued, "but what if something *does* happen to you?"

"Then you will be very well off, I should imagine. The estate brings me a tolerable income."

"Don't *say* that! I don't want to profit by your death," she cried, agitated now. "Alexander, you shouldn't have done it. It's all too much! You've paid me the two thousand pounds and paid all the dressmakers' bills and the rent. And the butcher's bills and the candle maker and the coal—"

"Confound it! You weren't supposed to know that!"

"Why did you do it? I don't understand!"

Alexander felt his face flush.

"I didn't want you to be forced into marriage as soon as I leave for Spain in order to pay your family's bills. Don't make a fuss over it, love. It is only money. If I'm dead, I won't have any use for it. And Cedric and Letitia already have more money than is good for them."

Vanessa caressed his cheek with one small, soft hand. He couldn't resist turning his head and kissing it.

"That was very sweet of you, Alexander. But I have no intention of crying off until after you return from the war."

"Do you mean it?" he asked, suddenly feeling happier than he had ever been in his life.

"Certainly." The roguish smile he loved touched her lips. "How could I jilt a war hero while he is fighting on foreign soil? Just *think* of the damage to my reputation! I intend to take your two thousand pounds and convince

Mama and the girls that it is our patriotic duty to return to the country and live quite retired until you return."

"You are going to wait for me!" he said teasingly as he hugged her again. "How very touching. One would surmise you cared."

She blushed and extricated herself from his embrace, then she reached into the pocket of her gown and took out the little square jewelers' box that Alexander knew contained the sapphire and diamond earrings.

"I was going to insist that you take these back."

"Why?" he asked, genuinely surprised. In his experience, women who refused gifts of jewelry were very rare.

"Because it wouldn't be proper of me to accept them."

"Nonsense. You've already accepted the necklace. By comparison the earrings are nothing but a little keepsake."

"The necklace is paste!"

"Not paste," he said, grinning.

"Don't quibble. Crystal then."

"Not crystal."

Her big, blue eyes grew as round as saucers.

"It's real," she breathed.

He nodded, grinning at her discomfiture.

"For heaven's sake! I have been leaving it lying about in my bedroom as if it were the merest trumpery. I even let the girls wear it around the house a time or two! Why didn't you *tell* me it was real?"

"Would you have accepted it?"

"No," she admitted. "But, Alexander! What am I going to do with the wretched thing?"

"If it looks like you're going to have to marry a merchant to pay your family's debts, you may sell it for all I care. It has served its purpose."

"But—"

"Keep the earrings, Vanessa, if you wish to please me."

She would have argued, but she was interrupted by an orderly.

"It's time, Captain Logan," the man said. His voice was polite, but firm.

Alexander kissed Vanessa on the cheek and closed her fingers over the little black box.

"Keep them," he told her. "I will be back after the French are beaten, and I want you to wear them the next time we dance the waltz together. Promise?"

Her eyes filled with tears, and she nodded.

Cedric, seeing that Alexander was about to get on the ship, came to join them.

"Where is Busby?" Alexander asked, referring to the footman who had escorted Vanessa to the docks. "I wanted him to escort Vanessa to her home."

"I sent him back to Stoneham House," the earl said. "I will take her home in the carriage."

"I will go home in a hackney carriage," Vanessa said defiantly, giving the earl a look that should have felled him where he stood.

"No," Alexander said. "You'll take care of her, sir?" he asked his father.

Cedric gave him a curt nod.

"I would rather walk," Vanessa said, continuing to glare at the earl.

Alexander laughed.

"No. You will go home with my father, or I will worry about you. Promise me?"

Vanessa looked mutinous, but she nodded.

"Very well, then," Alexander said, smiling. "Goodbye, sir." He was going to shake hands with his father again, but Cedric surprised him very much by giving him a hug.

"Come back alive to us, do you hear me, Alexander?" Cedric said gruffly, giving his son a final pat on the back.

Alexander raised his eyebrows at him.

"I shall do my poor best," he said.

Then he turned and accompanied the orderly toward the ship. His heart was lighter than it had been in years.

* * *

"I wonder if you realize what you have done," Cedric said to Vanessa once the carriage was in motion. "Or, if you *do* realize, I wonder if you care."

Vanessa gave him a defiant look from where she sat in the corner of the carriage as far away from Alexander's father as she could get. The earl looked fierce, a lion defending his cub. But Vanessa wasn't about to let him intimidate her.

"*You* are the one who used his influence to have Alexander recalled to Spain," she pointed out.

"And I suppose you hate me for it."

"What you have done is despicable." Vanessa knew it was unladylike in the extreme to say such things, and with every word she was confirming the earl's bad opinion of her. "I can't imagine how you managed to father a decent, honorable man such as Alexander. You don't deserve him."

"I quite agree," said the earl with a brittle smile. "But neither do you. If you truly loved him, my dear, you would let him go."

Vanessa wouldn't have admitted that her engagement to Alexander was a pretense for all the gold in the world.

"At least I am capable of love!" It felt good to say so, right out loud, even if she wouldn't have dared admit her true feelings to Alexander himself.

The earl's social mask slipped and for a moment he looked his true age.

"Love! What would a silly chit like you know of love? If he dies, you will shed a few tears and miss a few balls, but you will have Alexander's estate and fortune to console you. With a comfortable income at your disposal, you soon will take a better place in society than you deserve and find some other gallant fool to marry you. You will have forgotten all about Alexander within a year of replacing him."

"You're wrong," Vanessa said angrily. "No one could replace Alexander."

"I have no doubt you would regret the loss of the coronet that might have come to you as Countess of Stoneham. But that would be the extent of it."

"You have no heart!" she cried. "How can you speak so callously of your own son's death? You don't care about him at all!"

"You couldn't be more mistaken. If my son dies, my future dies with him."

"The future of the House of Stoneham, you mean. It is hardly the same thing."

"It *is* the same. Alexander was not like other children. He was big for his age and strong. He is a natural athlete, so I made sure he had the best of instruction in fencing, riding, and all of the military arts. His intellect is formidable, so I hired the best tutors I could find. And I sent him to the best schools and universities I could afford. He was the first in his class wherever he studied. He has studied law and political history and all of the natural sciences. What a statesman he would make. His country needs him, Miss Whittaker. *I* need him."

Vanessa could not believe the audacity of the man.

"Do you expect me to believe that when it is *you* who sent him to fight the French?" she asked.

"Only because I had to prevent him from making a mistake that would have cost him his future. If I had permitted him to marry you, it would have been the same as putting a bullet through his brain. Married to a nobody from Yorkshire, he would have been no good to me or to anyone. *You* as a political hostess? The notion would be laughable if it weren't so pathetic."

"How curious," Vanessa said. "Alexander has never expressed any interest in a political career. To me he always talked of returning to his regiment."

"It's this cursed war. He was perfectly willing to take the road I had chosen for him until he had his mind filled with all this patriotic nonsense about the war with the French. I thought some military service would be an asset to his political career, so I arranged for him to become a member of the Tenth Hussars."

"The Prince Regent's regiment?"

"Yes. He would have learned protocol there. Become acquainted with the right people. But he started believing all that thrilling propaganda that they issue out of the war office and he requested a transfer to an active unit behind my back."

"I honor him for it."

"Bah! You are exactly like all the other stupid young girls sighing over a redcoat. I warn you, I won't give up my son without a fight."

"It appears to me," Vanessa said, fully aware that she was delivering a formal declaration of war, "that you already have lost him."

"Do you think your mother was happy in her marriage?"

"I beg your pardon?" Vanessa asked, certain she could not have heard him correctly. "What is that to the point?"

"Your father was a member of my club. He moved in the very best circles before that unfortunate day when he met your mother. After their marriage, he might have been dead to his family for all the notice his relatives paid him. He defied them all to marry her."

"I don't understand . . ." But Vanessa was all too afraid she *did* understand.

"Would you say your father was happy, Miss Whittaker?"

Vanessa looked down at the hands clasped in her lap.

"He was content, I suppose," she said in a small voice, knowing it to be a lie.

"Content?" The earl lifted one eyebrow. "On the occasions that I did see him in London toward the end of his life, I would not have described him in quite that way. He died a very unhappy and disappointed man, Miss Whittaker. He regretted the breach with his family that his marriage to your mother caused. Did you know your father once had political ambitions?"

"He did?" Vanessa asked, surprised. "He never spoke of this."

"No. I imagine he did not. His marriage to your mother put an end to any political aspirations he might have had. Do you think your mother took a great deal of joy in her marriage? Was she content? I would imagine she expected that she would be able to command every luxury once she was married to a man so far above her in station. Would you say her expectations were realized?"

Vanessa remained silent, remembering her mother's constant complaints about their lack of money. She thought of her father, whose last days were spent in bitterness. Her parents, it seemed to Vanessa, had never been a comfort to one another. They were too little alike.

After a moment she looked up.

"I am not my mother," she told the earl.

"No. I give you credit for a great deal more common sense or I wouldn't waste my breath trying to make you see reason," he said. "Do you honestly think that marriage to you will make up to my son for the loss of his standing in society and the end of his political ambitions? I hold the purse strings until my death, Miss Whittaker. I can force Alexander to live on his own income from that pretty little estate his grandfather left him. Believe me, he is accustomed to so much more."

The little flame of hope that had sprung to life in Vanessa's breast when Alexander kissed her so tenderly at the London docks died.

Vanessa and the earl continued their journey in tight-lipped silence until Vanessa was set down in front of the house on Hans Crescent. She did not invite the earl inside. He did not wait until she had safely entered her front door to drive off.

Alone in her room, Vanessa took the sapphire and diamond earrings out of the jewelers' box and studied them. She would keep them to remind her of Alexander when she was old and gray . . . and alone.

Pride had forbidden Vanessa to admit it to the earl, but he was right. She didn't deserve Alexander. She could offer him love and loyalty, but nothing else.

In Alexander's world, it would not be enough.

Tears rolled down her cheeks as Vanessa realized the earl had misjudged her.

She *did* love Alexander enough to let him go.

FOURTEEN

June 1813 to June 1814
Yorkshire, England

The victory at Vitoria was a triumph for General Arthur Wellesley and for England, but Captain Alexander Logan's role in the conflict was the only one that interested Vanessa. For a month she had searched the published lists of war dead with anguished eyes, feeling giddy with relief at not finding his name.

Now, it seemed, Alexander was one of the heroes of Vitoria. The dispatches were full of him.

Putting the London newspaper down with hands that shook, Vanessa took a deep breath to compose her racing emotions.

At least now she knew he was alive.

The Whittakers had repaired to the country at Vanessa's insistence, for there seemed to be no point in remaining in London. Annabelle had become more and more concerned when no formal announcement of Alexander and Vanessa's engagement was issued from Stoneham House to be published in the London papers. Finally, Vanessa had been forced to admit to her family that her supposed betrothal to Alexander was a sham.

"We should take action against him for breach of promise," fumed Annabelle when she found Vanessa sitting at the library table with the paper spread in front of her. It seemed all the household knew where to find Vanessa after the newspapers had arrived.

"No, Mother," Vanessa said, trying to be patient although the argument was an old one. "Captain Logan made me no promises. And if he had, the two thousand pounds he gave me more than compensates me for my inconvenience."

"And you are determined to squander the whole upon— upon *chicken* feed!" Annabelle mourned. "I never dreamed that any daughter of mine would be so wasteful. Then you built a *barn*. I ask you, what does any marriageable lady in her right mind want with a barn?"

"For the cows, of course, Mother," Vanessa said. "The estate has been sadly run down, and it never will bring us a decent income unless we make some improvements to it."

"Better you should take the money, as I begged you, and go to Brighton. You aren't going to find a wealthy nobleman in search of a wife in the neighborhood at this season, I promise you. These are all good and worthy men in their own way," Annabelle said, dismissing the gentry of Yorkshire with one negligent sweep of her hand, "but with your beauty and two thousand pounds to lend you consequence, you could aim as high as you please."

"Mama, I don't want to look for a husband! Please believe that nothing you say will convince me to go to Brighton. I hold the purse strings now, and I won't let this family fall back into its spendthrift ways."

"*My* spendthrift ways, you mean!" Tears of anger and hurt gathered in Annabelle's eyes. "You might as well give me the word with no bark on it, you disrespectful baggage! I am no longer the mistress of my own home!"

"Of course you are, Mother," said Lydia, just entering the room. "There is no reason to berate Vanessa over a few sensible little changes. Come spring, we'll be ready for the planting season, I promise you. A good crop will have us in plump currant."

"A good crop!" Annabelle was beside herself with indignation. "Oh, that I should live to hear my daughters talking like a pair of farmers! How is a good crop going to find Vanessa a proper husband? Or the rest of you, for that matter? We haven't even a housekeeper to lend us consequence."

"Now, Mama," Vanessa said. "I know it was hard for you to part with Mrs. Grimsby, but if we are to stay out of debt we have to make all the economies we can. You won't see a great deal of change in the running of the household. Lydia and I between us will manage the staff. And Sally has been very helpful in making suggestions on how to economize."

"And no butler to answer the door," Annabelle sniffed, refusing to be placated. "Your father would turn over in his grave!"

"Of all the unjust things to say!" Lydia put her hands on her ample hips and scowled at her mother. "If Papa hadn't spent his whole fortune on the gaming table, we wouldn't be in this difficulty to begin with. We had to let the butler go *before* Papa died, if you will recall. He was so inebriated most of the time toward the end, I rather doubt he noticed."

"Unnatural girls," Annabelle snarled. "I had *respect* for my mother when I was your age. When it was time for me to look about for a husband, I followed her advice and was grateful for it! I am going to my room to lie down until dinner. The two of you have given me a headache!"

"Mama, please . . ." Vanessa began, starting to follow the older woman. Lydia reached out to catch her arm.

"Save your breath," Lydia said, her voice brittle.

Annabelle turned at the door, gave a sniff of derision, and left.

"She just doesn't understand," Vanessa said.

"Did you think she would? All Mama thinks about is recapturing our family's past glory by marrying you off to a rich man. Too bad your Captain Logan cried off."

"He didn't cry off!" Vanessa said, glaring at her. "And

you know it. There never was an engagement to begin with."

"For someone who isn't guilty of breach of promise, he certainly paid off handsomely," Lydia observed. "Two thousand pounds. A diamond necklace—positively garish, I'll grant you, but a diamond necklace just the same. And those lovely sapphire and diamond earrings. Quite an impressive collection of mementos, I'd say, from a gentleman whose attentions were not serious."

"Just what are you suggesting?" demanded Vanessa, rounding on her sister.

"Nothing as crude as you obviously are thinking." Lydia's smile was half affectionate, half mocking. "I merely suggest that Captain Logan did not appear to be entirely indifferent to you. Nor you, to him."

"Don't be ridiculous." Vanessa turned her face away. "I am not foolish enough to aim so high. Alexander chose me for his little deception precisely because he knew his father never would accept me as his daughter-in-law. Our arrangement is over, and that is an end to the matter. I am nothing to him. I should be surprised if he remembers my name after all this time."

"Oh, is that why you take the newspapers into the library and shut yourself up alone with them as soon as they arrive? And why you've told every one of the perfectly unexceptionable gentlemen who have shown an interest in you since we have returned to the country that you are betrothed?"

"*Someone* must keep up with what is going on in the world," Vanessa said. "And how could I possibly jilt a war hero while he is serving his country and retain a shred of reputation?"

"I see you've cut something out," Lydia said, gesturing to the newspaper scraps on the table. "Was his name mentioned in the dispatches again?"

"Yes," Vanessa said, avoiding her sister's eye.

"You take an unusual amount of interest in Captain Logan's welfare for someone who claims he means nothing to her."

"I didn't say he means nothing to me. I said *I* mean nothing to *him*," Vanessa said softly.

Alexander leaned back on the hard, lumpy cot and thought about the first time he had seen Vanessa Whittaker. It probably was the stale air inside the tent that reminded him, he decided, of the squalor of Chelsea Hospital. That, and the decidedly unsavory stench of whatever was boiling on the campfire outside.

God, she had been beautiful. Even feverish and drunk he had recognized that she was something out of the common way. Those few months he was reunited with her in London while they pretended to be in love had made him human again.

Pretended? Whom was he trying to fool? The hardest thing he ever had done was to leave her. Ironically, his love for Vanessa had made him all the more determined to return to Spain. If Napoleon were allowed to win, the England he knew would be destroyed.

Alexander had seen what happened to young innocent girls at the hands of the French, and he gladly would give his dying breath to keep those monsters from England and his Vanessa.

He thought of the meticulously manicured grounds of his father's primary seat, the flowers covered with dew in Hyde Park on cool spring mornings, and the way it had felt to hold Vanessa in his arms.

The cynical, dissipated son of the Earl of Stoneham realized that his love for Vanessa had somehow awakened his long-buried love for his country.

He should have asked her to marry him that day on the London docks. Instead, he left without making his intentions clear. It would be no more than he deserved if he returned from war to find her affianced or even married to another.

The earl no doubt would say the word of a fortune hunter was worthless, but Alexander clung to Vanessa's promise not to repudiate their engagement until he returned from war as if it were a lifeline.

It was the only thing that kept him sane.

In October, all of England rejoiced in Napoleon's defeat at Leipzig. Vanessa rejoiced that the end of the war was inevitable, and that Alexander might soon be on his way home, although he wouldn't be coming home to *her*. Their parting had been emotional and bittersweet, but, after all, he had made her no promises. He had not mentioned marriage. Only a waltz. She had no right to expect anything else.

The winter was lean for the Whittakers, but they managed to pay their remaining servants' wages with some regularity and stay out of debt somehow. Annabelle continued to bemoan the fact that the budget Vanessa and Lydia enforced so religiously did not allow for any of the luxuries to which the family had become so accustomed in London. Vanessa hoarded the remainder of the two thousand pounds, determined not to be forced into marriage with a man she couldn't love. Annabelle spent nearly two days in her bedroom recovering from the vapors when Vanessa began to talk of pawning or selling the diamond necklace in order to buy more seed, stock, and equipment for the farm.

Alexander's generosity had made it possible for her family to achieve some economic independence. It also had bought Vanessa freedom.

When several gentlemen from the neighborhood continued to show interest in her, Vanessa politely rebuffed their overtures. She once would have been willing to marry any man who offered her family financial security. Now she refused to give these perfectly acceptable gentlemen a second look. After all, *they* had been unwilling to give *her* a second look when her family hadn't had the proverbial feather to fly with.

One of her last promises to Alexander was that she would not sell herself to a rich merchant or aging peer for the sake of financial security. Vanessa never again would permit herself to be treated as if she were a marketable commodity.

If it meant she would spend the rest of her life alone, so be it.

In the spring of 1814, all of England and Europe rejoiced because the defeated Napoleon had abdicated and was on his way to Elba. And the victorious General Arthur Wellesley, created Duke of Wellington by his grateful nation, soon would return to England with his army.

Vanessa continued to read the society columns daily, hoping for a glimpse of Alexander's name. Surely an occasion as significant as the return of the Earl of Stoneham's son from war would warrant a mention in the newspaper.

Lydia pointed out that having the London papers sent down every day was a wicked extravagance. But the newspaper was Vanessa's last link with Alexander's world, and she refused to give it up.

In the middle of April, the Whittakers received a surprise visitor.

The fashionably dressed, heavily veiled lady stepped down from an elegant equipage drawn by four matched chestnut horses and refused to give the housemaid her name. She simply identified herself as a friend of Vanessa's and asked to be shown to a parlor where she could wait for either Vanessa or Mrs. Whittaker to join her.

"She would not leave her name?" Vanessa asked, puzzled when the housemaid came to find her. Vanessa had been helping Lydia inspect the linen to see which could be darned and which must be replaced.

"No, miss," the girl said. "The lady is dressed ever so fine, miss. Oh, miss! You should see the coach she arrived in. All painted in white and gold, it is, with a crest on the door. And four horses!"

Vanessa couldn't suppress a smile at the servant's excitement. Not since the family's return from London had the Whittakers received any visitors from outside the immediate neighborhood. Extending hospitality required money, staff, and leisure time that the Whittakers didn't have, so the entire household was eager for any diversion from the monotonous routine of daily life.

"I shall just step up to my room and tidy myself first, then, before I join her."

"Yes, do that, Vanessa," said Lydia. Then she gave the servant a straight look. "And you will return to your duties now, Meggie, instead of gossiping with the others, if you please."

"Yes, Miss Lydia," the cowed servant answered.

When Vanessa stepped into the parlor and her visitor threw off the veil that had been covering her face, Vanessa gave a shriek of joy and held her arms out wide.

"Oh, Vanessa!" cried Diana, her face crumpling as she ran into Vanessa's embrace. "It has been so horrid! To think that Rupert would use me so! I never have been so deceived in a man!"

Vanessa didn't know what to say. During the little season of the previous year, Diana Lacey had married Rupert Milton, Viscount Dunwood, a splendid match for a girl of merely respectable birth and fortune. Lord Dunwood not only possessed an impeccable pedigree, but also vast wealth and a position in the first circles. Vanessa had received an invitation to the wedding, but had regretfully declined it. She hadn't a cold-weather wardrobe fit to be seen in the City. Even if she had, her conscience would not permit her to incur the expense of a trip to London and the ensuing cost of lodging herself there in a hotel while her family remained in Yorkshire and endured the spartan economies being enforced in their household without her. By all reports, however, Diana had been a radiant and unabashedly triumphant bride.

"Diana, please calm down and tell me the whole. Surely it can't be as bad as all that."

Her friend blew her nose in the lace-edged handkerchief she had been clutching in her gloved hand.

"He said I was a disgrace to him!" Diana said. "I went to a public masquerade with some friends. Well, they weren't *friends*, precisely. Just some people I met at a party. I never had been to a public masquerade before because Mama was dreadfully strict with me when I was growing up."

"Yes, I see," Vanessa said. "Do go on."

"Well, Rupert caught wind of it and he stalked into the ballroom and *dragged* me out as if I were a naughty child of two years old. I was never so embarrassed in my life."

"What did he do to you?" asked Vanessa, horrified. No lady who wished to retain her reputation would be caught dead at a public masquerade. Vanessa could imagine Lord Dunwood's reaction to finding his bride of six months in such compromising surroundings. Another horrible thought occurred to her. "You weren't in the company of another, um, gentleman, were you, Diana?"

"Of course not! What kind of an abandoned hussy do you think I am?" Diana exclaimed. "I would never embarrass Rupert by going about with another man, although the wretched creature hardly deserves such consideration! Oh, who would have thought my own husband could behave so cruelly!"

"Diana!" Vanessa cried, expecting the worst. *"What did he do to you?"*

"You won't credit this, Vanessa, but he made me leave London—a month into the Season!—and go to Kent."

"Is that all?" Vanessa was greatly relieved. "Isn't his principal seat in Kent?"

Diana gave her friend a look of exasperation and began pacing the room.

"Is that all?" she said, mimicking Vanessa. "Haven't you *any* imagination? His horrid mother is serving as his hostess at the townhouse in London, while I, *his wife*, am cooped up in Kent with no one for company except the servants." Diana clutched Vanessa's hands. "You must help me!"

"I? What can I do?" Vanessa asked, surprised. "I hardly know your husband, so I can hardly intercede for you."

"No, silly. I want you to go with me to Kent for a few weeks, just on a visit. Please? Rupert said I might invite a guest to relieve the tedium of the country, and everyone else I know is in London for the Season."

"That was very considerate of your husband," Vanessa said. "Obviously he is not *very* angry with you."

"Yes, he is," Diana said, her voice tragic. "He said I am a disgrace to his name and he should have listened to his *mother* when the old harpy warned him that I wasn't good enough to marry a Milton."

"How dreadful," Vanessa said, pressing her hands to her suddenly flushed cheeks. She couldn't help thinking of her last conversation with the Earl of Stoneham and his contention that Alexander would regret it if he married a woman as far beneath him as Vanessa. And now here was Diana, telling her of her own unhappiness in her marriage to a wealthy peer of the realm. Vanessa's heart was moved to pity for her friend.

"Oh, Diana, love," she said. "I am so sorry."

"You must come to Kent with me," Diana said. "I know you are in reduced circumstances now, and I thought perhaps you would not want to go to the expense of a coach ride to Kent so I borrowed the traveling carriage and came to fetch you myself."

"I don't know," Vanessa said slowly. "I don't feel quite right about leaving my family."

"Oh, please! They have one another, Vanessa," Diana said, her eyes glittering with tears, "but I have no one."

It was true.

The poor, rich little viscountess was all alone in her misery. Vanessa couldn't turn her back on her friend, especially now that she knew what it was like to be disappointed in love.

It didn't take Vanessa long to explain things to her astonished family, pack a few clothes suitable for a short stay in the country, and join her friend in the coach.

FIFTEEN

Vanessa soon learned that she had been lured to Kent under false pretenses.

"I wish I could be there to see Rupert's face when he realizes what I've done," Diana said gleefully as she indicated the large pile of elegant note cards on the top of the white gilt writing desk in her boudoir.

"I'm rather glad I won't," Vanessa cried. "Diana, how can you even think of such a thing! He will be furious."

"Of course, he will," Diana agreed with what Vanessa considered quite foolhardy calm. "I think I have been positively Machiavellian."

"Machiavellian!" Vanessa scoffed. "I should be surprised if you can spell it."

"Hardly the point," Diana said with a satisfied smile on her face. "After I have sent out all of these invitations to a ball to be held in Rupert's townhouse, he can hardly expose me as a liar without looking like a complete fool. When you and I arrive in London next week, he probably will hail me as a savior, for his horrid mother is perfectly useless when it comes to making arrangements for entertaining guests on a grand scale. A modest dinner party is about all she can manage."

Vanessa shook her head.

"Diana, sometimes you frighten me. You truly do."

"Nonsense. Are you going to help me with these invitations or not?"

"I couldn't possibly be a party to this," Vanessa said. "Your husband would be perfectly justified in throwing me out in the street upon learning I had collaborated with you in such a scheme. I suppose I shall have to leave for Yorkshire at the same time you leave for London."

"I never thought you would be so poor-spirited!" snapped Diana. "Very well, then. I shall do them all myself."

"Diana, I'm sorry," said Vanessa, not sure whether she should offer to leave Kent at once. "But my conscience won't let me—"

"Oh, no," Diana said, her voice thick with sarcasm. "Don't give it a second thought. Just because I happen to be your best friend, and it probably will take me until midnight to write out the directions for all of these invitations all by myself, there is no reason for you to inconvenience yourself!"

"Diana—"

"Oh, just go into the library and read your stupid old newspapers. It is all you ever want to do, anyway," Diana said.

Observing the sad droop to her friend's mouth, Vanessa almost capitulated. Then she bit her lip and went on to the library to scan the newspapers for any mention of Alexander, as was her habit.

This time she found what she was looking for, but it brought her no satisfaction.

According to the society pages, Captain Alexander Logan, also known as Viscount Blakely, the hero of Vitoria, had returned to England from Spain a month ago. His proud father and aunt were to host a ball later in the month to honor him and Lady Madelyn Rathbone, a lovely heiress who, according to several stories circulating around town, was the most likely candidate for the honor of becoming Viscountess Blakely and, later, the Countess of Stoneham. It seems, the columnist went on, that rumors of an unofficial engagement between the gentleman and a certain young lady from Yorkshire that were flying about London during the previous year were quite unfounded.

Lady Madelyn was currently a guest at Stoneham House, and had been seen often, of late, strolling through the park and enjoying ices at Gunters in the company of the dashing Captain Logan.

Vanessa crumpled the newspaper in her hands and marched back into Diana's boudoir.

Diana glanced at the wreckage of the London paper.

"Did you find what you were looking for?" she asked.

"You knew he was back in London, didn't you?" Vanessa demanded.

"He has been back for almost a month," Diana admitted. "I didn't know whether to tell you or not. On the few occasions I've met him, he hasn't mentioned you at all, and I didn't feel I should bring the subject up."

Vanessa set her jaw to keep from bursting into tears.

"Have you seen *her?*" she asked.

"Lady Madelyn? She is very beautiful and has rather a high opinion of her own consequence. Lady Letitia's goddaughter, I believe. Before I left London, Lady Letitia told my mother that Lady Madelyn is the daughter of a general and would make a splendid political hostess. Naturally, she and the earl invited the young lady to visit them in hopes she and Captain Logan would make a match of it."

"He didn't even write to tell me he was back in the country," Vanessa said. The disappointment almost threatened to choke her. Vanessa had not gone a single day without thinking about Alexander since he left for Spain. He must have known she had been in Yorkshire all this time. It would have been a simple matter for him to discover her direction, yet he didn't bother to do so.

"All men are beasts," said Diana, obviously thinking of her husband as well as Alexander.

Vanessa gave her friend a straight look.

"Yes," she said. "You are perfectly right."

Vanessa pulled a straight-backed chair over to the little writing desk and picked up one of the small cream-colored cards.

"Well," Vanessa said, looking up at her friend with a

little nod of her head toward Diana's vacant chair. "If we are going to finish these invitations in time for dinner, we had better stop procrastinating."

Diana clapped her hands with glee.

"Does this mean you will go to London with me as well?" she asked.

"Certainly," Vanessa said, her voice a trifle too bright. "The gentleman owes me a waltz."

Alexander turned over the delicate silver filigree comb on the top of his desk and wondered if Vanessa was happy with the well-to-do country bumpkin she had married a mere six months after he left for Spain.

For someone who promised she would wait for him, Vanessa had been surprisingly efficient in finding another man to marry her. And Alexander, meanwhile, had been carrying this little silver comb all over Spain with him, day-dreaming like a callow youth about placing it among her dark, lustrous curls.

What a fool he was.

Unfortunately, he couldn't forget her. His brain had assimilated the fact that Vanessa Whittaker was lost to him, but his heart was being quite stubborn about the matter. The comb had become a talisman, and he had taken to carrying it with him everywhere and toying with it in idle moments. Seeing it still gave him pleasure, as if the bright metal retained some of the delight he had felt upon seeing it among the silversmith's wares in Spain and recognizing it as the very thing to set off the beauty of his beloved's dark hair.

Nevertheless, he was determined to hide his hurt deep inside as he had done from the time he was a child and pretend he didn't care. After all, Vanessa was perfectly justified in trying to find happiness with a gentleman who would appreciate her as she deserved. A man who could give her a home and children. *He* certainly had offered her nothing of the kind. Vanessa had made it clear from the beginning that the only reason she had embarked upon her association with him was to save her family. She hadn't pretended to love him.

And he had pretended *not* to love her.

If he had allowed her to see the love in his heart, would she have been faithful to him? Alexander had been torturing himself with that question ever since his father had mentioned seeing the notice of Vanessa's marriage in one of his letters.

"A pretty thing, that," said the earl.

Alexander started. He had been so lost in his thoughts of Vanessa that he hadn't heard his father enter the room.

Cedric reached over and picked up the comb.

"A present for Madelyn? It certainly would become her."

"You know very well for whom it was intended," Alexander said, his voice harsh.

"The less said about *that*, the better." Cedric said. "*She* is in your past now, thank heaven. I won't pretend to be sorry. Why not give the comb to Madelyn? She'll be much obliged to you, I am certain."

"Madelyn is a delightful young lady, but I don't wish to give her the mistaken impression that there could be anything but friendship between us. I have known her since we were children, Cedric. It would be like paying court to my own sister."

"Balderdash. She would make you an excellent wife. Madelyn is beautiful, her breeding is impeccable, and she is an accomplished hostess, having run her father's household for years after her mother's death. Her manners are perfection itself. Her fortune is large, and she is heiress to a valuable estate and some of the finest horsebreeding stock in England. What else could you possibly want?"

Alexander gave his father a thin smile.

"It is rather too soon to discuss this," he said. "I have only just returned to England, you know."

"You are still languishing over the Whittaker chit, you mean."

"We shall leave Vanessa out of this discussion, if you please."

"Nonsense! Put the two of them side by side and there is no comparison. Madelyn is by far the better choice."

"I have told you I am not in the market for a wife," Alexander insisted. "While I admire Madelyn greatly, I rather doubt I could ever love her."

"Marriage is a serious matter, Alexander," Cedric said, his tone stern. "One requires a cool head to make the right decision. Love is a fleeting state of mind, I assure you. You still lust after the chit because she was clever enough not to let you have your way with her. If she had, she would be just another past conquest to you now."

"You speak from vast experience, I presume?" his son asked. "You never married again after my mother died. Why?"

Cedric looked decidedly uncomfortable.

"I already had an heir," he replied. "There seemed to be no purpose in it."

"Did you love my mother?"

"What has that to do with anything? We got on well enough, I suppose. You sound like one of those silly novels all the young girls read nowadays," the earl said in disgust.

"Do you still have that rather highly finished piece of nature who used to dance at Covent Garden under your protection? I remember her as being quite remarkably pretty when I was a youth, although she has grown blowsy in later years. I can't quite recall her name. Miranda, was it?"

The earl's eyes widened in shock and anger.

"How *dare* you speak of her?" he demanded. "Have you no sense of decorum whatsoever?"

"Did you think I wouldn't know about her? I should imagine the Earl of Stoneham could have replaced his aging bird of paradise with a younger, much more beautiful opera dancer any time these twenty years."

"How dare you sneer at a woman you never have met?"

"I've seen her. That's enough to tell me that she isn't nearly good enough for my father."

"You go too far, Alexander!" the earl shouted. "I won't have you malign the good name of a woman who has never done you the least harm. Miranda is a person of great sweetness and charm, and if it has been my great good fortune to have had her friendship in the years since your mother's death, it is none of your business!"

"Precisely so, sir," Alexander agreed, satisfied that he had made his point. "If you will excuse me, I believe I promised Aunt Letitia and Lady Madelyn that I would escort them to the park this afternoon."

When Lord Dunwood's coach bearing Diana and Vanessa to London drove up to the front door of the Dunwood townhouse, the viscount himself came down the front stairs to greet them.

His expression was grim, although his greeting was civil enough.

"Good afternoon, Madam," he said in the polite tone of voice one would use to a perfect stranger. Neglecting to let down the steps, he reached into the carriage, grasped his wife by the waist, and set her down on the ground. His hands didn't linger. "I trust you had a tolerable journey from Kent."

"*We* did, thank you," Diana said, her voice calling attention to the pronoun.

He looked past Diana and saw Vanessa.

"I beg your pardon, Miss Whittaker. I didn't see you at first," he said. "I wondered if you would be coming to town with my wife. Welcome to London."

"Thank you, Lord Dunwood," Vanessa said. She felt ready to sink. It was obvious that Diana's husband was quite angry, only he retained enough dignity not to show it in front of an outsider. Vanessa didn't envy Diana when her husband got her alone.

Lord Dunwood let down the steps and offered Vanessa the support of his hand as she alighted from the carriage.

"I feel certain you would like to go to your room and rest after your journey," he told Vanessa, his tone making clear that this was not a suggestion, but an order. "You will excuse us, I hope, for Diana and I are long overdue for a discussion, is that not so, my love?"

A mocking intonation underscored the endearment.

"*Long* overdue," Diana agreed. To Vanessa's surprise, her friend didn't seem in the least cowed.

After being shown to a delightful room done in wallpaper the color of raspberries and cream picked out in gold, Vanessa was glad to remove the dirt of travel from her person with the help of a well-trained and attentive housemaid and watch the servant unpack her clothing from the vantage point of the comfortable bed. Vanessa's eyelids were so heavy she was almost asleep by the time the housemaid took her gowns away for pressing.

Dinner, which was served to the three of them from a massive baroque-style table in the impressive formal dining room of Dunwood mansion, was decidedly strained. Diana had dressed bravely in diamonds and silver tissue. Vanessa felt rather under-dressed in a demure blue muslin dress with white ribbons and regretted she had not thought it necessary to pack any of the evening gowns from her season in London for a short visit to Kent. She had brought the sapphire and diamond earrings with her, mainly because it comforted her to look at them when she was alone. But they would have looked ridiculous with the plain blue gown.

"I suppose you haven't forgiven me yet," Diana said to her husband.

Lord Dunwood at first didn't seem to know what to think of this audacious statement, then he shook his head and for the first time since their arrival a smile cracked the granite facade of his disapproval.

"Diana, what am I going to do with you?" he asked.

Vanessa, who had not known the viscount well before

his marriage to Diana, was surprised to observe that the rather taciturn young man was quite attractive when he smiled.

"I had planned to let you cool your heels in Kent for at least a month to teach you a lesson," he admitted, "but I nearly weakened last week and sent for you. The house seems rather empty without you setting everything at sixes and sevens. But Mother said if I relented now, you probably would walk roughshod over me for the duration of our marriage. It appears, however, that you are going to do so anyway, so I may as well enjoy your company."

At the mention of her mother-in-law, Diana's warm smile grew stiff on her lips.

"I see Edith doesn't join us tonight. Dare I hope that she is indisposed?"

The viscount gave his wife a small frown of disapproval.

"As a matter of fact, she is attending a card party this evening. I must say this animosity you have toward my mother is quite incomprehensible, my love. She is not the most tactful of ladies, I will admit. But I am certain that not one word of censure has ever crossed her lips except for the purpose of molding you into the kind of chatelaine my estate deserves."

Diana rolled her eyes.

"Your mother *hates* me, Rupert."

"Nonsense, you are simply too sensitive. If you will allow me to say so, you have been permitted an injudicious amount of liberty in your upbringing, which was no doubt the influence of, er, a lady who is quite admirable in her way, but was unequal to the task of preparing you for your role as mistress of a great household."

"You are speaking of my mother," Diana said, throwing her napkin down on the table. She stood up so abruptly that some of the porcelain dishes rattled. "And I won't sit here and listen to you make cutting remarks about her."

Vanessa was acutely uncomfortable.

"Diana, I am certain Lord Dunwood didn't mean—"

she began in a foolhardy attempt to mediate what promised to be a very unpleasant scene.

"And I am equally certain he did," snapped Diana, turning on her. "I will not sit here and listen to this well-fed, pompous hypocrite sneer at my mother simply because she was an actress before she was married to my father. How dare you judge her because she turned to the stage, Rupert! She was a young widow, left impoverished by her husband, with my half-brother still in leading strings to support. What would you have had her do? Starve in the gutter and her child with her?"

"Calm yourself, my dear, you know I have the greatest affection for dear Rosemunde, but—"

"I am proud of her, do you hear me?" Diana shouted. "I am proud of her talent and her courage and her willingness to do anything she had to in order to survive. She is worth a dozen of that spiteful, lazy old cow who gave birth to you!"

"Diana, we have a guest," the viscount said, his voice heavy with disapproval. "Miss Whittaker, I apologize for my wife. She is not herself tonight."

Before Vanessa could think of something to reply to this, Diana rounded on her husband.

"Don't you *dare* apologize for me as if I were a badly behaved child. Vanessa is my dearest friend. I have no secrets from her."

"Diana," her husband said, tight-lipped. "You will go to your room at once and remain there until you recover your composure."

"And you," his wife replied with a smile of false sweetness, "may go straight to—"

"Diana!" the viscount shouted, shocked.

Diana gave a heavy sigh, sat down in her chair, and placed the napkin in her lap.

"Don't look so distressed, Vanessa," she said with a bleak little smile. "I am quite finished making an exhibition of myself." She turned to her husband. "Sit down, Rupert, and eat your turbot. Cook made it especially for my homecoming because he knows it is one of my favorites. There is no reason to let his efforts go to waste. Indeed, we can fight anytime."

"I don't know what Miss Whittaker must think of us," he said, obeying his wife.

"If she thinks the worst, you have only yourself to blame," said his unrepentant spouse. "You *would* make those unkind remarks about my mother, even though you know perfectly well it always sets me off."

"You were equally uncomplimentary about *my* mother, Diana. It is no doubt ungentlemanly of me to mention it, but you *did* make a cutting remark about *my* mother first."

Diana leaned forward, her eyes dancing with mischief.

"Not so, Rupert. It is true I called Edith a lazy, spiteful old cow, but that was *after* you said my mother was unequal to the task of preparing me to be the kind of chatelaine your estate deserves. That is absolute rubbish, and you know it. My father is a *viscount,* for pity's sake. His rank is equal with yours. And you may be sure that my mother, for all that you disparage her, made sure that I would be the most accomplished young lady ever to embark upon a season in London. She knew well that fusty gentlemen like yourself would look askance at any lady whose mother once had been an actress, even if she did leave the stage twenty years ago and has led a life of unexceptional virtue ever since."

"All right!" Rupert said hastily, throwing one hand up in surrender. "Let us not begin fighting again."

"Yes, let's not," Diana agreed. "Cook said he would make a raspberry syllabub for dessert. It is quite one of my favorites."

Rupert rolled his eyes.

"I don't know how you are going to learn the proper decorum required by your station if you persist in allowing the staff to make a sort of pet of you. If you will permit me to say so, it is quite undignified for the lady of the house to linger in the kitchens sampling the glazes on the cakes."

"And what should I have been doing instead? Sitting in the parlor sewing a fine seam?"

"You could have been keeping your husband company," Rupert said, giving his wife a wistful smile. "We have been separated for nearly two weeks."

Diana raised her brows.

"And whose fault is that, pray?"

"My dear, I am not going to permit you to cast yourself as the injured party. I have done what any rational man would have done in my place."

"And I have done what any lady of spirit would have done in my place," Diana said, throwing down the gauntlet. "So, what shall it be? Shall you send me packing off to Kent again and explain to the people invited to our ball that your rebellious wife issued the invitations without your knowledge? Or are you going to admit defeat gracefully and act the part of the genial host to all our acquaintance?"

"Fortunately for you," Rupert said between gritted teeth. "I am not the sort of man who beats his wife."

"Fortunately for *you*, you mean," Diana said sweetly.

By then, Vanessa had consumed her dinner without tasting a bite, and Diana directed a footman to remove all the plates. Diana had eaten most of her food with good appetite during the argument, although Rupert had eaten only half of his.

"The syllabub!" Diana exclaimed in delight when the servant bore the dessert to the table with a flourish. "You will present my compliments to Henri," she said, closing her eyes in rapture after taking her spoon and tasting the treat. The servant obviously was struggling not to smile at her enthusiasm.

"Yes, my lady," he said, bowing. Then he began to cut the dessert and take the plates to each diner.

Rupert gave a heavy sigh, obviously disapproving of his wife's informal behavior.

Diana gave her husband a sharp look.

"What I don't understand, my *dear* husband," she said,

her eyes glittering with defiance, "is why you married me when what you obviously wanted in a wife was one of those over-bred, horsey creatures from your own set who wouldn't have had the temerity to say boo to a mouse without your permission, let alone commit the unpardonable sin of taking a bite of her own dessert at her own table in her own dining room before you deem it proper for her to do so."

"Neither do I, *darling*," he said, his tone malicious. "Neither do I."

Vanessa felt her stomach knot, even though the aroma wafting from the hot syllabub was intoxicating. Suddenly she was back in Yorkshire, squirming at her place at the dining room table as she witnessed other scenes equally as unpleasant. Upon attaining her fourteenth year, Vanessa sometimes was permitted to join her parents at dinner instead of taking her meal in the schoolroom with the other children. Mr. and Mrs. Whittaker's arguments were even more acrimonious than the one Vanessa had just witnessed.

No doubt Annabelle, like Diana, had been thrilled to better her position in society by marrying above her. And, like Diana, Annabelle had fallen far below her husband's standards of behavior once his initial infatuation had worn off.

Vanessa looked at her friend—really looked—and was horrified to observe that the formerly vivacious and sweet-natured Diana had a petulant look on her face that was most unattractive. Only six months of marriage to a man who constantly belittled her had transformed Diana's formerly sunny disposition into that of a bickering, defensive shrew.

No doubt the viscount's mother, who had made no pretense of approving the match, reminded her son daily that she had warned him against espousing this unworthy bride.

Is this the inevitable result, Vanessa wondered bleakly, *of marrying above one's level of society? Would it have been like this for me, even with Alexander?*

For the first time, Vanessa's heart accepted what her head had known all along.

The earl was right.

A match between Vanessa and the man she loved was doomed to unhappiness because one day she would look into his eyes and find him regarding her with all the censure of a man who was ashamed of his wife. The disdain Rupert exhibited for Diana's family chilled Vanessa. Would Alexander eventually have treated Vanessa's little sisters with contempt, even though their eyes shone with hero worship every time they saw him?

Would he have made rude remarks about *her* mother?

Vanessa looked up to see both Diana and Rupert looking at her with curious expressions on their faces. Obviously one of them had just addressed a remark to her, and Vanessa hadn't the least idea what had been said.

She smiled wanly and forced herself to take a bite of the sweet, fruity dessert.

It turned to ashes in her mouth.

SIXTEEN

"I wish you would reconsider," Diana said, laying her hand across Vanessa's. They were seated in the breakfast room, having tea and toast. Vanessa had just announced her intention of returning to her family in Yorkshire within the week. "It seems a shame for you to leave London before the ball when you have done so much of the work. I don't know what I would have done without you."

"I'm sorry to disappoint you," Vanessa said, "but I just can't face him."

Diana pursed her lips in annoyance.

"If I had known it would upset you so much, I would not have sent him an invitation. I thought you would *want* to see him. And *her.* Will you tell me now, that you have no interest in seeing your rival?"

Vanessa averted her gaze, embarrassed. In the past few weeks, she had found herself searching for Alexander whenever she and Diana went out in public. Not once had she seen him, possibly because the only time she left the house was to accompany Diana on errands or to walk in the park at an hour when she knew the fashionable world was still abed. Vanessa certainly had read all about Alexander in the newspapers, however.

"Captain Alexander Logan, hereafter to be known by his courtesy title, Viscount Blakely, has resigned his commission

*after distinguishing himself both at Salamanca and Vitoria,
to accept a prestigious government post. . . ."*

*"Viscount Blakely, son of the Earl of Stoneham, escorted
his aunt, Lady Letitia Logan, and his aunt's houseguest,
the ravishing Lady Madelyn Rathbone, to a musicale at
the home of Lady Sarah Jersey on Tuesday evening. Lady
Madelyn performed an aria in a voice her impressed audience declared was as good as Madame Catalani's. . . ."*

*"Lady Madelyn Rathbone, a young lady who seems to
have taken society by storm this Season, attended the Prince
Regent's soiree last Wednesday evening in the company of
The Earl of Stoneham, his sister, Lady Letitia Logan, and
their son, Alexander, Viscount Blakely. A reliable authority
close to the earl's family has revealed that an Interesting
Announcement is expected to be issued from Stoneham
House in the near future."*

No. Vanessa *could* not face him.

"I am disappointed in you, Vanessa," Diana said, dis-
tracting Vanessa from her reverie. "I never have known
you to be a coward. Even when all of society was whispering
about you behind your back, you held your head high and
refused to be cowed. Did you not say the gentleman owed
you a waltz? What better place to collect it than at a ball?"

"You don't understand."

"No, I don't," Diana admitted. "Why should you leave
London just because Captain Logan—Lord Blakely, I
should say—is making up to some heiress? We are nothing
to men but game pieces, interchangeable and disposable
if a better comes along. Why should we not regard them
in the same way?"

"You have grown cynical," Vanessa observed.

Diana's soft pink lips hardened at the corners.

"Marriage to Rupert would make a cynic of the most
romantic woman, I assure you," the viscountess said.
"When he courted me, he declared I was perfect for him.
He admired my spirit. My playfulness. My affectionate nature. But now that we are married, nothing I do or say

pleases him. He doesn't like the way I dress. He doesn't like the companions I choose. He doesn't like the way the servants defer to me rather than to his horrid old mother. He doesn't like the way I *laugh*. In short, I am a *wife*, now. Not a sweetheart. The scales have fallen from his eyes and he realizes he is married to a woman who is undeserving of the lofty position to which he has raised her."

"Oh, Diana," Vanessa cried, casting aside her own un-happiness. How could she have been so selfish? She put her arm around her friend's drooping shoulders, aware of how much it had cost Diana to make her sad admission. "I am so very sorry."

"Sorry?" Diana said with a bitter smile. "You have no cause to be sorry for me, my dear. True, I was blinded by Rupert's polished manners and the promise of becoming a viscountess. The man told me he was my slave, and in my innocence I believed him. However, I have no real cause for complaint. Do I not possess exactly what I have been bred to seek in marriage—privilege, wealth, a house so full of servants they are tripping over one another, a wardrobe that would rival that of a crown princess?"

"Is it not vastly uncomfortable to be married to someone with whom you do not get along?"

"Because we argue, do you mean?" Diana asked with a flippant wave of her hand. "*All* married couples argue. My parents certainly did, and I would wager yours did, too. My mother tells me matters will improve after I have given Rupert a son or two. Then, if you please, I may take *lovers* as long as I am discreet. I suspect Rupert already has done so. He certainly has far less enthusiasm for exercising his husbandly rights than he did in the early days of our marriage. In that arena, too, it seems, I am found lacking."

Vanessa could have wept.

Diana must have sensed this because she forced a smile to her lips and patted Vanessa's hand lightly.

"Don't look so sad, Vanessa. I did not mean to weigh down your spirits with my self-pity. Perhaps you are more fortunate than I. The man you love has merely broken your heart, but that will heal. At least you won't have to watch him transform before your eyes into a *husband.*"

She wrinkled her nose prettily.

"Now, let us talk of something pleasant. My housekeeper tells me your ballgowns have arrived from Yorkshire. Your mother, it seems, is delighted that you will have this opportunity to attend a ball in London and, perhaps, meet some eligible marital prospects. It would be a pity to disappoint her by returning to Yorkshire prematurely after she has gone to the trouble and expense of sending your gowns here, don't you agree?"

Vanessa gave a heavy sigh.

"I suppose you are right," she admitted.

"That's the spirit," Diana said.

"Perhaps when I see him, I will find my feelings for him quite changed," Vanessa continued, without much hope. "And he may not come, after all."

"Very good." Diana clapped her hands in approval. Her tinkling laugh sounded almost as it had when they conspired together at boarding school after they were supposed to be in bed. "Now, what shall you wear? Let us go upstairs and go through your trunk at once. You must look absolutely stunning at the ball."

"We will do so if you wish," Vanessa said. "But it hardly matters. No doubt he has forgotten my very existence."

After his casual announcement at dinner that he had decided to accept Lady Dunwood's invitation to her ball, Alexander had to escape to the library in order to avoid the inevitable objections.

Madelyn had pouted at him. His father had raged at him. His aunt, finding her efforts at cajoling him into doing her wishes in vain, simply had looked martyred.

They might as well have saved their breath.

Alexander was going to the ball at Lady Dunwood's house no matter what anyone said because there was the chance that *she* would be there.

He was a romantic, masochistic fool, but he had to see Vanessa one more time. Even if she was lost to him forever.

"I suppose there is no changing your mind," the earl said belligerently.

Alexander looked up, annoyed to see his father had followed him into the library and was about to pour himself a glass of port from the decanter standing upon the desk. Alexander extended his own glass for a refill. The earl hesitated, then obliged him by pouring Alexander two fingers of the liquor.

"No," Alexander said, sipping from the crystal glass. He peered over the rim at his father.

"You would do well to forget that wretched little chit and marry Madelyn," Cedric said with a sneer.

"I am not going to marry Madelyn, so you may as well stop planting those preposterous little innuendos in the newspapers. It is appalling to consider what sort of trash the columnists will print if someone with a title suggests it to them."

"Madelyn will be disappointed."

Alexander scowled at the earl.

"And whose fault is that? *I* did not invite her here and fill her head with nonsense about becoming the next Countess of Stoneham. Madelyn is far too convinced of her own worth to let the loss of a mere man undermine her self-esteem. Accepting your invitation to Stoneham House was the only way the little manipulator could think of to get away from her strict guardian to spend a season in London, and she grabbed it with both hands. She would have accepted a proposal of marriage from me in precisely the same spirit. You will forgive me if I am not precisely flattered by her attempts to captivate me."

"She is genuinely attached to you," the earl protested. "And you have not precisely discouraged her."

"I could hardly repulse a girl staying under the same roof as myself. I have taken lodgings in the city near Whitehall, by the way."

"What?" demanded the earl, outraged. "Why should you do any such thing?"

"What better place for a political appointee to live?" Alexander replied, lifting his brows.

His father gave him an impatient look.

"No one actually expects you to haunt the place, as if you were some insignificant clerk," he said. "You would be very much in the way."

"No doubt," Alexander said dryly. "Nevertheless, I intend not only to *haunt* the place, but also to perform the responsibilities *personally* to which I have been appointed. You astonish me, Cedric. *You* were the one who was so keen upon my pursuing a political career."

"Nonsense. You merely want to be out from under my thumb."

"That, too," Alexander agreed.

"What about Madelyn? She had her heart set on attending General Mayhew's reception. She had promised to sing afterward."

"Ah, now I see the attraction. The girl does like to play to an audience. Very well. Since you are so anxious to oblige Madelyn, *you* may escort her to the general's house. I am going to Lady Dunwood's ball, and, if I don't miss my guess, Letitia will insist upon accompanying me to make sure I don't make a cake over myself over Vanessa— no, not Whittaker. She would have taken her husband's surname. What is it, by the way?"

"How should I know? I don't remember the fellow's name," the earl said, looking annoyed. "Some country squire, I imagine."

"No matter," Alexander said, his jaw hardening. "I am for Dunwood House."

"She has been in the country, breeding heirs for the yokel she married," the earl said, his tone brutal. "Do you suppose she is still the pretty little debutante you knew all that time ago? She has grown fat and coarse, you mark my words."

Alexander gave his father a rueful half-smile.

"I am very much afraid," he said quietly, "that it wouldn't make the slightest difference."

The earl drank the last of his port in one swallow, slammed his glass down on the desk, and stalked from the room to find his sister.

"What are we going to do if he finds out?" Letitia said, looking distressed when her brother told her the outcome of his conversation with Alexander.

"We have to make sure he *doesn't* find out," the earl said, his mouth hard. "Damnation! Who would have thought he would persist in his ridiculous fascination for Vanessa Whittaker! I was certain he would have forgotten all about her by this time, and he never would need to know we lied to him about her supposed marriage."

"It was for his own good," Letitia said. "When he finds out what we have done, he probably will marry her out of hand just to punish us."

"He won't get the chance," Cedric growled. "We are all four going to that deuced ball, and if the wretched chit is there, we must keep them apart. Perhaps we are worried for nothing, and Vanessa Whittaker *won't* be there. No one has seen her in London since Alexander left for Spain, after all."

"She is here, a guest at the Dunwood mansion, although she hasn't gone out much at night for some reason," Letitia informed him, her eyes hard. She gave a cynical little laugh. "Did you think I would not have my own sources of information? She will not have him, I tell you! No daughter of Annabelle Whittaker's is going to take *my* place as mistress of Stoneham House!"

SEVENTEEN

Determined to put on a brave face despite the fact she was quaking inside, Vanessa wore the sapphire blue gown with the daringly low neckline Madame Celeste had created as a setting for the diamond necklace.

The necklace had been sold to buy livestock for the estate, so now the dress showcased an indecent amount of white bosom. Diana's dresser had pulled Vanessa's hair up in a Psyche knot and allowed one long curl to fall over one shoulder. The sapphire and diamond earrings were her only ornaments.

She needed all the false courage she could get to face Alexander again. And, as Diana had suggested, Vanessa supposed she *did* want him to suffer, just a little, for breaking her heart.

However, when he entered the room with a perfectly ravishing young lady on his arm, Vanessa was the one who suffered.

Carefully, she searched his person for any injury he might have suffered in the war, but she found none. He was as handsome, as *perfect,* as he had ever been.

Vanessa swallowed hard as she watched Alexander bend his head slightly to listen to something the beautiful girl was whispering in his ear, for she was almost as tall as he. Vanessa had known Lady Madelyn would be lovely. But nothing had prepared her for this magnificent, Junoesque goddess with her glorious, flaming hair and enchanting face. She had *dimples,* Vanessa observed in despair. What man could resist dimples? No wonder it had not occurred to Alexander to write to her when he returned to London.

Who would look at an ordinary, dark-haired girl like Vanessa when he could have this exquisite creature?

"Stop staring at him," hissed Diana at her side.

"She is so beautiful," Vanessa said, looking at Diana.

"So are you. There are the earl and Lady Letitia," Diana said, making a face. "If you will excuse me, I shall have to collect Rupert and greet them. For pity's sake, go find some other man—it makes not the slightest difference which one—and *flirt* with him! And *smile!*"

"Yes, Diana," Vanessa said absently, looking about her for a susceptible male. All too soon, one found her.

"Vanessa, my sweet," said Sir Gregory Banbridge, taking her hand and raising it to his lips.

Vanessa snatched her hand away and drew back.

"You," she said bitterly. "I am surprised you have the gall to approach me."

"That was a long time ago, sweetheart," he said.

"Don't call me that!"

"As you wish. You heard that Susan died of the influenza last year."

"Yes. Your mother told mine. I am very sorry, Gregory."

"Thank you," he said, as if the wife that brought him a fortune and the influence that would earn him a government post was of no particular import. "Would you care to dance?"

The way the man was leering at Vanessa's bosom made her go hot with embarrassment. Had he no decency?

"Gregory, please go away," Vanessa said.

In response, he gave an unpleasant bark of laughter and took her arm in a grip she felt sure would leave bruises. He was very sure of himself, Vanessa realized, now that Alexander was no longer her self-appointed protector.

"Don't you understand, you little fool?" he said under his breath. "I have no wife now. There is no longer any reason for you to reject my advances. You loved me once."

"Let go of me!"

"Damn it, Vanessa," he growled, giving her a savage shake. "I will *make* you love me."

Seeing her captor's face distorted with passion, Vanessa knew fear. She tried to wrench her arm free, but he was too strong for her. How could she get away from him without making a scene?

"I believe the lady asked you to release her," a calm male voice said, deadly with menace. "I should do so *now,* if I were you."

She heard Gregory mutter a curse under his breath, then his arm relaxed its hold on her. Pulling away from him, Vanessa rubbed her abused arm and looked into the eyes of her savior.

"Robert Langtry!" she exclaimed, breaking into a relieved smile. The last time she had seen Robert was in Yorkshire and he had been on one knee before her in her mother's parlor, proposing to her at the time. Considering how genuinely disappointed he had seemed at her refusal, she was surprised and touched that he had come to her rescue.

"Damnation, Langtry," Gregory snarled. "What business is it of yours?"

"That of a nearly affianced husband, so take yourself off, Greg, or I'll tell your mother," said Robert with the easy familiarity of a man who had grown up in the same neighborhood with his rival and had, occasionally, been led into scrapes by him. "You can't bully Vanessa into marrying you. Or even dancing with you. Not in public."

Gregory glared at Robert, who laughed in his affronted face.

"Go away, Greg, there's a good fellow," he said.

In high dudgeon, Gregory stomped away. Vanessa looked after him in astonishment.

"Don't stand there with your mouth open, girl," Robert said, his voice sounding lazy and amused.

She turned to him, tears of relief standing in her eyes.

"Oh, Robert, how can I ever repay you?"

"You could marry me."

Vanessa frowned at him.

"Merely jesting, my dear," he said drawing her hand through her arm and leading her to the dance floor. "The minuet will do nicely."

"I must say you don't seem to be too brokenhearted."

"Well, I'm not about to wear it on my sleeve. Give me credit for *some* pride. I see Lord Blakely is here. I do trust I won't have to fight him off, too. Really, my girl, you appear to attract the most *violent* people."

The smile was quite wiped off Vanessa's face.

"Ah," Robert said softly. "The wind blows in that quarter, does it? I'm afraid you will have to battle the magnificent amazon for him."

"I wish it could have been you instead," she said, and she meant it.

The laughter left his eyes.

"So do I," he said.

Vanessa was saved from the necessity of making a reply by the opening chords of the dance.

From his vantage point near the wall, Alexander watched Vanessa take her partner's hand and burst into laughter at something he said.

A memory stirred.

Langtry. That was his name. Robert Langtry. The young man whom he had scared off with a single mean look at a ball when the fellow had dared approach Vanessa for a dance. Vanessa had said at the time he was one of her neighbors from Yorkshire.

This, then, was the country squire who had persuaded Vanessa to marry him. From the looks of it, not much persuasion had been necessary. They seemed entirely comfortable in one another's company.

There had been nothing hesitant in the way Langtry had extricated Vanessa from that bounder Banbridge's grip. Alexander had muttered an apology to Madelyn and been halfway across the room to plant the cad a facer when Langtry intervened.

Langtry's post-adolescent figure had broadened, and his calm assurance told Alexander that he would not be as easily intimidated now as he was a year ago. Even so, Alexander could break him with one hand. But what was he thinking of? Vanessa was *married* to the man. Perhaps she even loved him.

"I suppose that is your little nobody from Yorkshire," Madelyn said.

Alexander blinked at her. He had forgotten her very existence.

"So *this* is my rival," Madelyn continued, a pensive look on her face. "She is rather pretty if one has a taste for squabbish little females with dark hair. Not much of a figure, has she?"

Madelyn preened, taking a deep breath to show her most spectacular assets to advantage.

"Behave yourself, brat," Alexander said, trying to repress a smile. "I suppose you have been charged with the duty of keeping me away from her."

"Of course. Really, Alexander, this is most unflattering to me. I had thought she would be something quite out of the ordinary."

"She is, Maddy. Now be a good girl and find some other poor man to drive out of his wits for love of you."

"Where are you going?"

"To collect my waltz."

Madelyn rolled her eyes.

"If I really meant to have you, she wouldn't stand a chance."

"We'll never know, will we?" Alexander said with a grin.

"Here he comes," said Robert as he escorted Vanessa to a chair at the side of the ballroom.

Alarmed, Vanessa saw that Alexander was purposefully making his way toward them. He looked so formidable that Vanessa clutched Robert's hand, as if for support.

"Here, none of that, my girl," Robert chided her, only half serious. "Stiff upper lip, and all that."

"How dare you laugh!" she said out of the corner of her mouth.

"I am weeping inside, I assure you," he said dryly. "Must the man be so confounded handsome?"

Vanessa made no reply, for Alexander had arrived before them and his dark, stormy eyes were fixed on her face.

"I believe I am owed a waltz," he drawled.

Vanessa's throat was so tight, she could only nod.

Alexander glanced at Robert, who was eyeing him with all the fascination of a spectator at some sort of sporting event. "You have no objection, I trust?" Alexander asked, his tone barely civil.

"None in the world, old man," Robert said. "Steady on, my girl," he whispered under his breath to Vanessa as he stepped back from her.

Alexander took Vanessa's hand in his and led her to the dance floor, unpleasantly aware of the way conversations all about them had stopped.

Then Vanessa was in his arms and he forgot all else.

"How are your sisters?" he asked, feeling like a fool. He had dreamed of waltzing with Vanessa every night since their separation. In his dreams, however, it hadn't been necessary to make polite conversation with her.

"They are well, I thank you," she said, finding her voice at last.

What on earth was wrong with the girl? It was almost as if she feared him. But that couldn't be, he assured himself. She probably felt guilty. After all, she had promised to wait for him.

"And your mother?" he persisted.

"Also well. Alexander—"

"Vanessa—" he said at the same time.

"I'm sorry," she said. "What were you going to say?"

"Nothing of consequence. You were saying?"

"I read about your government appointment," she said.

"I just wanted to congratulate you. And to tell you I am glad you returned safely from the war."

"Kind of you," he said, his voice dry. "I am surprised the news of my activities reached you. You must be very busy tending to household matters in—Yorkshire, is it?"

Vanessa gave him a straight look.

"Alexander, you know very well I live in Yorkshire. Yes, I have been very busy. I did have to sell the necklace, but I will be happy to reimburse you for it after the rents are collected. We needed livestock for the farm, and you *did* say I could sell it if I had need."

"Is he that poor, then?" he asked, frowning. Langtry had a look of prosperity about him, and he would have supposed him rather well to pass.

"Who?" asked Vanessa.

"Never mind. I don't want to talk about him now," Alexander said, tightening his grip around her waist. She still wore orange blossom scent. She may as well have produced a bludgeon and knocked him over the head with it.

She was just as slender, just as beautiful as she had been a year ago. And she was wearing the sapphire and diamond earrings. Seemingly of itself, his hand crept up her back to touch the soft skin left bare by the low-cut gown.

"Alexander," she said, her voice choked.

"Not now," he murmured. He didn't want to talk about her family. He certainly didn't want to talk about her husband. He just wanted to hold her in his arms for one last time. One waltz. Then he would find the courage to let her go from his life forever.

He felt her body lean into his and knew that they were dangerously close to crossing the line of propriety. Vanessa gave a soft shudder, and he looked down to see that her eyes were half closed and her lips slightly parted.

Alexander lost his head.

With a savage growl, he abruptly halted their progress around the dance floor and, imprisoning her in one arm, led her toward the French windows which led to the terrace. He could hear the whispering voices all around him. From the edges of his vision, he could see the stares.

"What are you doing?" Vanessa asked, her voice breathless. "Have you gone mad? Alexander—?"

Without answering, he led her into the darkness beyond the French windows and pulled her roughly into his arms.

Vanessa gave a soft sigh of surrender and melted against him, just as he knew she would. Then he was devouring her soft, sweet lips and running his hands over her beautiful, languid body.

"Alexander, darling. It has been so long," she whispered when he stopped to draw breath. In the moonlight he could see her face was transformed by passion. "We mustn't do this. But I can't seem to stop."

Vanessa's slender fingers tangled in Alexander's hair and she drew his face down to hers. Willingly, he took her sweet lips again and again. He displaced one of the small sleeves of her gown and kissed her bare shoulder. Then he came to his senses.

She was married to another man.

Married!

"No," he rasped, releasing her so quickly that she stumbled.

Vanessa opened her eyes and stared at him, as if in bewilderment.

"Alexander—" she whispered, reaching for him again.

"No," he said, louder this time. He stepped back. "Vanessa, forgive me. This should not have happened. This must not happen again."

"You don't care for me, then, after all?" she asked.

"Damnation, Vanessa. How can you ask me that? Have you no shame?"

"Have *I* no shame? How *dare* you, Alexander, when you are the one who dragged me out here and began—" She made a helpless, fluttery gesture with her hands and pushed her sleeve back into place. Tears filled her eyes. "It was a mistake to come here," she said brokenly. "I should have stayed in Yorkshire. I knew it then. But I wanted to see you again. I wanted . . . *this!* I am so ashamed!"

She buried her face in her hands and turned away from him.

"Don't cry," he said, feeling like a monster. He put his hands on her shoulders, but took them away at once. He couldn't trust himself to touch her now. "None of this was your fault."

For a mad instant it occurred to Alexander that Vanessa could dally wherever she chose now that she was a married woman as long as she was discreet. In his world, such arrangements were commonplace, although Alexander himself never had been a part of one. For all his cynicism, Alexander considered the nuptial vow sacred, and he always had intended to remain faithful to his wife should he marry. Conversely, he knew he could never be a complaisant husband, content to pursue his pleasures outside the marriage bed while his wife pursued her own.

Briefly, he entertained the notion of sharing Vanessa with her unsuspecting husband. Then he discarded the notion. He wanted more than Vanessa's body. He wanted her love. He wanted her faithfulness. He wanted her, God help him, to be the mother of his children. He would not persuade Vanessa to cuckold a decent man for the sake of his own pleasure.

Besides, she probably would break a chair over his head if he even suggested such a thing. And he would deserve it.

"Here, we must go back inside," Alexander said, turning Vanessa around to face him and handing her a white handkerchief from his pocket.

She dried her eyes and blew her nose into the snowy linen. Then she gave the handkerchief back to him.

"Thank you," she murmured. "I'm sorry."

"Are you ready to go inside now?" he asked.

"Yes." He saw her straighten her spine with an effort. "Will he be angry?"

Vanessa looked surprised. She was beautiful even when

her eyes were swollen from weeping. Alexander felt his throat grow tight with the need to comfort her, yet he managed to keep his hands at his side.

"Who do you mean?" she asked.

"Your Robert Langtry."

"*My* Robert—? Do you mean because I came out here with you? No, of course he will not be angry. He understands about . . . us. When he proposed to me I told him all. I owed him that."

It seemed her Mr. Langtry was of a generous disposition, damn his eyes!

"Do you love him?" Alexander could not stop himself from asking, even though he knew whatever answer she gave would cause him pain.

"Robert?" she asked, as if the idea were a curious one. "No. We are good friends, of course. We have known one another all of our lives."

"I see." Alexander didn't want to hear anymore. In his heart he couldn't blame Vanessa for making a marriage that promised security and the ease of old friendship. Alexander himself had not offered marriage. The fact that she had been forced to sell the necklace to pay for livestock was curious, but he had, after all, told her she could do as she wished with it. She still had the earrings. It had brought a lump to his throat to see them in her ears, looking as exquisite as he knew they would on her. But he couldn't help being glad that she hadn't sold them. Perhaps whatever financial difficulties Vanessa and her Mr. Langtry had experienced were behind them now.

"It's time to get you inside," he said. "I think I have damaged your reputation enough for one evening."

Vanessa nodded and allowed him to take her arm.

"It's for the best," she said, her expression tragic. "It would not have worked . . . between us."

"No," Alexander agreed. Irrationally, he was glad she retained enough integrity to be faithful to her country yokel. "It is common in my world for husbands or wives to seek their pleasures outside their marriages, but I could never reconcile it with my conscience to do so. Not even for you, my dear.''

"No. Of course not," Vanessa said, looking so sad that he had to fight an urgent desire to take her in his arms again. Instead, he escorted her back to the ballroom, forcing himself to smile at the curious faces turned to them. Vanessa, he noticed, held her head up high and was doing the same.

What a proud, courageous woman she was.

Alexander scanned the faces of the guests for Vanessa's husband and saw him standing by the punch bowl talking to Madelyn with an enraptured expression on his face.

Well, Alexander thought. Madelyn *did* have that effect on healthy males. Alexander glanced quickly at Vanessa to see what she thought of her husband's obvious pleasure in Madelyn's company and surprised a look of such naked hopelessness on her face that he turned away quickly.

Apparently, despite her words to the contrary, she cared for her husband. As she should, he told himself firmly as he walked up to the other couple, relinquished Vanessa into her husband's care, and practically dragged Madelyn away from the Langtrys.

"All right, minx," Alexander said in a savage undervoice as he walked Madelyn to the other side of the room. "What have you been up to?"

"Skullduggery," she replied, her green eyes dancing with mischief. "He is a very nice man, your *inamorata's* husband. We had the most interesting chat."

"Shame on you," Alexander said sternly. "What did he say?"

"Not much about your precious little nobody, actually." Madelyn preened a little. "He appeared to be much more interested in *me.*"

Alexander's brows drew together, and he turned Madelyn to face him.

"What do you mean?"

"What do you think?" She gave him an arch look from beneath her thick, dark eyelashes. "At first I thought him rather ordinary-looking, but he is such a charming flirt that after a while I began to think him quite as handsome as yourself, my dear Alexander."

"You cannot be serious," he said, feeling indignant on Vanessa's behalf.

"I must say, you aren't at all modest or gallant," she said with a mocking smile. "I begin to wonder what I ever saw in you, quite apart from the fact that you will be an earl someday. Mr. Langtry, I'll have you know, has the greatest admiration for a woman built on queenly lines. He has the most flattering way of trying *not* to stare at one's bosom with those positively *worshipful* blue eyes of his. My eyes, by the way, are quite the most beautiful he has ever seen."

"That unprincipled philanderer!" Alexander exclaimed, roused to fury on Vanessa's behalf. "How dare he make a cake of himself over a woman he has just met while his wife is in the same room?"

"She wasn't precisely in the same room, was she?" Madelyn pointed out. "Actually, she was out in the moonlight with you. He *could* have been flirting with me in order to make her jealous, I suppose. But I don't think so. At the risk of seeming immodest, I can tell when a man is interested in me, and your little friend's husband is *definitely* interested."

Alexander clamped his jaws shut to stop himself from saying something he would regret and seated Madelyn in a chair by the side of the ballroom so she could watch the dancing. At her suggestion that he take her out onto the floor, he scowled at her.

Instead, he stood watching the couples perform the steps of the country dance in progress, aware that Robert Langtry had led Vanessa onto the floor. Then he took an involuntary step forward when Vanessa suddenly stopped dancing and covered her face with her hands. Alexander could see the way her shoulders were shaking, but he could hardly make his way across the room to take her in his arms. That was for her *husband* to do.

Raging inside, Alexander saw Robert Langtry solicitously put a comforting arm around Vanessa's waist and, after a whispered conversation, lead her away from the room.

"Well," said Madelyn with a piqued expression on her face. "One would hardly guess that a few minutes ago he was staring at my bosom with all the longing of a starving man."

"Shut up, Madelyn," Alexander snapped.

"Vanessa, what is wrong?" Diana asked when she encountered Robert and Vanessa outside the ballroom. Vanessa tried to answer, but her throat felt as if there were a live coal lodged in it and no sound came out. Diana looked alarmed. "Mr. Langtry, what has happened? Is she ill?"

"No, but she is very upset," he said. "You had better take her to her room."

"Thank you, Mr. Langtry," Diana said, putting her arm around Vanessa to lead her away. "Come with me, dearest."

"I will take my leave of you now, Lady Dunwood," Vanessa heard Robert say to Diana. "Thank you for a delightful evening. It was kind of you to invite me."

"Not at all," Diana said. "Must you leave so soon, Mr. Langtry?" she added, apparently remembering her manners.

"Yes," he replied, sounding a little sad. Fresh tears sprang to Vanessa's eyes. She couldn't seem to stop them. "I'm afraid I must."

He left them, and Diana quickly walked Vanessa up the stairs and into the bedroom. Vanessa collapsed onto the bed and began to weep in earnest. Her ribs hurt from the effort of trying to control her sobs.

"My dear, tell me at once what that beast said to you!" Diana demanded, sitting beside Vanessa and wrapping her arms around her. "I shall find Rupert and demand that he turn the horrid man out of the house at once!"

"No, no! It is not Alexander's fault. Only mine, for behaving like a fool. I *threw* myself at him in the most brazen fashion. It was shocking! I don't know what came over me."

"I can hazard a guess," said Diana. "Vanessa, what did he *do* to you?"

"He kissed me. And he *touched* me—" She buried her face in her hands again. Diana patted her back in an effort to console her.

"There, there," Diana said, her voice soothing. "It is all right now."

"No," Vanessa said, sitting up and taking a deep breath to steady herself. "It will never be all right again. Diana, he is going to marry her."

"Did he *tell* you that?"

"Yes. He said it was common in his world for men to seek their pleasures outside marriage, but he could never reconcile it with his conscience to—"

"I should hope not," Diana said, her voice tight. "That red-haired vixen of his would probably claw his eyes out. He deserves the harpy. You should have seen the shameless way she was flirting with Mr. Langtry while you were out on the terrace with Lord Blakely. *She* didn't seem to mind that her precious Alexander was out walking with another woman in the moonlight. It is going to be one of those marriages of convenience, you mark my words."

"He must love her a little," Vanessa said, annoyed with the way her voice trembled. "You should have seen the way he seized her arm and dragged her away from Robert when he saw them in conversation together. He was positively *seething* with jealousy."

"Well!" exclaimed Diana. "It sounds to me as if the man is a perfect dog in the manger! Now, I want you to dry your eyes and not give him another thought. You are well rid of him!"

EIGHTEEN

The afternoon after the ball, Alexander walked into the parlor where Madelyn and Letitia were entertaining callers and stopped dead in his tracks.

There, sitting on the sofa with Madelyn, was Robert Langtry. They were flirting so shamelessly with one another that they didn't take notice of Alexander until he lifted Langtry bodily from the sofa by grasping a handful of his shirt and frog-marched him out of the room.

"Alexander!" cried Madelyn, following behind them. "What are you doing? Let go of Mr. Langtry *at once!*"

"This doesn't concern you, Madelyn," Alexander barked. He slammed the front door in her face with his free hand when she would have followed them outside.

When Alexander released him, Langtry stood back and straightened his shirt.

"What the devil is wrong with you?" Langtry demanded. "Do you have something specific against me, or do you treat all of Lady Madelyn's gentleman callers this way?"

"Only the married ones," Alexander said through gritted teeth.

"Very proper. That hardly pertains to me, however, so why don't you stop glaring at me as if you would like to draw my claret and tell me in round terms what I have done to offend you?"

Alexander gaped at him. For sheer crust, you couldn't best the man!

"What do you mean it doesn't pertain to you? Do you think I'm a fool?"

"Yes," Langtry agreed at once. "However, that is none of my concern. I haven't the slightest objection to indulging in a bout of fisticuffs with you. I am said to be handy with my fives, and I should enjoy trying to plant you a facer. God knows, you deserve one. However, damaging your handsome face is unlikely to endear me to the lovely Lady Madelyn, so let us try to settle this in civil fashion. Why don't you point out which of the ladies you want for yourself, and I'll confine my attentions to the other."

Alexander blinked and dropped his hands.

"What are you babbling about, Langtry?"

"Let me put it in plain words," Langtry said with a long-suffering sigh. "You can have Vanessa *or* Lady Madelyn. You can't have both. Just make your choice, and I'll engage to comfort the other one. However, if you make Vanessa cry again, I shall most likely forget my noble resolve and call you out."

"Are you mad?" roared Alexander. "You are *married* to Vanessa. Do you think I'm going to let you trifle with an innocent young girl who is a guest in my father's house?"

"Married to Vanessa? I?" Langtry shook his head. "Old boy, you can't imagine how much I wish you were right. The lady turned me down flat. Didn't even pay me the compliment of a moment's hesitation."

"But she said—"

"Vanessa told you we were *married*? If she did, she was probably trying to make you jealous. But I've never known Vanessa to play a fellow such tricks, and I've known her all my life."

"You mean she's married to someone *else*?"

Langtry rolled his eyes.

"Not precisely needle-witted, are you, Blakely?" he said. "Listen to me. Vanessa is not, nor has she *ever*, been married. Do you think for one moment she would have let you drag her out onto the terrace if she were? You don't know her at all, old man, if you think that."

"You must be mistaken," Alexander said, feeling his world rock about him.

Langtry gave him a look of pure disgust.

"Vanessa is *not* married. She has been in Yorkshire for the past year, working like a stevedore in order to build the estate back up and take care of her mother and sisters. It will be years before the ramshackle place turns a decent profit, but between them she and Lydia have managed to keep a roof over their heads. Ours is a very small neighborhood composed mostly of busybodies and gossips. Believe me, I would have known about it if Vanessa were married."

"But—"

"And you made her cry, you blackguard!" Langtry said, his eyes narrowed in anger. "Make Vanessa cry again, and I'll plant you that facer, I promise you."

He started down the steps, but he turned when he reached the bottom to deliver his parting shot.

"Pray present my apologies to Lady Madelyn," he said, his voice thick with sarcasm. "Tell her I'll send around a note the next time I intend to call on her so she can have her guard dog chained up!"

Alexander stared after him in disbelief.

Vanessa was not married? Could it be true? If so, his father had much to answer for.

Alexander went back inside the house for his hat and was accosted at once by Madelyn and Letitia.

"Alexander!" Madelyn cried. "What have you *done* to him? If you've hurt poor Robert, I'll—"

" 'Poor Robert' has suffered no damage at my hands, damn his eyes!" Alexander said. "Get out of my way, Madelyn. I've no time to spare."

"Where are you going?" Letitia and Madelyn said together as he took his hat, threw his greatcoat over his arm, and opened the front door to go out again.

"To the newspaper office! Don't hold dinner for me. I expect I shall be very, very late."

Alexander spent the rest of the day poring over the past

years' issues of the *Morning Post, The Gazette,* and *The Times* for Vanessa's supposed engagement announcement at their respective editorial offices, assisted by curious employees of those publications. He returned to Stoneham House with his shirt stained with newsprint and his disposition a curious mixture of elation and murderous rage. No such announcement existed.

Cedric glanced up at the doorway when Alexander stalked into the library, then sat up straighter when he saw the look on his son's face.

"You look as if you have been shoveling out the dustbin," the earl said.

Alexander didn't bother to reply to this inane observation.

"You wrote to a man serving his country in a foreign land and told him the woman he loved had married another in his absence. Cedric, do you have any idea what that does to a man's concentration when he is trying to stay alive?"

"It was for your own good," the earl said, avoiding Alexander's eyes. "No one had seen the chit in London for months. For all I knew, it could have been true."

"And I, fool that I am, never dreamed my own father would lie about something so important to me. My lodgings in the City won't be ready for another week, so I am going to put up at a hotel for the night."

"No!" Cedric said, leaping to his feet with his hand outstretched. "Alexander, *listen* to me! I had to do *something* to stop you from making a mistake you would regret for the rest of your life. What do you think will happen to your political career with a wife like Vanessa Whittaker at your side? Do you think she is equal to entertaining prime ministers and royalty?"

"Vanessa is equal to anything!" Alexander declared. "In the morning I am going to the Dunwood mansion to beg her to forgive me for making her unhappy. You had better pray she accepts my proposal of marriage, Cedric, or there won't *be* any grandsons to carry on your precious name. I'll retire to my estate alone and wait for you to die."

"Alexander, wait! No woman is worth this!"

Alexander turned at the door and favored his father with a withering stare.

"If you believe that, Cedric, I truly do pity you."

Alexander spent the night at the Clarendon Hotel, and in the morning he sent to Stoneham House for his valet and his clothes. By the time these had arrived and Alexander had washed, shaved, and been dressed in his best coat, it was a little past the hour permitted for the beginning of afternoon calls.

When he arrived at the Dunwood mansion, determined to beg Vanessa on bended knee to become his wife, it was to find that she had departed for Yorkshire the day after the ball in Lady Dunwood's traveling carriage.

Lady Dunwood's tone was barely civil when she greeted him. Grudgingly, she provided him with Vanessa's direction in Yorkshire.

Before he followed Vanessa into Yorkshire in order to lay his heart at her feet, he penned a quick note to Robert Langtry, scrawled his name at the bottom, and paid a footman from the Clarendon to deliver it.

Robert, enjoying a glass of brandy with Gregory Banbridge at the club, tossed the crumpled note across the table.

"I am for Yorkshire," it said. *"You are welcome to try to fix your interest with Lady Madelyn. I wish you joy of the minx."*

Gregory squinted at it, then looked at Robert with a knowing eye.

"Ah, so that's why you haven't been your usual abstemious self tonight," Gregory said with a heavy sigh. He signaled a waiter for another bottle of brandy.

"To the future Countess of Stoneham," Banbridge proposed, raising his glass and downing the fiery liquid in one gulp.

"To Vanessa," said Robert, drinking his brandy as well. He fixed Banbridge with a silly grin on his face.

"What are you looking so happy about?" Banbridge demanded, entering the belligerent stage in his progress toward inebriation. "Blakely has as good as won her."

"Probably, but look at it this way," he said philosophically. "At least Vanessa will take the bloody idiot out of circulation, and maybe we'll have a chance at the ladies who are left. I don't know what they see in the curst-tempered brute."

Banbridge gave a short, unpleasant laugh and reached for his glass.

"I probably won't, either, when I'm as drunk as you," he said, looking glum.

Vanessa was picking flowers in the garden when she heard her little sisters shouting with glee about something. She forced a smile to her lips and stood, turning to see what it was that made them so happy. For herself, she would never be happy again. But for her sisters' sake she would pretend to take pleasure in whatever it was that caused their high spirits.

Her eyes widened when she saw Alexander enter the yard. Lydia, resembling nothing so much as a pugnacious little dog, was at his side, glaring at him. Self-consciously, Vanessa brushed the dirt from her skirt and clasped her hands in front of her.

Blast the man! He looked so handsome in his dark blue coat and gleaming boots. *She* had been working in the garden all day, and looked it. Like Lydia, her sleeves were rolled up and her hair had worked loose to hang in damp tendrils around her face.

"Alexander, what are you doing here?" Vanessa asked, annoyed by the way her voice trembled.

"He says he's here to ask you to marry him," Lydia said without ceremony before he could speak. She turned to Alexander and narrowed her eyes at him. "I told him if this was another one of his false proposals, he could take himself off again."

"Lydia, *please!*" whispered Vanessa, mortified.

"You can stay if you behave yourself," Lydia continued, giving Alexander a look that could curdle milk, "but if you make her cry again, I'm going to come after you with my broom. Do you understand?"

"Yes, Lydia," Alexander said. "Thank you."

He bent down and kissed Lydia on the cheek. Flustered, she pushed him away.

"Don't waste your time trying to turn *me* up sweet," she said, her voice dripping with sarcasm. "If you'll excuse me, I'll go tell Mama to kill the fatted calf."

"No, Lydia!" Vanessa cried, starting to follow her sister. "Don't go."

"I have to, darling. Fatted calves take time," Lydia said, favoring Vanessa with a wistful smile. Then she turned to Alexander. "I won't be able to hold Mama and the girls off for long, Alexander. So I'd advise you to get straight to the business."

She disappeared into the house.

"*Et tu*, Lydia?" Vanessa murmured.

"Remind me," Alexander said, sounding amused, "to give that girl a splendid come-out next season. With that mouth, I predict she will take the *ton* by storm as an original."

Vanessa was at a loss for words to do justice to this audacity, but Alexander didn't seem to notice. He stepped closer and took Vanessa's shoulders in his hands. She could smell the masculine scent of bay rum he used on his person. That did it. Her resistance collapsed like a house of cards.

She put her arms around his waist and rested her head against his broad chest. Vanessa felt as if she had come home after a long journey. She felt Alexander's lips against the top of her head.

"Thank God," he whispered. "I thought I had lost you."

She pushed herself away from him and looked up into his face.

"Taking rather a lot for granted, aren't you, Lord

Blakely?" she asked, proud of the perfectly calm way the words came out.

"Be reasonable, darling," he said, grinning. "Even Lydia called me Alexander. I'll get down on my knees, if you wish."

She started to shake her head, but reconsidered at once.

"Fine," she said, pointing to the loose dirt of the garden.

Alexander gave a wry glance at his spotless pantaloons and levered himself to the lumpy ground.

"Vanessa, will you marry me? Please?" he asked.

Tears sprang to her eyes and she turned away.

"What is it?" he said, leaping up and wrapping his arms around her as he pulled her back against his chest. He kissed her temple, then her cheek. Every part of her face he could reach from behind her. Then, impatient, he turned her around and took her lips with his in a kiss so hungry that it left her knees weak with desire.

"No, Alexander! What about Lady Madelyn?"

"Lady Madelyn? She is not your concern."

"But, I thought you were going to marry *her.* You said you couldn't reconcile it with your conscience to seek your pleasures outside of marriage that night at Diana's ball. Why did you say so, if you didn't mean to marry Lady Madelyn?"

"Because I thought you were married to Robert Langtry."

"Robert Langtry!" she exclaimed. "Did he *tell* you that? Of all the unprincipled—just *wait* until I see him again. I never would have thought him capable of such a dirty trick. And *you*—"

Alexander silenced this impassioned speech by pulling her into his arms and kissing her until she was breathless.

"Langtry is innocent, my love," he said when they had broken apart. "My father wrote to me in Spain that you had married in my absence, and when I saw you at Lady Dunwood's ball with Langtry, I assumed he was the lucky man."

"Your father told you . . ." The bottom dropped from Vanessa's stomach. His father. In her joy at seeing him again, she had completely forgotten her noble resolve to give him up.

"Alexander," she said, pushing him away. "If you marry me, you will regret it someday."

"What nonsense is this?" he said frowning.

"Our positions in society are too far apart," she explained. She could feel tears running down her cheeks. She had never cried so much in her life. "Your father is right. I would make you dreadfully unhappy."

"My father's opinion doesn't hold the least weight with me at the moment," Alexander said. "Now dry your tears unless you want Lydia to come back and chase me off with her broom. You heard what she said."

Vanessa was surprised into a watery gurgle of laughter, but she sobered immediately.

"Don't try to make me laugh," she told him. "Do you think I want you to end up like my father? That is what happens to men who marry beneath them."

Alexander took in a deep, ragged breath. His eyes were so dangerous at that moment that Vanessa cowered.

"Let me tell you something about your *father,* my love," he said, his voice menacing. "He was a bloody snob. And if you think he ended up the way he did because of your mother, you are a bloody snob, too! He should have gotten on his knees and thanked God for giving him a beautiful, affectionate family like yours."

"Alexander—"

"Be quiet!" he shouted, grabbing her shoulders. "*I* am not your father, Vanessa! I am not *my* father! It is a grievous insult for you to suggest I am. Now, are you going to marry me, or not?"

Vanessa looked up into his strong, passionate face and felt all the heartache inside her melt away. He was right. He did love her. And she loved him. That was all that mattered.

"Yes!" Vanessa cried, jumping up and throwing her

arms around his neck. For a moment, Alexander apparently was too stunned by her sudden capitulation to react. Then he laughed, picked her up so that her feet dangled several feet from the ground, and spun her around in joyful circles.

"Alexander! Stop it! You're making me dizzy!" she squeaked.

"I am glad to hear it. You've been making me dizzy for more than a year, my love!" he replied, still laughing.

Vanessa felt a soft body crash against the back of her legs.

"Alexander! Alexander!" cried Aggie and Amy as they lent their support to the mad dance.

Alexander gave Vanessa a smacking kiss on the cheek and put her down. Then he dropped to his knees and spread his arms wide. Without hesitation, the little girls fell on him, covering his face with fervent little kisses.

They squealed when Alexander lost his balance and fell flat on his back, sweeping them along with him.

"Alexander! Are you all right?" Vanessa cried, dropping to her knees beside him.

With one arm he reached up and pulled Vanessa into the pile of laughing, squirming bodies.

"I've never been better, love," he said as a big, glorious grin of happiness spread over his face.

NINETEEN

Eyebrows were raised all over London when the word spread that the heir to the Earl of Stoneham was going to be married, not at the fashionable St. Paul's, but at his bride's home in the wilds of Yorkshire.

The blissful couple cared not at all.

The parlor at the Whittaker home had received a new coat of paint and splendid velvet draperies picked out in gold for the occasion. The bride's little sisters, preening in matching dresses of primrose-colored silk created by no less a personage than the celebrated Madame Celeste herself, greeted guests at the door and led them to the chairs set in a semi-circle in the parlor.

Mrs. Whittaker shed happy tears, although she, for one, would have much preferred to see her daughter become a viscountess at St. Paul's. Lydia was decked out in an excessively flattering dress of amber, and pearls were threaded through her soft brown hair.

Vanessa, wearing a charming bridal gown of white voile trimmed in silver, stood at the top of the staircase and smiled down at everyone. Alexander, grinning like a schoolboy, took her breath away in his black cutaway coat. His usually unruly hair had been brushed to a fine gloss, and his eyes were sparkling.

He held out his arm, gesturing for her to come down.

Playfully, she shook her head no.

Those assembled in the parlor waiting for the ceremony to begin laughed.

Vanessa waved at them and went back into her room.

"Where were you?" Mary Ann asked, taking the wedding veil out of its protective cocoon of white tissue.

"Looking down into the parlor from the stairs," she admitted. "I know I wasn't supposed to let Alexander—or anyone—see me before the ceremony, but I just couldn't wait."

Mary Ann rolled her eyes.

"Stop fidgeting while I put this on you," Mary Ann said. "I declare, you are worse than Aggie! You know very well it's bad luck for the bridegroom to see the bride before the ceremony on their wedding day."

"I don't believe in that old superstition," Vanessa said.

Lydia and Annabelle Whittaker came running into Vanessa's bedroom with stricken looks on their faces.

"What has happened?" Vanessa cried, seeing their expressions.

"He's here," Annabelle said fretfully. "The earl has come to stop the ceremony!"

Mary Ann gave a heavy sigh.

"I *told* you it was bad luck," she said to Vanessa.

Downstairs, Alexander met his father at the door and guided him into a separate room.

"If you've come to stop the ceremony, you have wasted your time," Alexander said calmly, gesturing toward a chair. "You have interfered in my life for the last time."

Before the earl could open his mouth, Vanessa ran into the room, her veil streaming behind her. Quietly, she closed the door.

"Good morning, my lord," she said, pleased that her voice didn't shake. "Welcome to my home. Is Lady Letitia with you?"

"In the coach," he said tersely. He took a deep breath and gave Vanessa a rueful look. "We were somewhat unsure of our welcome."

Lydia opened the door and skidded in. There was murder in her eye.

"Lydia," said Vanessa. "Go outside to Lord Stoneham's coach and bring Lady Letitia inside."

"Are you sure?" the girl asked, her hands on her hips.

"Yes, Lydia," Vanessa whispered. *"Now,* if you please!"

Lydia hesitated, then she shrugged her plump shoulders and left to do her sister's bidding.

"Well, are we welcome?" Cedric asked Vanessa, his tone belligerent.

"Yes," said Vanessa.

"No," Alexander said at the same time, turning to stare in astonishment at his future bride. "Vanessa, he is up to something. Why would you even consider letting him stay after what he tried to do to us?"

"Because he is your father," she said. "And despite his faults, you love him. He and your aunt are the only family you have left."

She rounded on the earl.

"And *you,* you dreadful old man! You love Alexander. Don't bother to deny it. You wouldn't have come otherwise."

Both Alexander and his father looked embarrassed.

"Now, you listen to me," Vanessa told them. "My father had his faults. When he drank, he became sarcastic and rude to all of us. He regretted to his dying day that none of us had been sons, and he made my mother's life miserable by telling her that he should have married a rich heiress from his own class instead of sullying his noble bloodlines by marrying her. He was crusty and cantankerous and stubborn. But I'll tell both of you this. I would give anything I possess to have the stubborn old fool with me today."

She looked first at the earl, then at Alexander to see if they were listening to her.

They were. Neither said a word.

Vanessa went to the door, yanked it open, and turned to look back at them.

"I want you to think about *that,* my lords, while I go upstairs to finish preparing for the ceremony," she said.

Then she stalked out of the room, through the parlor, and up the stairs as several dozen pairs of curious eyes followed her.

A few minutes later, her mother came to the bedroom to tell her it was time to begin.

Flanked by her sisters, Vanessa stood at the top of the stairs and looked down, once again, into the flower-decked parlor. Robert Langtry winked at her. Diana and Rupert Milton, Viscountess and Viscount Dunwood, were holding hands, seemingly oblivious of everyone else in the room. Lady Letitia, sitting next to the earl, favored Vanessa with an apologetic little shrug of her shoulders and blew her a kiss. The earl, looking sheepish, gave her a brusque nod.

Then Vanessa saw Alexander looking up at her from the bottom of the stair with a beautiful smile on his face, and she knew everything was going to be all right.

LOOK FOR THESE REGENCY ROMANCES

SCANDAL'S DAUGHTER   (0-8217-5273-1, $4.50)
by Carola Dunn

A DANGEROUS AFFAIR   (0-8217-5294-4, $4.50)
by Mona Gedney

A SUMMER COURTSHIP   (0-8217-5358-4, $4.50)
by Valerie King

TIME'S TAPESTRY   (0-8217-5381-9, $4.99)
by Joan Overfield

LADY STEPHANIE   (0-8217-5341-X, $4.50)
by Jeanne Savery